THE WAY OF THE CUILLIN

Long, long and distant,
Long the ascent,
Long the way of the Cuillin
and the peril of your striving...

'S fhada, cian fada,
'S fhada an dìreadh,
'S fhada slighe a' Chuilithinn
Is cunnart bhur strì-se...

Sorley MacLean

IN MEMORY OF PETER HODGKISS

Roger Hubank

THE WAY OF THE CUILLIN

RYMOUR

© Roger Hubank 2021

ISBN 978-0-9540704-9-6

Published by Rymour Books
45 Needless Road,
PERTH
PH2 0LE

cover and book design by Ian Spring
printed by Imprint Digital, Exeter, Devon

A CIP record of this book is available
from the British Library

All rights reserved. No part of this publication may be reproduced, stored in a retrieval system, or transmitted, in any form or by any means, electronic, mechanical, photocopying, recording or otherwise, without the prior permission of the copyright holder or holders. This book is sold subject to the condition that it shall not by way of trade or otherwise be circulated without the publisher's prior consent in any form of binding or cover other than that in which it is produced.

The paper used in this book is approved
by the Forest Stewardship Council

ROGER HUBANK is a novelist whose work is largely devoted to risk-taking in a wilderness of one kind or another. *North Wall*, an Alpine epic, was described by the critic Al Alvarez as 'a genuine and moving work of imagination on a subject where true imagination is usually the one quality never found.' *Hazard's Way* won the Boardman Tasker Prize, the Grand Prix at the Banff Mountain Book Festival, and a special commendation from the Royal Society of Literature. Jim Perrin called it 'quite simply a masterpiece—the finest piece of fictional writing about the subject of mountaineering ever to have been published in this country.'

Other work includes *North*, winner of a Special Jury Award at Banff, *Taking Leave*, and *Evening Light*, hailed by leading Himalayan mountaineer Stephen Venables as 'that rare treat—a good climbing novel'.

ACKNOWLEDGEMENTS

I would like to thank the National Library of Scotland, the National Archives of Scotland, the Skye and Lochalsh Archives Centre, the Royal Commission on the Ancient and Historical Monuments of Scotland, the Scottish Mountaineering Club, and the Rucksack Club.

Among the books consulted for the writing of this novel were Hugh Thomas's magisterial *A History of the Spanish Civil War*, William Rust's *Britons in Spain: the History of the British Battalion*, David Faber's authoritative *Munich: the 1938 appeasement crisis*, and Colin Coote's *The Other Club*. Trish Hayes of the BBC Written Archives Centre provided essential details of the live broadcasts and special bulletins transmitted during September 1938.

I am especially indebted to Mrs Isabel MacRae of Glenbrittle House, and the late Charles Rhodes for invaluable information relating to an earlier period in the history of the glen.

I would also like to thank Chris FitzHugh for help in the preparation of the text, Colonel John Marsden for his reminiscences, and those fellow mountaineers whose writings and conversations about the Cuillin have contributed immeasurably.

Ian Spring designed the cover for the book and Calum Smith and Jim Perrin contributed their generous assessments of my work.

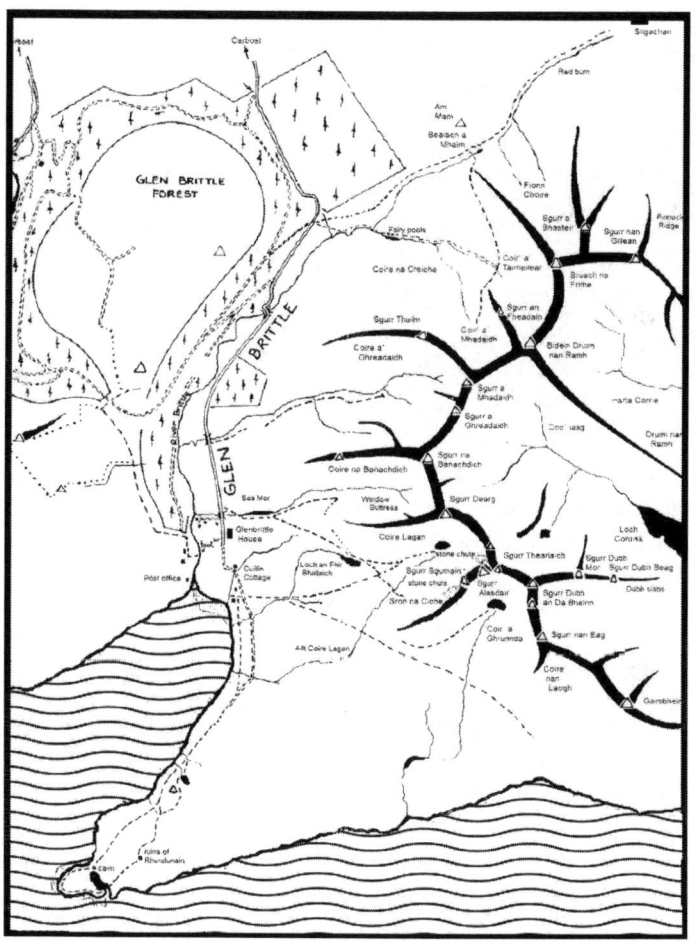

The Black Cuillin

CHARACTERS

Stephen Marlowe, a Professor of Greek.
Millie, his wife.
Robert Clarke, brother of Millie (deceased).
Henry Marlowe, an Archdeacon; Stephen's son.
Vanessa Marlowe, wife of Henry.
Leo Marlowe, MP, Stephen's son.
Lady Kitty Marlowe, wife of Leo.
Giles Marlowe, an undergraduate; Henry's son.
Nicholas Frost, an undergraduate; friend of Giles.
Miranda Marlowe, an art student; Henry's daughter.
Hugh Marlowe, a child, Henry's son.
Andrew Marlowe, a child, Henry's son.
Susannah Fleming, a widow; Stephen's daughter.
Richard Fleming, Susannah's son.
Adam Stone, undergraduate; friend of Richard.
Charles Bartrum, a literary wastrel.
William Coldstream, an artist.
Gideon MacRath, a farmer; tacksman to the MacLeod of Dunvegan.
MacRath's wife.
Euan MacRath, his son.
Jeannie, niece of MacRath.
Morag, a maid.
Lachlan, a shepherd.
Dr MacKay, a general practitioner.

Sundry others include mountaineers, fishermen, an innkeeper, an airline pilot and a passenger.

The action takes place in Glen Brittle, Isle of Skye, and in Cambridge, London, and Spain.

— CHAPTER ONE —

Marlowe was the last to board the plane. Missing by minutes the airline transport in St Enoch's Square he'd managed to hire a taxi which raced in pursuit of the coach all the way to Renfrew, swinging at last through huge doors into a cavernous hangar.

The old man found himself whisked instantly out through the doors at the further end to where the aircraft was waiting.

'We'd almost given you up,' said a cheerful voice. A small, clear-eyed man in uniform stood aside to let him board.

'Not much room, I'm afraid,' he said apologetically, following his passenger up the steeply inclined fuselage, allowing Marlowe to take his seat before squeezing through the cockpit door.

Marlowe glanced round the cramped little cabin, conscious of a reek of octane and leather. It was certainly a crush. Barely room for six passengers.

'Well, we've got a nice day for it,' said his neighbour. He was a bulky man, rather too large for the seat he occupied. he'd

'First flight?'

Marlowe smiled, nodded.

'A present from my son,' he said. He'd have preferred to have gone by boat from Mallaig with the rest of the family. It would have been just as exciting. Probably too exciting, he suspected, for one or two of them. At least Millie was a good sailor.

'We should touch down in Glen Brittle at 11.30,' the bulky man informed. He himself was flying on to Barra.

Marlowe unfolded his paper, resolving not to look out of the window.

'Wonderful machine, this,' continued his neighbour, raising his voice against the engine roar—'A great improvement on the old '89. Though of course you *do* have to fly her. Make no mistake, one lapse of concentration—especially on take-off or landing—and she will bite you. She'll sometimes drop a wing quite viciously on a three-point landing.'

Already they were in the air, the hangars falling away beneath them. Marlowe swallowed hard, glancing down despite himself at the tiny figures on the ground, half-expecting to see them scuttling for cover.

'Strong winds can sometimes be a problem. I've known a plane like this literally forced into reverse while airborne. Most of the time she had to crab along sideways at 45 degrees to the wind just to make progress.'

Tight-lipped, Marlowe nodded grimly.

Already the city skyline, the University spire, the cranes and steamer funnels on the Clyde, were visible through the forward windows.

'Don't worry. Barclay's top class. He's their Chief Pilot, you know. Very experienced man. Even in bad visibility he always knows when to land at Renfrew. Know how he does it? He opens the side window, and keeps popping his nose out. As soon as he smells the cornflour from the custard factory he puts the flaps down. Never fails. That chap knows every conceivable landing strip from the Mull of Kintyre to the Butt of Lewis.'

'I'm glad to hear it,' said Marlowe with genuine relief.

He was an old man, white-haired, apple-cheeked. Hale and hearty, according to his doctor. And pretty nimble for his age. He put it down to his build. Small. Wiry. Light on his feet. In his day an extremely hard goer on the hill, some part of the fire of youth remained. It worried his daughter, Susannah, who feared he might exert himself in excess of his capacity. *Your father will do as he pleases*, her mother sighed. *He usually does.*

He gazed down as the plane followed the river westward, banks of warehouses and factories giving way to sludgy, grey mud flats. Henry had been the prime mover in this celebration, the rest of the family endorsing it with, he suspected, varying degrees of enthusiasm. Leo, of course, had jumped at the idea. It was just the kind of stunt to get his name into the papers. Leo enjoyed cultivating his reputation as a politician-mountaineer. Young Giles had been quite starry-eyed about it. *Just think of it, grandfather. Three generations on the same climb.* For Giles, of course, it would be an adventure. For Henry too, perhaps. After all, the Church of England couldn't offer much in the way of excitement.

The old man, though, was not deceived. He was too old to relish former glories. Besides, he knew very well they would persist in badgering him to climb, if only the first pitch. And he was not sure he was up to it. For a while, though, he was content to let go of all that, his gaze following a bright, V-shaped wake crossing the dark waters of the Firth. The Greenock ferry? He closed his eyes, and settled back in his seat.

When he opened them again the earth below showed in irregular patches, a dense impenetrable green giving way to a brown, baked land of scarps and ridges picked out in slanting shadow by the morning sun.

'Loch Awe,' said the bulky man, nodding at a long arm of dark water, hemmed in by forest.

Marlowe smiled, nodded.

He glanced down at his paper. It showed a picture of the German Chancellor greeting the Prime Minister. Chamberlain waving his hat, umbrella dangling from one arm. It did not inspire confidence. Leo's words came to mind. *Winston thinks it's the stupidest thing he's ever done. Eden was furious.* Well, it was all of a piece with Chamberlain's vanity. Oblivious of a catastrophe until it actually happened.

'Lovely spot,' remarked his neighbour, glancing at the photograph. 'Berchtesgaden. Do you know it? The Königssee? Beautiful. Can't imagine anyone planning a war there.'

Marlowe smiled. 'I hope you're right.'

The question was certainly on everyone's mind. This was 1938, not 1914, yet the streets were beginning to take on an unpleasant resemblance to those last days before the outbreak of war. Looking at photographs of the crowds watching and waiting in Downing Street, he thought they seemed remarkably silent, which was not usually the case at times of political crisis.

He looked down to see a crescent of grey roofs and walls drowsing in the sun. That must be Oban. North and east, the high hills of Lochaber wrapped in peace.

'Been to Skye before?'

'I used to go a lot.' Marlowe turned his head to the window. Out in the Firth the thin, green fingers of Lismore quivered in the sun. 'Before the war,' he added distantly. It might have been in another world.

'Never been back?'

'Well, yes,' he said, hesitantly. 'I did go back again. Some years afterwards.' —

Though changed, he thought, *from what I was when first I came among these hills.* How did it go on? *More like a man flying from something that he dreads.* Yes, that was the year of the war memorials then springing up throughout the land. 'The glorious dead'. Only there was nothing 'glorious' about the dead. And there was nothing 'glorious' either about those words, of which 'love' was the most betrayed, which he'd heard so often, and seen set down in stone, lapidary inscriptions with which it was not possible to tell the truth.

A Greek scholar, he'd taken a copy of *The Odyssey* to war with him. In the trenches, as he'd turned the well-thumbed pages, he'd often reflected on the hero's long home-coming. There was something archetypal about a man's forlorn yearning for home; to escape at last the realm of the monstrous, to restore to himself the joy and treasure of familiar things. But what if a man brought it back with him, the monstrous, haunting his days, breaking into his sleep. No, better a wilderness as far from cultivated men and women, and the society that shaped them, as he could get.

So it was, after the war, that he'd come to this mountain fastness on the edge of the Atlantic to find out if he still had ground to stand on. It was either that, or go under. And yet the wilderness, as he'd discovered, had its demons too. At first he'd been overcome by paroxysms of weeping. Sometimes it seemed as if he'd come for no other purpose than to weep. Among the mountains a man might howl out loud his cry of desolation. Howl it to the sky. Once, in thickening mist, seeking the south-east ridge of Sgùrr nan Gillean, he'd gone astray, blundering blindly up wet, blocky scree. There, up against a streaming wall, he'd sat down and wept, his screwed-up eyes bubbling a grief that welled up endlessly.

But the great peaks refused to show themselves. In the hills was a darkness in which his spirit suffered its conviction of deserved expulsion from the place of fullness. Alone in the vastness of Coire na Creiche, with the rain hammering down, he found himself defenceless, wholly exposed to the void which regular contact with the routine of daily life had somehow kept at bay. At the foot of Sgùrr an Fheadain he'd sought shelter in the Waterpipe Gully, a variation of which he'd climbed with Millie's brother so many years before. There, peering up at the great cleft, he sought to revive memories of that time of fullness, only to discover he had lost all sense even of what fullness might consist. He'd feared it would be so. Only by not coming back had he, in some tortured way, maintained a tenuous contact with remembered fullness. All he'd found now, amid the drip of water, was accusing silence. And the misery of loss.

'Nearly there now,' informed his neighbour helpfully. 'There's Rum.'

'I thought it might be.' Marlowe gazed down on the green, lovely island afloat on a shimmering sea.

'Rhum can sometimes be tricky for turbulence. Plane once dropped like a stone. Man sitting next to me shot up to the ceiling. I had to reach up to pull him down. No danger of that today.'

There were deer running far below on a green slope of Askival, their shadows slipping ahead of them. Marlowe's heart leapt at the sight.

But within seconds the brightness which had filled the cabin was extinguished, the scintillations of Loch Scavaig suddenly dulled, as the plane flew into shadow. Now, emerging from the swelling land across the loch, a dark, triangular peak came into view, overcast by the cloud which was even then spreading like a stain across a steep massif of sombre rock. The two men, looking down, saw what might have been a long, irregular parabola of splintered teeth set in an ancient and gigantic jaw.

'The Black Cuillin,' said the bulky man impressively. 'Savage, what?'

Marlowe's heart tightened, stirred by an uneasy *frisson* to which he couldn't give a name, unless it was the old excitement.

Only on dark wet days are they truly black. Or against a louring sky of dark storm clouds. Or in winter, with the naked rock showing through a thin skither of snow. Often a hazy blue in summer heat, they turn blood-red at sunset, sinking to a dusky terracotta as the sun dips down. Or at nightfall in autumn, seen against a northern light, an inky prussian blue. Black, though, is the name that has stuck, perhaps because of some forbidding character that tends to swallow up the kindlier colours.

Now, as the little plane began to dip down and round towards Loch Brittle, a succession of harsh peaks and lonely corries swung into view: Garsbheinn, an isolated summit rising above grey slopes of shattered rock... then lonely Coire nan Laogh... Sgùrr Dubh Mòr... then Coir' a' Ghrunnda, cupped in its high hollow...

'I expect you've been up most of those,' said Marlowe's neighbour cheerfully.

Marlowe smiled. No, he should not have agreed to this. He should not have come. Too late now.

A blustery wind got up, buffeting the Rapide as it flew in over the loch, driving white-topped breakers onto a narrow strand. But there was brightness down below, sliding over a patchwork of little fields, lighting on white-walled cottages scattered here and there, brightness on the River Brittle, meandering through its boggy pastures, on the purple hills west of the glen where the heather was in bloom.

The little plane flew on over Glenbrittle House, sheltered in its belt of trees, following the white, dusty track winding down the long, green glen, then banking steeply over the forest, circling round, losing height steadily as it made for the Big Meadow.

In the garden of the Lodge were small figures waving up at the plane. Millie, instantly recognizable in black, looking up and waving briefly from a deckchair. Millie, of course, had been against it from the start. *I will go, Stephen, because whatever you may say, I know you want to go. But I think the whole thing is ridiculous. The past is not recoverable.*

He knew she thought he was selfish and self-absorbed. God knows she had reason enough to feel that. Ah, he felt a pang then. He wondered sometimes how she'd coped all these years. He remembered coming upon her once unexpectedly in the little box-room at the top of the house. After the war she'd turned it into a workroom. And he'd come upon her there without warning. Quietly, her sewing lying idle in her lap, she was weeping. He knew then that she went up there to weep.

Now, as the ground rose up towards them, Marlowe swallowed hard, and closed his eyes. *Make no mistake, one lapse of concentration—especially on take-off or landing—and she will bite you...* Then the plane touched down, bumping along the meadow for a couple of hundred yards before stopping.

'There, not a bad landing,' said the business-man. 'I told you Barclay was top-notch.'

As Marlowe clambered stiffly from the fuselage he saw a tall figure in boots and breeches limping towards him over the meadow. A little way back two small boys, arms outstretched, performed complicated aerobatics as they zig-zagged after their father. Evidently a sea voyage had done nothing to dampen the spirits of the twins. Snatched from their preparatory school due to an untimely outbreak of measles they were still unable to believe their luck. *I suppose there's nothing else for it*, said Henry resignedly. *We shall have to take them with us.* Their delight had not been universally reflected by the family. *The little beasts are supposed to be in quarantine*, said their sister Miranda. *I don't want them coming anywhere near me.*

The other passengers had already disembarked. Two of them,

like the business-man, were going on to Barra. The other two would be returning to their homes on Skye, via the saloon car which its owner had left garaged at the farm. All now were stretching their legs or, like Marlowe, waiting for the cargo to be unloaded. First, though, came a batch of that day's newspapers.

'Well, good luck,' said the business-man, offering his hand. 'And good climbing.'

Marlowe smiled doubtfully. 'Let's hope so,' he said as they shook hands.

Meanwhile Henry had arrived, with the twins in tow.

'Knee troubling you again?'

'Oh, just a slight twist. Caught my boot, coming off the hill yesterday. It'll pass.'

He shouldered his father's rucksack, and together they set off across the meadow, leaving the twins to watch the plane take off.

'As you know, we have the Lodge to ourselves,' he said. 'Though Charles Bartrum might be arriving in a day or two.'

Marlowe raised an eyebrow.

'Well, the family is greatly indebted to Charles,' said Henry apologetically. Though it might have been intended as a mild rebuke.

'Leo isn't here yet, I'm afraid,' he went on. 'Pressing affairs of state, or something of the sort. But he hopes to come on later.'

Marlowe grunted.

'I hope you've brought your boots. Giles is determined to get you up something.'

'How very good of him,' murmured Marlowe dryly.

Henry sighed inwardly. Father maintained a space around him it was sometimes difficult to cross. A distant warmth, at most, was all one could expect.

'Well, you should be able to manage Collie's route on the Cioch,' he said cheerfully. 'I was hoping we might do it together.'

His father, though, made no reply.

Henry sighed again. *How is it you manage to get through to your grandfather?* he'd once asked his son. *Oh, I just climb over the wall*, said Giles cheerfully, and grinned. *He's not a bad old stick.*

In the glen they still walked in sunlight, but up above the moorland Coire Lagan was filling with cloud. Of the great precipice of Sròn na Ciche only the Western Buttress was still visible.

Down on the strand, beyond a line of scrawny trees battered by Atlantic winds, a young man was picking up stones, tossing them into the breakers. Eventually he sank on to a boulder and sat motionless, a solitary figure, staring out to sea. An image, it seemed to Marlowe, of utter dereliction.

'He seems to have the weight of the world on his shoulders.'

Henry sighed. 'He is as you see him, father. Susannah was hoping a few months at home would see a change in him. But it wasn't to be. And it's breaking her heart.'

Marlowe shook his head. He was filled with anxiety for his grandson. Millie had been dead set against inviting him. But of course Susannah wouldn't have come without Richard. He'd had to put his foot down about that. *Susannah is my only daughter, and I want her there.*

'I expect you've heard the news,' his son went on. 'The BBC are reporting that if need be the Czechs will go it alone. It's very worrying. '

Marlowe thought of Chamberlain waving his hat—of Herr Hitler's outstretched hand. What if Richard perceived the present more acutely than any of us? Suffered it, one might almost say.

Here, though, the soft air held a faint scent of second hay. MacRath's men were taking another mowing from the small meadow; beyond, the peaceful farmhouse in its belt of trees, proof against Atlantic storms.

'Haven't we come here,' he said shortly, 'to get away from all that.'

— CHAPTER TWO —

From time out of mind the MacAskills of Rubh' an Dunain had farmed land in Glen Brittle as tacksmen of the MacLeod of Dunvegan. From their ancestral home out on the point beyond the glen they'd kept watch on the coast, finding safe anchorage for their galleys in the channel carved from little Loch na h Airde to the sea. In those days the farm east of the river was known as Leasol. When, towards the end of the seventeenth century, the tack of MacAskill of Rhubh' was merged with that of his kinsman and neighbour at Leasol the entire holding became known as 'Rhundunan'. Some years later the lease was extended to take in much of Glen Brittle and the Cuillin forest as far north as the Red Burn. There for two hundred years the MacAskills reared their black cattle, their goats and horses, and manufactured kelp from seaweed collected from the shores of Scavaig and Soay.

When Donald, last of the Rhubh' MacAskills, gave up the tack, it was taken on by his kinsman Hugh. Hugh it was who brought stone quarried on Soay, and built the cottages to one side of the farmhouse to accommodate the many relatives and servants who made up his household. A road of sorts was made into the glen. Not long afterwards, as the royal passion for stalking deer took hold among the English, a Georgian-style shooting lodge of pink ashlar was built on to the rear of the farmhouse. When Hugh died, the last link to the MacAskills broken, the tack passed to an outsider and 'Rhundunan' became known as Glenbrittle House.

As the years passed it was not for the stalking of deer that Glen Brittle became celebrated. Rented season after season by Professor Collie, the Lodge became a home from home for the mountaineers who came in increasing numbers to climb in the Cuillin. For Collie was a generous host and held open house for his friends. Marlowe himself had been one of those who, in the years before the war, had found a bed on the floor of what was then the smoking room. And when Gideon MacRath took over the lease of the farm, and opened the Lodge as a boarding house, the Marlowes, father and sons, had been among the first of his guests. And now the Marlowes had themselves taken the Lodge for their family celebration.

On that September day in 1938, nowhere could have seemed further from the threat of war. The sudden, swelling note of the little Rapide, taxi-ing towards its take-off, achieved no more than a momentary disturbance of the tranquillity which, as the engine drone faded westward, settled again over the wooded garden at Glenbrittle Lodge. It looked out across the moor towards the long green shoulder of Sgùrr Dearg and the peaks beyond. Early risers in the eastern bedrooms would contemplate the high, black, fretted outline of the Cuillin, enigmatic against the dawn light, and wonder what the day might bring. At dusk, striding down the long green slope, they would see in the lights of the Lodge windows the promise of a hospitable welcome; a hot bath for tired limbs, dry clothes, and food for hungry bodies.

It was late in the season. Already the larches bordering the Banachdich burn were turning gold. The burn itself, a pretty sight in spring and summer, ran along the northern edge of the garden. Later, when the first winter storms came howling out of Coire na Banachdich, the inhabitants of Glenbrittle House would hear it roaring over the rim of Eas Mor and into the cauldron eighty feet below, and roaring through the channel above the sheep pens, tumbling the boulders in its rocky bed. Such storms were always a cause of anxiety for dwellers in the glen. Memory still told of the catastrophe less than a century before, a torrent of water rushing over the rim of the cauldron, pouring in one broad sheet of foam down the steep rise above the house. The inhabitants barely had time to open the door and fly for their lives before the deluge was upon them, smashing through the building, filling the lower rooms up to the ceilings. Garden, trees, cultivated fields were swept away, covered with a debris of silt and stones more than a foot deep.

That morning, though, the burn ran peaceably enough in its shallow bed down past the garden on its passage to the River Brittle. The sun was still warm for the time of year, and the three women gathered in the garden might have been intent on making the most of it while it lasted. The youngest of them sat a little way apart from the other two. Sketching block propped in her lap, her tongue caught between her teeth, Miranda Marlowe was attempting to reproduce the play of light and shadow on the forms of things up in the corrie.

Miranda's attendance at the School of Painting and Drawing had not been entirely without misgivings on her mother's part when she got to hear of the kind of people who inhabited the studios in and around Fitzroy Street. Certainly, they were a racy lot.

'Well, Virginia Woolf's niece is one of the pupils,' said Henry shrewdly, who knew his wife. 'Isn't that so, Miranda?'

'Angelica? Oh yes. She's awfully nice.'

It went some way to reassuring the mother.

In the short time since her arrival the young woman had been overwhelmed by her surroundings. Here were none of the rounded summits of the mainland she had travelled through, but real mountains of naked rock rising out of the Atlantic. Here she felt freed at last from the dreary warehouses and railway stations, drab streets and sunless back alleys that so obsessed her teachers at the School of Painting and Drawing. 'Squalorscapes,' she called them, painted with such a miserly dole of pigment they seemed barely scraped on to the canvas. A dutiful pupil, she duly scraped away herself. Sometimes, though, she longed for colour, for thick impasto, for bold strokes with loaded brushes. Now, filled with excitement, she drank in all she saw: the spaciousness, the constant play of sun and shadow, the warm earth-reds and ochres, the olive greens and *terre verte* of moorland, the cool grey-blues and greens of the sea, and all of it her own newly discovered continent that seemed to cry aloud to her, *Look! Look!*. And then the sky, for it was boundless; miles and miles and miles of it. It needed a Turner to do justice to it all.

Miranda's mother lounged in a deckchair under the larches, glancing negligently at the magazine lying open in her lap. Her round, rather complacent face had lost its youthful outline, and was already falling into middle age. Long corn-coloured hair—fading now—she wore caught up in twists and coils, and pinned behind her head. Vanessa Marlowe had chosen to appear that morning in a white, flowered dress, a repudiation, it might have been, of the tattered coats, the heavy sweaters and ragged cord breeches favoured by the men of the party. Though resigned now to making the best of a bad job, the truth was she'd never wanted to come to Skye. It was thoroughly irresponsible, she'd protested, to go on holiday at such a time. Well, for one thing, explained her husband, they couldn't let down Mrs MacRath, who was expecting them. Besides, he added obscurely, a time of crisis was precisely when one should elevate the gods of hearth and home. *'But we won't be at home.'* Really, Henry could be so obtuse when it suited him.

'And in September,' she said again. 'Why *September*, for Heaven's sake?' The small, rather prim mouth above the small, plump chin, wore an expression of weary disapproval.

'Believe me,' said her mother-in-law, 'September is infinitely preferable to July or August when the midges are at their worst.'

Millie Marlowe lay back in her deckchair, eyes closed, her face raised to the sun.

'You married into a family of mountaineers,' she went on. 'I did warn you at the time. I do believe Henry's father only courted me so that he could the more readily go climbing with my brother.'

'That's as maybe,' declared the younger woman. 'As you know, I've always believed Henry's mountaineering to be a foolhardy pastime.'

The truth was the Cuillin frightened her. She thought them cruel, oppressive.

'Besides, what might be excusable as a youthful recreation is scarcely suitable for an Archdeacon of the Church of England.'

'The present Pope, I would remind you, was a keen mountaineer,' retorted her mother-in-law, who might have been playing a trump card.

'The Pope is a Roman Catholic,' replied her daughter-in-law firmly, 'and, of course, they do things differently.'

Millie Marlowe's lips tightened a shade. She had herself converted to the Church of Rome twenty years before.

She was clad as usual in black. Miranda would have it that since the news of her uncle Robert's death in the first months of the war her grandmother had worn nothing but black. Raven hair—dyed, according to her daughter-in-law—and large sombre eyes invariably ringed with *kohl* completed the suggestion of a face somehow suited to tragedy. *I don't believe I've ever seen grand-mama smile,* young Giles once remarked to his sister. *Do you suppose she always looked like that?* It was an arresting thought. Certainly, it was a face the passing years had pared to the bone. Once thought beautiful, in old age it suggested an uncompromising strength of character none who knew her would have denied. A mouth, full-lipped once, shrunken now, seemed to reflect what might have been scorn, or stoic indifference.

At that moment a dark-haired girl came out from the Lodge bearing a tray laden with cups and coffee pots. She set it down on a wicker table, smiling shyly at the guests as she did so.

'Thank you, Morag,' said Vanessa.

She rose to see to the coffee. At the same moment two small boys came racing round the side of the Lodge.

'He's here... he's here... ' they shouted, jumping up and down.

'Captain Barclay let us sit in the pilot's seat,' burst out Hugh, the taller of the two.

'I hope you didn't touch anything,' said his mother anxiously.

'Where's Giles?' asked Marlowe. 'Has he gone off with his friend?'

'With Nicko? Yes.' Henry sank down in a wicker chair, stretching out his gammy leg. 'Young MacRath gave them a lift to Sligachan. Apparently he drives up and down the glen several times a week. He'll pick them up from the road on his way back, if they're lucky. Otherwise they'll have a long walk.'

'Well,' Marlowe went on, gazing round at his family. 'How are we all? I'm glad to see you survived your sea trip.'

'Hugh was awfully ill,' said one of the twins gleefully.

'So were you.'

'Not as bad as you.'

'Well, almost everyone was ill,' said their mother pulling a face, it might have been at the lurch of enormous seas.

Marlowe suppressed a smile. No, he couldn't imagine his daughter-in-law taking the Atlantic in her stride.

'It was four hours of sheer hell,' Vanessa went on, passing round cups of coffee. 'I have never been so frightened in my life. And all the while Henry was distributing ham sandwiches, and giving us a guided tour. Look at this… look at that… '

Her husband, who was a good sailor, smiled apologetically.

'Then, to cap it all, Andrew fell in the loch.'

'Well, I thought it was wonderful,' said the young woman, holding her sketching block at arms' length, examining it critically. She was a headstrong girl.

'Oh Miranda,' said her mother. 'You were greener than the sea.'

'Perhaps I was. But it was still wonderful,' she insisted, looking up. She'd always longed to climb snow-capped peaks and icy glaciers like her grandfather, to outface storms and lightning, and brave the perils of mountainous seas. 'You were all too sick to notice,' she added scornfully.

Marlowe looked fondly at his grand-daughter. She had her mother's corn-coloured hair, only warmer, richer. When lit by the sun, as it was now, it seemed all a-flame.

'How did you find it, Millie?' he asked, turning to his wife.

'Well, it was perhaps a little too bumpy to be entirely comfortable. But certainly nothing to make a fuss about.' She proffered a cheek for him to kiss. 'I understand Henry has devised more adventures for us,' she went on. 'But what terrors they might hold, we know not. We're all agog, aren't we, Vanessa?'

Vanessa sipped her coffee, reflecting that her mother-in-law's waspishness was no more than she expected.

At that moment a young man appeared around the side of the Lodge. His face, deeply burnt by suns decidedly not of home, wore a strained, haunted look. Richard Fleming looked far older than his years.

'Have the papers arrived?' he asked.

Later that afternoon Marlowe set off across the moor towards the long, green shoulder of Sgùrr Dearg. He'd declined his son's offer of company.

'No, no. I'll be all right. I shan't go far. Besides, you'd do better to rest your knee.'

It was a long time since he'd come face to face with the Cuillin, and he wanted the encounter to take place in private. He was none too sure what ghosts might rise to pluck at his sleeve. Besides, Henry would want to talk, and he needed silence. He wanted to listen to his thoughts. What he heard though, amid the crunch and clatter of scree, was only his own harsh breathing as, checking, sliding, he tried without success to strike a rhythm. How long since he'd done this kind of thing? Too long.

A basalt dyke made for easier going up the first steep rise. Beyond that, a vast expanse of stones led him gently up to a turreted rampart set high astride the ridge from side to side. Any hopes of a view looking south had seemed likely to be dashed by the cloud swirling fretfully over the black cauldron of Coire Lagan. But he'd been forgetting the fitful mood of these mountains, for the cloud now seemed to be lifting. In moments, as the mist swept upwards, a subdued radiance, filtering through the corrie, shed on the great buttresses of Sròn na Ciche a soft, silvery-grey lustre, as if the rock was lit from within.

He gazed at the thin grey trod of the Sgumain Stone Shoot, a ribbon of scree and boulders toiling up from the corrie. He picked out the Terrace, rising out of the Stone Shoot and climbing diagonally across the Central Buttress to the stony plateau which formed the summit of Sròn na Ciche. Harsh, inhospitable, its naked rock forbidding even in the kindliest light, the very antithesis, it seemed, of all that was human. Yet there had been a time, before

—24—

the war, when this was holy ground. That was what Robert used to call it. The Holy Ground. A ribald joke, really, since it was the ironic name for an area of dockside bars and brothels in what used to be known as Queenstown. *'And still I live in hope to see the Holy Ground once more,'* Robert used to sing. An image of the longed-for place. Each visit, for sea-farers and climbers alike, a home-coming. And afterwards, the long journey south to the tedium of one's humdrum self.

He tried to pick out the line of *Marlowe's Variation,* his own climb up to the Terrace so many years before, remembering the joy of that day. Oh, and the fear too. Up to that point, all he'd encountered in the mountains had seemed to him the gift of a benevolent Nature. For to climb then was to experience the innocence and freshness of the early world. But he'd been badly frightened up on that wall. The severe shaking he'd received that day had woken him from his slumbers. It brought home to him, as nothing short of a war had ever done, the radical insecurity of his own existence.

He turned to look north, across Coire na Banachdich. Somewhere up there in the mist, where the ridge began to swing north-east, beyond the three teeth of Thormaid, was the scimitar sweep of Sgùrr a' Ghreadaidh. That was the place where he'd learned to accept the gift of life again, since he could not let go what his fingers held in their grasp. And maybe it was enough to live in the body, and trust the witness of the heart.

Yet in those first visits after the war he had driven himself relentlessly, climbing alone, indifferent to the danger, not much caring whether he lived or died. He had no right, anyway, to be alive. Once, traversing the razor-edge of Ghreadaidh, gazing into Coruisk 2000 feet below, he'd felt an urge to leap down into clean air. Yes, *'like swimmers into cleanness leaping...'* Never before had he been tempted to such a thing in the mountains. And it frightened him. He was, he knew, teetering along a brink. Sometimes, in his distress, he would mutter 'Hold on... hold on... ' feeling the gabbro biting into his finger-tips, as if to reassure that the rough rock would not let him go.

—25—

One night, sitting at Sligachan, gazing at the darkened hills, he knew the grief had finally dissolved. Here there were no guns, no bugles, no tramp of marching men, nothing on which to hang a flag. Only sea and rock, and those abrasive truths which could be grasped in the hand. He had become that simple thing again, a man of flesh and bones.

Sitting there absorbed, with Sròn na Ciche glowing like a furnace as the westering sun slipped behind the heather hills, he'd lost all track of time. At length, as the glow slowly faded, he rose to begin his descent, turning for a last look at the ridge. The cloud, breaking as it often did late in the day, seemed to be in slow retreat towards the north, a long, single file of cumulus dragging over Ghreadaidh, and the tops of Mhadaidh. To the south and west, where isolated stragglers were sinking down, Rhum and Canna might have been floating on a sea of vapour under bars of golden light.

He thought of the preparations for war he'd left behind in London. Was it true, he wondered? Had Chamberlain already offered the surrender of the Sudetenland? Hardly surprising the Czechs wouldn't agree to that. If, as Henry claimed, they were prepared to go it alone against Hitler, would Britain and France really stand by and see them overwhelmed?

A twilight hush lay over the glen. A quiet land at peace with itself, it seemed to him a place inaccessible to evil. He thought of the kindly folk who lived there: Mary Campbell, the white walls of her cottage showing dimly through the trees by the sea-shore, Mrs Chisholm at the post office across the river, no more now than a pale ribbon of light. What had they to do with Czechoslovakia? The thought of men and women subject to the operations of a crisis which they were powerless to avert filled him with anxiety for his family. How foolish to think they could leave all that behind them, like those Florentine notables, telling stories in the hills of the Campania as they sat out the plague. This was a plague no one could run away from. He thought of poor Vanessa's terror at the very thought of war. Her fears were for her children.

What might suffice, he wondered. In a corrupted world in which evil was rampant, what might suffice? In Richard's book nothing short of smashing the Fascists would do any good. For Henry the solution lay in sensible negotiation. Dear, decent Henry, all for peace and disarmament. No man expressed better the confused emotions of the times. For Millie only Rome, whose truths she saw as absolute, final, offered a bulwark against the gates of hell. *Civitas Christiana.* Yet it was that same civilisation which had sowed the seeds for a wasted world.

He came down the last green slope in ever-deepening twilight, the windows of the Lodge showing brightly, pinpoints of light in the darkened glen. As he climbed over the stile into the garden he saw a figure by the dog-kennels.

'Susannah?'

'I was looking out for you.'

'You worry too much about me,' he said dryly.

'I don't want to lose you,' she said, putting her arm through his as they set off across the garden. She'd spoken in all seriousness. He knew it. He gave her arm a squeeze

'How's Richard?'

She hesitated. 'He's up and down. Some days good, some not so good. At first, when he came home, I really feared for his state of mind.'

'Spain?'

She sighed. 'It's as if he never left,' she said, as they made their way round to the porch. 'I had hoped, if he came to Skye, we could get him climbing again. It might take his mind off things.'

As they reached the porch, they heard voices.

'That'll be Giles,' said Susannah. She stood waiting while Marlowe took off his boots. Leaving them in the porch they went together into the hall.

Standing by the hall table was a well-knit youth whose dishevelled mop of corn-coloured hair, paler than his tan, declared his kinship with Vanessa. Though the wide, dark eyes—an unexpected shock in so fair a face—proclaimed the grandmother. A shade taller than his companion, he seemed to flash with strength and vigour.

'Well, what did you do?'

'The Pinnacle Ridge, of course,' said Giles excitedly. He was clearly still full of it. 'We climbed up a rib on the north-west side to get to the top of the first pinnacle. There were some awkward wet patches, but Nicko did awfully well. Oh—this is Nicko, by the way. Nicko Frost. He's reading Classics.'

Marlowe smiled, shook hands with a slim, dark young man.

'How did you find it?' He was thinking it must have seemed a hostile place to a novice. Parts of the ridge were quite exposed. Not a place for the nervous.

'I quite enjoyed it, in a dry-mouthed sort of way.'

Giles was generous in his praise for the beginner.

'Nicko's never climbed before, you know. He did awfully well.'

There was no doubting his sincerity. Running through Giles was a core of artlessness no one could mistake for anything less than truth.

'The view from the summit was tremendous. We could see Blaven, and Loch Scavaig, and all the wild country in between. And the Hebrides, across the Minch. Portree gleaming miles away to the north. And so many peaks. Oh, wonderful… wonderful! You must tell me what they are. We must go over it together on the map.'

He still had something of the spontaneity, the uncorrupted wonder of the child. The world for him had not yet lost its strangeness.

'You came down the west ridge?'

'That's right. It's terribly shattered. You can actually see right through it, you know. *Really*! There are *holes* in it. As for the *gendarme*—it's like the tooth of some fearsome dinosaur completely blocking the way. Horrendous drops on every side. It's really quite alarming.'

'I didn't look,' confessed Nicko. 'I simply closed my eyes, put my arms around the thing, and sort of shuffled round it.'

'Gosh, but I'm tired, though,' he added, yawning.

The old man smiled. He recognised that note of deep content at the day's end when one had spent all of oneself, when one felt subdued to the earth, at peace with it, and ready for rest.

'You should sleep well tonight,' he said.

heer overflow of delight caused Giles to repeat his account of the day's events to the rest of the family gathered in the drawing room. Again he was especially warm in his praise of Nicko, who stood shyly before slipping away to change.

'That young man evidently adores you,' said Millie dryly.

'Grandmother!' Giles looked shocked.

'Oh, you know he does, Giles,' said Miranda maliciously. 'He'd do anything for you.'

'Poor Nicko only goes climbing in the hope of impressing Giles,' she went on, turning to her grandfather. 'It's what young men do,' she added sweetly

---

For dinner there were sea-trout fresh from the river. Morag carried them in on a great dish decked with parsley.

'Mr MacRath caught them himself,' she said shyly.

'Apparently they'd been trapped for days in a deep pool further up the glen,' said Henry. 'With the river as low as it is the poor creatures stood no chance of escape.'

He slid his knife deftly along the flank of his fish, exposing the bony spine, prising it away from the flesh.

It was not a dish to everyone's satisfaction. Andrew, who detested fish, began poking at it gloomily.

'Nothing from Godesberg,' continued Henry.

It was a statement, rather than a question. There had been no report on the Second News at seven-thirty.

'As I understand it, those areas having a majority of Sudetens are to be turned over to Germany,' said Vanessa, who'd been looking at the *Daily Mail* brought on the plane that morning.

'Not Sudetens, dear,' admonished her husband mildly. 'The Sudetens are a range of mountains.'

'Andrew!' a sharp voice interjected. 'You really are making the most extraordinary dog's breakfast of that fish. Give it to me.'

Shamefacedly, Andrew passed his plate to his grandmother. The old lady set about picking what bones she could from the mangled carcase, collecting them on the side of the plate.

'The Sudeten *Germans*,' Henry continued, 'like other nationalities, have a right to self-determination.'

'What if the Czechs refuse?'

'Then the Czechs will have to be made to see reason.'

'*Made*? Did you say '*made*'?'

'Deeply unpleasant though they may be to our way of thinking, Richard,' Henry went on, 'I believe Hitler and Mussolini are rational men. Or, at any rate, they must be treated as such. I believe their grievances can be settled by rational discussion and the rule of law. After all, what is the alternative?'

The Archdeacon's principal weapon was his sharp rationalism. He used it to fend off all opposition.

'Hitler should be hit on the head,' said his mother firmly, picking away at the bones.

'Perhaps the French should have stopped him when he marched into the Rhineland,' suggested Nicko, thinking he should contribute something.

'You're assuming the French army was capable of offensive action,' said Marlowe, pouring himself a glass of water. As usual, the old man did little more than push around the food on his plate. With a digestive system permanently damaged as a result of the war, he'd been advised by his doctor to eat small quantities at frequent intervals, and to have little or nothing after four o'clock in the afternoon.

'There,' said Millie, returning her grandson's plate. 'Now eat it properly.'

'Well,' sighed Vanessa, 'there's nothing we or the French can do to stop Hitler if he chooses to march into Czechoslovakia. Not without threatening to go to war with Germany. And who would want that?'

'What's for pudding,' asked Andrew plaintively. 'Clooty dumpling,' whispered his Aunt Susannah, who'd been in the kitchen. 'You'll like it. It's like Christmas pudding.'

'Andrew can't have any, can he, unless he cleans his plate,' put in Hugh, who was washing down his own trout with frequent gulps of water.

'The Versailles Treaty was an appalling mistake,' said Henry, helping himself to more potatoes. 'Keynes said so at the time, and he was right. It was punitive and it was unjust. And now it has to be rectified. I'm pleased to see that for once Britain has taken the initiative.'

Richard shook his head. His face wore a look more eloquent than any words.

'Say what you like, Richard,' said Vanessa mildly, 'surely it's more sensible than war?'

'You think so, do you? You think Hitler will settle for that?'

In the uncomfortable silence that followed, the scathing question seemed to hang menacingly over the table. It seem to suggest a possibility none of them wished to contemplate.

'I simply can't believe,' exclaimed Vanessa suddenly, with forced gaiety, 'that mankind is shortly to commit suicide over the troubled affairs of Czechoslovakia.'

'*TRUST CHAMBERLAIN*' she'd read in the *Mail* that morning. In a bid to give weight to that advice the paper had published an extraordinary photograph to accompany its 'day-in-the-life' piece on the PM. There, as if peering at her through the slit of a letter box, were the eyes—just the eyes—of the Prime Minister which, it was claimed, showed '*fierce concentration on one subject to the exclusion of all others*'.

'I'm sure the Sudeten German crisis of 1938 will mean as little to our descendants as... as... ' Vanessa floundered to a halt.

'I don't suppose,' said Marlowe, seeking to change the subject, 'anyone read the report of Strutt's address to the Alpine Club?'

It was a clumsy manoeuvre, but one in which his son was happy to join forces.

'Yes, I did,' said Henry, setting a foot firmly on the safer shores of mountaineering. 'He didn't seem to think much of those goings-on on the Eiger. *An obsession for the mentally deranged*, I think were his actual words.'

'Then Strutt, whoever he is,' exclaimed Giles hotly, 'is an ass.'

'Who *is* Strutt?' asked Miranda.

'He is, or rather *was*, the editor of the *Alpine Journal*.'

'How many lives have been lost so far on the Eiger?' Millie turned towards her husband.

'Eight.'

'Then perhaps Colonel Strutt has a point.'

Marlowe hesitated. Profoundly affected by the slaughter on the Western Front, the old man feared that this post-war generation who came to throw themselves at the Eiger Nordwand remained in thrall to the same inadequate mysticism of heroism and suffering, the same preparedness to sacrifice themselves and others.

'German alpinism has a different tradition from ours,' he said at last. 'For us mountaineering has always been a reasonable activity, and isn't perhaps justified when it ceases to be so.'

Giles leant forward, aflame with eagerness.

'Of course people sometimes get killed in the Alps. But they did in your day too, grandfather. And they always will. It's what happens. We can't be satisfied repeating your climbs. We have to set our own standards. You mustn't try to hold us back.'

'Perhaps you're right,' the old man smiled.

'I read somewhere,' remarked Vanessa, 'that they were simply obeying an order from on high.'

'No doubt they were expecting to get a medal,' said Millie dryly.

'Oh, for heaven's sake!' protested Giles. 'Why can't it just be what it was? Wonderfully brave. A wonderful triumph of courage and determination.'

'If you'd been on the receiving end of Fascist courage and determination,' said Richard quietly, 'you wouldn't be quite so loud in their praise. '

'Oh, that's unfair. '

'I don't believe for a moment,' said the Archdeacon in his quiet, firm way, 'that those young men were seeking to present themselves as Nazi heroes. They were simply attempting to restore national pride after defeat in war, and the humiliation of the peace settlement.'

He looked round the table meaningfully.

'And we bear some responsibility for that,' he added mildly.

'And was that what they were doing when they flattened Guernica?' muttered Richard, his fingers working nervously at his napkin. 'Restoring national pride?'

'There are those,' said his grandmother, very decidedly, 'who think that the most likely culprits were actually the Basques' own shady friends in Catalonia.'

Marlowe sighed, reflecting that Millie could be relied upon to add fuel to any fire she came across.

'They *were* German planes, mother,' said Henry soberly. 'Heinkels and Junkers. *The Times* published an eyewitness account.'

'Perhaps they were Government planes got up to look like Heinkels,' said Richard, with withering sarcasm. 'Is that what it said in *The Tablet*, grandmother? I wouldn't put anything past Woodruffe and his Fascist chums.'

'I think you're a very disturbed young man, Richard.'

'Yes, I'm disturbed,' he cried, getting to his feet. 'It disturbs me that you're *not* disturbed… '

'Oh but I am, Richard. I'll tell you what disturbs me. Nuns violated. Priests nailed to beams of wood, their eyes gouged out. Shall I go on?'

Flinging down the napkin her grandson stumbled from the table and blundered over to the window. Henry, who'd been raising his fork to his mouth, lowered it to his plate. Susannah cast an imploring look at her mother who continued, imperturbably, to eat her dinner. Miranda sat motionless, her eyes cast down. The twins, too appalled to snigger, glanced furtively at one another, while Giles and Nicko, their eyes fixed uncomfortably on their plates, might have been wishing themselves anywhere but where they found themselves.

Then, in the fraught silence, came the sound of a voice crooning softly:

'There's a valley in Spain called Jarama,
It's a place that we all know too well...'

Suddenly, the singer swung round to face his family.

'But of course, you *don't* know, do you, grandmother? None of you know.'

With that he strode from the room, slamming the door behind him.

'Why must you be so beastly to him, mother?' Susannah burst out. 'He does nothing to hurt you.'

Eyes filling with tears, she got up from her chair, and hurried after her son.

— CHAPTER THREE —

If the Marlowes were, for the most part, solidly Conservative it was perhaps less from political conviction than from a sense of what was fitting for people like themselves. They belonged to that comfortable class flourishing within a social order which was Anglican, monarchist, and thoroughly law-abiding. They looked to the police for the protection of their property, and to Oxbridge for the education of their children. Of course, like any other family, they had their black sheep. Millie had defected to the Church of Rome, while Henry had declared himself a Christian Socialist. Yet in all other respects even they conformed to the *mores* of their class. They read the weeklies. They went to the theatre. They attended concerts at the Queen's Hall, and always visited the Summer Exhibition at the Royal Academy. They were prosperous. They were cultivated. Above all, they were English. They viewed the rise of Hitler with distaste, and his occupation of the Rhineland had alarmed them. But the Great War had shaken them as it had shaken many other families. No sensible man wanted war. Like most of their countrymen they were firmly opposed to anything that might embroil the country in another European conflict. Events in Spain, a country, as it seemed, on the brink of falling into the hands of the Bolsheviks, only intensified the instinct to keep clear of Europe. And when at last a civil war broke out the Marlowes, in common with many families of their class and background, shook their heads while reflecting, with the complacency of a nation several hundred years removed from a like calamity, that it was only to be expected of a country which had for decades been sliding into anarchy. Neither side had anything remotely in common with what they regarded as proper to a civilised country. Even so, it was not their business. Even Henry, despite his sympathy for the Republican cause, fully supported the Labour Party's endorsement of the policy of non-intervention.

Throughout that autumn, as the war in Spain grew increasingly savage, they were appalled by the atrocities reported in the Press: men crucified, men flung from balconies, men flung over cliffs, flung into corrals of fighting bulls, men drenched with petrol, flaring like torches, corpses castrated, the sick shot in hospital beds, hundreds turned out in a bull-ring to face the machine-guns, blood ankle-deep in the streets…

'Well, what do you expect?' said Leo Marlowe. 'It's a mistake to think of Spain as a modern European country. It isn't. It's still the Middle Ages over there.'

Then, with Franco's army on the outskirts of Madrid, came news of the first British volunteers going into action. They'd suffered heavy casualties. Cambridge men, it was reported, among them.

Then Richard dropped his bombshell.

'I'm going to Spain.'

He'd been intended for the law. It was all but settled that he would go from Cambridge to Lincoln's Inn where he would eat his dinners as his father and grandfather had done before him. In due course a place would be found for him in chambers, where he would knuckle down to the routines and disciplines of the Bar. It would be a future which, to all intents and purposes, had largely been lived for him by generations of his predecessors.

So when he announced his intention of joining the International Brigade the response of his family was one of complete bewilderment.

'I'm pretty sure it's illegal,' said Henry cautiously, when he was told. Since the death of Susannah's husband he had done his best to keep a fatherly eye on his nephew.

'It *is* illegal,' said Leo. 'The Foreign Enlistment Act makes it unlawful to enlist in the armed forces of a foreign power.'

And the Government, he added, were very likely to enforce the Act.

Shortly after Christmas Richard left for Barcelona. It was, he told his mother, a matter of conscience. Either Fascism was stopped now, or there would be a great European war. Since Britain and France would do nothing, it was up to people like himself. He and his comrades. It was as simple as that. Nothing Susannah could say would deflect him from his purpose. He loved her, but he was firm. He must go to Spain.

All Miranda's sympathies were with her cousin. She had mild left-wing sympathies herself, and had painted banners for the Popular Front. And yet her heart was with her Aunt Susannah.

'She thinks he will be killed,' she confided to Giles. 'Oh, she hasn't said anything. But I know that's what she feels.'

Millie was appalled. Her grandson's politics were detestable enough. But that Richard could inflict this terrible anxiety upon his mother was utterly incomprehensible to her.

'And where did he learn all this?' she raged. 'He learnt it at Cambridge. A hell-hole of Bolsheviks and atheists.'

In his own eyes, though, Richard's decision was morally irreproachable. Swept along by the sheer generosity of his own response, he believed he had received a kind of absolution from the justice of the cause.

Henry suggested that there were perhaps other, better ways to support the Spanish people in their struggle. He had himself been collecting tins of milk and other foodstuffs for shipment to Barcelona, delivering them into a dustbin outside the Co-op opposite Campden Town tube station.

Susannah, though, sprang to her son's defence.

'I'm proud of him,' she said defiantly. 'At least he's doing what he believes in.'

Yet in truth she was terrified. For the losses on both sides were fearful.

He'd warned that letters were likely to be few and far between. And what letters Susannah did receive told very little, except to say that he was safe. It was very cold, though. Hard frosts every night, and of course they slept out of doors, with not much in the way of blankets. *'On the whole, things aren't too bad. Some of it's grim, of course, but the less said about that the better.'* Such reticence did nothing to ease her fears. Then, reading in a newspaper that a mother somewhere in the north of England had indentified her son on a newsreel of prisoners captured at Jarama, she became a constant attender at cinemas, waiting for the newsreel, hoping to catch sight of him.

Her father had little sympathy for Communism. It seemed to him the most sterile of human creeds. A void of abstract words. Yet for Richard it was the discovery of his life. *'I never dreamed,* he'd written to his mother within days of arriving in Barcelona, *that such fraternity was possible.* The old man thought of the volunteers immersed in that sea of tumult. They seemed to him like children. Excited children, for whom nothing else was real. Only their own great-heartedness. Only the reality possessing them.

Then, shortly after the battle of Jarama, Marlowe received a letter from his grandson. He was touched that Richard should want to write to him. At the same time he was troubled, for it was not a letter he could possibly have shown to Susannah. It was too alarming for a mother's eyes.

'I dare say you'll have heard what happened at Jarama. Those losses are not important, except that they hinder the struggle. It's what we must learn to put up with. In the British battalion there are gentlemen and there are soldiers. But the soldiers aren't gentlemen, and the gentlemen aren't soldiers. We've much to learn and little time to learn it. What we hadn't bargained for is the terror. No, we can cope with the losses, but whether or not we can cope with the terror none of us know. Being bombed and shelled is sheer hell... '

Yes, he'd been there too, long before Richard was born. He was struck then by a sense of helplessness, as if he'd somehow arrived ahead of his grandson at the wrong destination, the end-place where Richard had yet to arrive. He thought again of those flying banners, the clenched fists, the *Internationale* roaring up from lorry-loads of men. The culprit was the myth of human perfectibility, a delusion which answered the need to believe in something. To belong to something.

How little, he thought, we have given him. How little England has given him.

The war was extremely newsworthy. Once the rebellion had started there was a rush of correspondents to Spain. Many of the newspapers concerned were hardly friends of the Republic. *The Times*, having erroneously predicted the imminent fall of Madrid, and arguing on that basis that the British Government should recognise the Nationalists, now carried extensive accounts of the conflict.

Within weeks the papers were reporting that the long-expected counter-attack by Government forces had been launched on the village of Brunete, west of Madrid. After ten days of ferocious fighting, subjected to overwhelming air and artillery attack, they were gradually forced back. As was always the case after reports of a major action involving the International Brigade the anxiety of the families of volunteers was intense. So Susannah was overjoyed to hear in due course that Richard was safe and well. Yet knowing he was still alive, while it afforded a temporary relief, only served to prolong her torment.

As the months slipped by and the Government forces suffered further reverses Marlowe continued to hear intermittently from his grandson, dispatches that had the urgency of a voice calling across the wastes of war, laying claim to a kinship deeper than ideological difference. They were, the old man recognized, letters only a soldier could have written to another soldier.

'Our losses in this last affair have been heavy, our CO among them. He was the best of men. Bravest and best. Mortally wounded, we sang him out of life, just as he ordered us to do, and buried him that night by the Guadarrama river under the olive trees. The brigade commissar gave the funeral oration. Many of the men stood by with tears running down their cheeks...'

For a moment Marlowe closed his eyes, remembering the simple comradeship of war, and the fidelities it bred, and the pain of loss that undercuts all else. Random lines from a schoolboy poem sprang suddenly to mind: *'We buried him darkly at dead of night, the sods with our bayonets turning...'* That, too, was in Spain.

'To tell the truth, it's shaken me a bit. It's always the best blokes that seem to come off worst. We were ordered into some abandoned trenches, taking up position at precisely the worst time just before sunset. The Fascists' gunners had the range to a T, and fairly plastered us. Half a dozen killed around me in a matter of minutes. One of them a close friend. But it doesn't do to let your feelings show. You have to keep a tight rein. We had a nasty night of it before we got out. We couldn't even recover our casualties.

'I don't know how things will turn out, but I think we're in for a bad time. I know you'll look after mother. You will, won't you?'

Marlowe folded the letter, the desperation of that final plea a heavy weight on his mind. As he did so a further fragment of that old poem rose unprompted from the depths. *'We steadfastly gazed on the face that was dead, And we bitterly thought of the morrow.'*

Towards the end of the year came news of a fresh Government offensive, this time in the harsh, high hills of Aragón. It was launched in ferocious winter weather. For once the superior force of Franco's army counted for nothing. All his engines of war were frozen. His German bombers were locked in ice. His trucks and armoured cars couldn't move on the snow-filled roads. The worst winter, the correspondents wrote, in living memory. The mountain streams silenced. On both sides men slept, where sleep was possible, huddled together for protection against the cold. Some froze to death. Others, who drank to get warm, died in their sleep as the effects of alcohol wore off. The Republicans were forced to use dried oranges for kindling. The bitter tang of their fires wafted across the frozen fields.

For two months the battle raged around the walled city of Teruel. Fought out street by street, house by house, it was taken eventually by the Government forces, only to fall again to Franco. The losses on either side were enormous. And though Vanessa declared repeatedly that no news was good news no one really believed that.

With the fall of Teruel, the Aragón front collapsed. A hundred thousand Nationalist troops, backed by tanks and planes, began a massive advance towards Catalonia and the sea.

The Government army fled before them. Exhausted, short of arms and ammunition, demoralised by defeat, they were in full retreat. The newsreels showed vivid scenes of the rout. Roads choked with refugees fleeing the terror to come; a jumble of carts, donkeys, old men, weeping women, babes in arms; littering the roadside a pathetic flotsam of pots, pans, abandoned mattresses, crates of chickens, sticks of furniture. And overhead, the strafing Messerschmidts and Heinkels. The Fascists were in full cry.

Amidst all this, half out of her mind with anxiety, Susannah received a telegram. Steeling herself to face the worst, she tore it open.

'*Madame*,' she read. '*Your son is safe. He will be at frontier on 30th. Send your agent to Bar Cathar in the village of San Vicente. Ask for Primitivo. He will do what is necessary.*'

Susannah, perplexed, bewildered, her head in a whirl, consulted her brother.

'My agent? What does it mean? I have no agent.'

'I think that much is fairly clear. We are to send someone to meet Richard and bring him back.'

To his father Henry was more guarded.

'What do you make of it? Do you think it's genuine?'

'Whether it is or not, someone must go if only for Susannah's sake.'

The older members of the Marlowe family met to decide what should be done. They all agreed that someone should be sent. But who? Marlowe himself was too old. And Leo, as he was quick to point out, couldn't possibly embark on some cross-border smuggling expedition.

'Just think of the consequences were I to be arrested. It could be extremely awkward for the Government.'

'I'll go,' said Henry.

'Don't be ridiculous,' said his mother. It was a rebuff so self-evidently justified, no one sought to contradict her.

'Charles Bartrum might do it,' suggested Henry hesitantly, after some reflection. 'He knows the Pyrenees. He also speaks excellent French. Some Spanish too, I believe.'

'But he's completely irresponsible,' protested Vanessa.

'In some things, yes,' said Henry. 'Not in all.'

'He's nothing but an adventurer,' his wife persisted.

'Perhaps an adventurer is what is needed,' said Millie. She could be surprisingly tolerant of desperadoes.

So it was agreed that Bartrum should be approached.

It proved easier said than done. A tour of the usual haunts failed to bring him to light. Annie at the Fitzroy Tavern said to try the Duke of York.

'No, he's not been in,' said Alf, the landlord. 'I do know he was hoping to buttonhole Guy Burgess at the Beeb. Try the George.'

Henry finally ran him to ground in Bertorelli's. He was dining on a very basic plate of pasta. Evidently Charles was strapped for cash.

Yes, he'd fetch Richard, he said, forking up the last of the spaghetti. Though of course he'd need some funds for the journey.

It was agreed, after some discussion, that he should take the Lagonda, a more discreet way, Charles had argued, of transporting a man without papers back through France. Though anything less discreet than Bartrum's great scarlet motor-car was difficult to imagine. It remained a sore point with Vanessa.

'It's simply an excuse to go on a motoring jaunt. They'll have to load it on to the ferry with a crane. Think of the expense.'

In due course, handsomely provided for by the Archdeacon, the hired man prepared to set off for the channel ports.

Vanessa was appalled. 'There'll be drinks all round at the Fitzroy for a fortnight.'

'I don't believe that for one moment,' said Henry just as firmly.

Bartrum was as good as his word. In little more than a week Richard Fleming was restored to his mother.

Though pressed repeatedly Richard refused to speak about his time in Spain. Indeed, the whole affair had turned into something of a mystery. Nor could Bartrum be any more enlightening.

'I've no idea,' he said. 'He spoke scarcely a word all the way back. But if you ask me I should say he's had a pretty rough time.'

Not unnaturally this prompted speculation among his family. Since he'd been recovered from territory held by the Fascists they assumed that Richard, having perhaps escaped capture, had been sheltered by peasants. But, as Miranda pointed out, peasants don't send telegrams. She thought it all very romantic.

Only his mother realised how distressed he was. How close to breakdown.

It soon became evident that something was wrong with Richard. Though Millie, it was considered, had been unnecessarily brutal in her diagnosis.

'If Richard's going off his head,' she said, 'he's only himself to blame. '

If some of the family thought they saw in Richard's troubled state a sickness of the mind, it was as something exterior to them, peculiar to him. If questioned, he seldom answered. Or, if he did, it was with a monosyllable, turning away from contact.

Once, though, he did appear to attempt something approaching an explanation.

'I can't speak about it,' he said. Said it—and faltered, as if thwarted by some kind of breakdown, frowning, gesturing with a cramped motion of the hand as if constrained by the impossibility of saying anything.

His mother tried to reach him by involving him in simple household duties, tasks with which he would help readily enough. Sometimes, though, he seemed borne down by a burden that couldn't be cast off. And it was pressing him to death.

'What is it? What's wrong?'

At which he suffered one of his dislocutions, making odd little noises, gesturing, struggling for words, while she watched tensely, in a sweat of anguish.

'It's as if he never came home,' she said to her father. 'As if for him the war is still going on. Only it's going on in him.'

Or else she saw him teetering along an edge, poised at the brink of an abyss, fearing that a fraction more, a millimetre…

'Sometimes I'm not even sure he knows I'm there,' she confessed to Marlowe. 'Or even where he is. Or maybe who I am and where he is just don't matter any more.'

As if he had gone beyond her. Sometimes she feared he was lost to her altogether.

— CHAPTER FOUR —

For Marlowe the day began long before sunrise. A faint mist hung over the dewy grass of the garden. It was still several hours till dawn. For years after the war, night-horrors had robbed his sleep of most of its value. He still suffered intermittently from bouts of insomnia, and slept now apart from his wife. He sat, well wrapped in muffler and dressing gown, watching the fretted line of the Cuillin taking shape above the glen. The new moon, pale and clear, threw into sharp relief the black silhouette of Sròn na Ciche. A treasure trove, so it was said in ancient times, of all that was lost on earth: men's dreams, their wasted youth, their fruitless tears, their unfulfilled desires. Now, under its influence, the top-most flanks of Sgumain and Alasdair seemed to reflect a faint phosphorescence. Mountains of the moon, they might have been. Remote. Not of this world.

The unpleasant scene over dinner continued to resonate; Richard's harsh contempt, Millie's withering rejoinders—she could be so withering—raw and fresh in his mind.

Not for the first time he regretted that fierce Catholicism of hers. It was something to which she'd migrated after that irreversible eruption of evil, his 'war to end all wars'. A choice, she said, between Christianity and Chaos. She'd wanted a rock to stand on. A surer rock than he'd proved to be.

His translation of *The Odyssey*, still a work in progress, lay open on the table at his side. He'd brought it thinking he might tinker with it during the long sleepless hours. Softly he recited to himself the opening lines.

'Of that resourceful man, the wide world roaming,
War-weary after Troy's bitter, bloody sacking,
At length to his last, long-delayed home-coming,
I beg the Muse to aid me in my tale… '

Yes, he thought, home is the heart's true longing. A safe anchorage in the world. Whatever the history of it there was no doubting that the Trojan tragedy recorded a collective experience of disaster. What followed was an impoverished world. Troy… Mycenae… Pylos… One by one they went down the dark paths of decay; the frescoes, the carved ivories, the exquisite gold and silver—within a hundred years it had all gone. Vanished under dust. Illiterate shepherds lit their fires under the vaults of Atreus. A dark age fell on Greece. For ever, as it seemed. And what of the war now fermenting in Europe? He thought it likely Britain might have to go to war with Germany. His own war, shot through with horrors though it was, would be as nothing compared with what was to come. What will survive, he asked himself, amid the rubble of our own cities? What epic stories? What heroic deeds? What will survive of us?

The party were to set off in two groups after breakfast, Giles and Nicko to Coire na Banachdich, the rest of the family to Coire Lagan where they would all meet up again to lunch together beside the lochan. Susannah, not wishing to risk her son in further hostilities, had improvised her own expedition down to the Rubh'.

'There's a Neolithic burial site,' she'd remarked over breakfast. 'It was excavated only a year or two ago. I'd really like to see that.'

'I do hope we're not to be subjected to some rocky horror,' remarked Vanessa, as she stood waiting in the hall. Miranda was delaying them as usual.

'Not at all, not at all,' said Henry, bustling about with packed lunches. 'Believe me, an easy day for a lady.' He positively beamed with anticipation.

His father suppressed a smile, recalling that the expedition which first prompted that celebrated quip had been far from easy, and the lady in question no ordinary lady. Fortunately, the walk up to Coire Lagan was not such as to try the powers of any of the party.

Henry led them at a gentle pace, less out of consideration for the ladies than for the sake of his knee which was playing him up that morning. He still cherished hopes of climbing something before the end of the holiday, and was anxious not to aggravate the damage. ...

First, though, he led them to inspect one of the sights of the district, Eas Mor, that day a narrow torrent crashing down over its lip of rock. They halted close to the grassy rim, and peered into the dark, green depths of the ravine.

'Not too near,' said Vanessa, yanking back Andrew.

'Ah, that deep romantic chasm,' exclaimed Henry. 'A savage place! As holy and enchanted as e'er beneath a waning moon was haunted by woman wailing for her demon lover! '

They all agreed it was very fine.

The lack of rain had rendered the usually squelchy moorland path pleasurably dry and springy. Henry pointed out things of interest as they went.

'Loch an Fhir-bhaillaich,' he informed, as they approached a low-lying reedy lake. 'The lake of the little spotted folk.'

'Not fairies,' exclaimed Hugh scornfully.

'Trout, actually,' said his father.

'Ugh!' said Andrew.

It was a warm, sunny morning, one of those soft September days, with a gentle breeze to cool flushed faces, and stir the tufts of cotton grass around the margins of the lake. The party halted there, and stood a moment amid the silence of the mountains, that silence heard so deeply you *are* the silence, until broken by the lecturer's voice.

'The genesis of these mountains—for they are mountains, not hills—belies the peaceful scene you see around you.'

Henry told of gigantic upheavals deep down in the earth's mantle; of plutons and basoliths—legendary monsters they might have seemed to the rest of the party—rising from infernal depths; of colossal forces, as billions of cubic feet of molten rock erupted from unimaginable regions. In all, an event of inconceivable violence. A cataclysm which, the way Henry told it, might have occurred almost overnight.

'There's nothing like it anywhere else in Britain,' he concluded. 'In geological time, it could have happened yesterday.'

His listeners, staring up at the steep southern flank of Sgùrr Dearg, a chaos of scree and vertical crag, at the black, still smoking bulk of Sròn na Ciche opposite, at the piles of debris scattered everywhere, might have agreed that it all looked very fresh and raw.

Above the reedy lochan the path divided. They followed a line of cairns climbing the left hand slope of the corrie. The path grew steeper, stonier, twisting this way and that. Heather moorland and aromatic thyme gave place to expanses of bare rock, the way ahead seemingly cut off by great boiler-plates of ice-ground gabbro barring access to the upper corrie. As they climbed higher they saw, rising before them, beyond the facade of slabs, a high skyline of jagged rock topped by a grim tower.

Then, passing beyond the last of the slabs, they entered into a scene of desolate grandeur: a wide sanctuary surrounded on three sides by walls of rock from which vast slopes of scree tumbled down to the emerald waters of a little lochan. They saw that the tower high on the ridge a thousand feet above their heads was itself overlooked by two great pyramidal summits, their looming bulk all the more imposing in the long shadow cast by the low September sun. But beside the lochan where they stood were unexpected grassy banks among the boulders where, sheltered from the wind, one might bask in the sun.

'What's that?'

Hugh, it was, pointing across the lochan to a deep, dark chasm rising from the shadows of the corrie floor. The hall of some mountain god it might have seemed to an awestruck boy.

'That's the Great Stone Shoot, Andrew,' his grandfather informed gravely.

Rearing up above the chasm enclosing the Stone Shoot was the north-west face of Sgùrr Alasdair. Marlowe tried to pick out the line of *Abraham's Climb*, an insecure adventure on fracturing basalt, with little in the way of belays, running steeply up the crest of the huge right wall of the Stone Shoot, over which it flung an enormous shadow. The insecurity, he remembered, was part of the deep experience. Not visible in the shadow, that little recessed ledge before the traverse, a welcome respite amid testing rock.

Miranda, toiling up with easel and satchel, was the last to pass beyond the slabs. While the rest of the party arranged themselves among the boulders, she wandered here and there searching for a subject. Eventually she chose a position facing the sea, with the shadowy bulk of Sròn na Ciche looming in on the left, the sun just above its shoulder, the slanting light throwing into deep relief the cracks and gullies seaming the huge western buttress.

Knowing that Turner often used a figure in the foreground to lead the eye, she persuaded her grandmother to act the part, setting her on a rug in a grassy alcove among the slabs below the lochan. Then, facing the sea, holding a brush upright at arm's length, one eye closed, she began to take a measure of the shore-line. She was doing her best to follow her teacher's instruction, since it was all she knew. Assembling the data, William called it. Really, there were times when William seemed to live in a world of dead matter, as if fate had somehow contrived to keep him at the barren surface of things, when all around her everything seemed to vibrate as if it were alive: hazy islands floating on a shimmering sea, the glint and flicker of white horses, breakers bursting on a beach of dazzling sand, tiny lochans like jewels in a patchwork, all set dancing under the play of light. *Too much imagination*, William would have said, 'imagination' being with him a term of abuse. He hated anything that smacked of the 'artistic'. So, sighing, she pushed on with her task of assembling the data, aligning her ticks and crosses vertically over and under, or horizontally opposite, each other.

Ah, how to lay hold of Life? Oh, but there was a way.

'Grand-mama,' she blurted suddenly, 'I love someone.'

It was out before she could stop it. The old woman smiled.

'Of course you do. Do I know the young man?'

Miranda took a deep breath.

'Yes.'

'Are you going to tell me his name?'

There was a pause.

'No.'

Then, after another pause, 'I'm afraid he's not very suitable.'

'Very well. I won't pry. But does he love you?'

'Oh yes!'

Such fervour there was in the young woman's voice. Her grandmother suppressed a smile.

'Does your heart tell you this?'

'Yes.'

'Then you must follow your heart. But remember—your heart may turn out to be wrong.'

'No, he loves me. Just as I love him. I'm certain of that.'

In life, my dear, Millie was about to say, *nothing is certain*, when a sudden rattle of stones caused them both to turn their heads. High up to one side of the slopes tumbling down to the lochan, a short distance below the headwall of the corrie, a tiny figure could be seen clattering down a pale runnel amid the debris. Giles was running the An Stac screes. Long-striding, bending low, he rode the stones with the fluent ease of a practised skier flicking this way and that through powder snow, every now and then stopping abruptly with a swing of the hips, heels digging into the rubble, to check on the progress of his friend. Slowly, painfully, as it seemed to the watchers far below, Nicko was picking a laborious, uncertain line over the loose, unstable scree. At length, as if satisfied that Nicko was heading roughly in the right direction, Giles rode out the last few hundred yards of scree, arriving at the corrie floor with whoops of delight, and so to the lochan where the family were gathered.

'I'm starving,' he announced. 'I hope these two brats haven't scoffed my lunch.' He reached out a playful hand to ruffle Andrew's hair. 'I think we ought to wait for Nicko, though, before we start. Don't you?'

Looking at him, Marlowe was put in mind of the saying of some saint of the early church: that the glory of God was man fully alive. He could not begin to imagine in what that fullness might finally consist. Yet the lit eyes, the shining face seemed to look out at them from another world.

The party settled themselves on the grass among the boulder as Henry, delving into his rucksac, distributed the packed lunches. *The loaves and fishes*, as he put it, to tease Andrew. Though there was no need for any multiplying miracle, the thick ham sandwiches, generous slices of Dundee cake and oranges provided by Mrs MacRath sufficing to satisfy the appetites of the hungriest boys. There were, too, flasks of coffee for those who preferred it.

After a leisurely lunch Henry insisted on leading the party over to Sròn na Ciche to inspect *Marlowe's Variation*.

'If Giles is to climb it he needs to know where it goes.'

The wives, though, having had enough of rock, elected to return to the Lodge. Miranda went with them. She wanted to look again at her picture. Already in her mind's eye she saw the glint and glitter of rock and water transfigured as the light moved over it, matter itself dissolving, the play of light being all there was. She knew now how it must be done.

'We can save ourselves a long descent,' suggested Marlowe, 'if we take the rake across the Western Buttress. It'll bring us out in the Sgumain Stone Shoot.'

'An excellent idea,' said Henry. 'The boys will enjoy that. They've been agitating to scramble up something ever since we got here.'

'They'll be perfectly safe,' he assured his wife. 'If necessary we'll rope them up for any difficult bits.'

Seeing their women-folk safely embarked on their descent, the men traversed the glaciated slabs above the lip of the lochan and descended a short distance to an obvious break above the apron of steep slabs marking the edge of the western buttress of Sgumain. They climbed steadily up the ascending line of the fracture between the overlapping slabs, clambering past whatever obstacles presented themselves, boulders blocking the way, and then an overhanging wall, where the upper slab leant outwards. Here and there, where the fracture narrowed, steeper sections with patches of greasy rock found the boys in need of aid.

Now, halfway across the traverse, they were several hundred feet above the floor of the lower corrie. Directly ahead, concealed beyond the curve of the buttress, was the Sgumain Stone Shoot, above which lay the six hundred feet of *Marlowe's Variation*, the climb they were bent on inspecting. Here, at the highest point of the crossing, it was as if they'd been raised up to gaze straight into the huge, blank face of the Cioch slab, from which the Cioch itself projected, or rather hung suspended, like a gigantic nose. Directly above the slab, steep, intimidating, hung the Upper Cioch buttress, a pattern of dark cracks, of shadowy grooves and overhangs. So immediate and extraordinary was the sight, so close at hand, a pebble picked up at their feet and hurled into the air might have bounced off the rock confronting them, or so it seemed.

Gradually the line began to flatten out until the fracture eventually debouched into the wide, boulder-filled gully that broke the line of crags between the great mass of Sgumain to the left, and the eastern buttress of Sròn na Ciche. At this point the party began picking its way down the large blocks which comprised the greater part of the Sgumain Stone Shoot.

The twins had stopped at a spring bubbling out from the boulders, and were scooping up mouthfuls of icy water.

'That's the original route up to the Cioch,' said Marlowe, nodding towards the foot of the buttress directly across from where they stood. 'It was climbed by Harland and Abraham a year or two before mine.'

Giles weighed up the corner set in an open gully.

'Have you done it?'.

'As a matter of fact I have. Your father and I climbed it some years ago. That was before his accident, of course.'

A few yards further down the scree they arrived at the foot of *Marlowe's Variation*.

'It starts here,' began Henry, indicating a steep groove, 'gets into that chimney you can see above—quite hard, as I remember it—

then follows the same line for several pitches, before breaking out right.'

He retreated a little way from the face in order to point out the various features of the climb, while Giles listened, trying to identify the awkward slab, the horizontal ramp that led to a flake, then the long sensational traverse—very exposed—the airy ledge, the corner, the final steep wall, all of them jumbled together in his head, and located, as it seemed, an immense distance up the cliff. He'd never climbed on so great a crag before, and was somewhat overwhelmed.

'You did it with grand-mama's brother, isn't that right,' he said, groping for something to say.

'With Robert, yes. Our aim was to find a way directly to the Cioch. Of course, we didn't know then that others had already succeeded in doing so, and by a finer course than ours.'

'Yes, and it all but cost them their lives,' added the Archdeacon.

'Through no fault of their own,' Marlowe thought it fair to point out. 'Some of the rock in the Cuillin,' he turned to explain to Giles, 'is not altogether above suspicion.'

He did not add that his own attempt had not been without incident. He'd gone astray, having mistaken the line, and had been lucky to have got away with it.

He was gazing up at what might have been the fatal wall, seemingly lost in memories of that day thirty years before, oblivious of his grandson's smiling regard. It looked very bleak and bare up there.

Yet it might have been a flicker of desire the young man thought he saw in the old man's face, for he grinned, and said cheerfully, 'We'll get you up it, grandfather.' His natural buoyancy was never dashed for long.

The old man smiled.

'I don't think so, Giles.' And yet… and yet…

'Oh, come on. The Fell and Rock chaps got dear old Limpet-Smith up the Needle, and he's older than you.'

'The name,' said Marlowe reprovingly, 'is Haskett-Smith, not Limpet-Smith, as you very well know. Besides, *Marlowe's Variation* is a lot longer than the Needle. '

And that was certainly true. Indeed, it was longer by a hundred feet than Harland and Abraham's more direct route.

They resumed their descent of the corrie, the two young men striding ahead, the Archdeacon instructing the twins in the history of climbing in the Cuillin. Henry, his father was reflecting, would like to think that *Marlowe's Variation* represented a Golden Age of joyful innocence. Well, there was joy, certainly. Such a joy as seemed at times almost one's natural condition. What one was called to. But that was not all, he reflected. Yet it had seemed straightforward enough to start with. After three hundred feet of immaculate rock he'd found a comfortable grass ledge for another stance from which Robert had belayed him as he tackled the steep slab above. After all, it seemed the natural line. And perhaps might have been, for a better man than himself. A Kirkus, an Edwards. They might have got up it.

He, though, had found it increasingly taxing. Finally, at a point some dozens of feet above his second, and confronted by a line of overhangs, he'd simply run out of rock. There was only one thing for it, daunting prospect though it seemed. He would have to climb down. He'd looked in vain for a friendly spike over which he might loop the rope. He was a long way from safety.

Collie used to say that he'd never climbed up anything he couldn't climb down. It was all about the precise distribution of weight. A question of simple mechanics. The whole downward thrust of the body focused vertically on a single nail at a time. Would he have thought as coolly as that? Hardly. He'd been badly frightened up on that slab. Even so, some kind of autonomic self-protective system had evidently taken over, bringing him down step by step, hands resting on the rock, serving little more than to keep him in balance. *Don't lean in… don't lean in…* looking down between your boots for the next foothold… seeing only that…

I must remember, Marlowe told himself, to warn Giles about that false line.

The meal that evening was a much more tranquil affair. No one wanted a repetition of the previous night's unpleasantness. Besides, appetite sharpened by fresh air and exercise, they were too intent on their dinner to fall out over politics.

Even Millie confined hostilities to the twins, who were wolfing down the mutton.

'Hugh, don't gobble! You should chew each mouthful forty times.'

Susannah was full of enthusiasm for her walk to Rubh' an Dunain.

'It really is a delight. The views are quite wonderful. There were seals on one of the skerries. We even saw an otter.'

'We saw the Cioch,' said Hugh importantly

'It was discovered by Professor Collie,' added Andrew, not to be outdone.

'Your grandfather knew Professor Collie. He was a colleague of yours. Isn't that so, father?'

'Well, only in a manner of speaking. He's a scientist. Besides, I never actually climbed with him.'

'I expect he went too fast for you,' quipped Giles,.

'Hugh!' cut in a warning voice. 'Forty times!'

'I know all about the Immortals of the SMC,' went on Giles, who'd been studying the guide-book. 'They covered the ground at speeds not possible to ordinary men.'

'Collie was certainly a prodigious walker,' said Marlowe mildly.

He went on to tell of an epic day. Collie and his guide had set out from Sligachan towards Glen Brittle as far as the Mhaim. There they turned aside to go up through Coire na Creiche to the Bealach na Glaic Moire, then over all the peaks of Mhadaidh, Ghreadaidh, Banachdich, up the Inaccessible Pinnacle, and on along the ridge to Thearlaich. They were stopped at the Thearlaich-Dubh gap. So it was back to Alasdair, then over the scree to the Bealach Coir' an Lochan, a descent into the corrie—dreadful place for tired legs—and down in fading light to the Coruisk river. Then straight up over Druim nan Ramh—very steep, that—down the other side into

Harta Corrie and back by moonlight along Glen Sligachan.

'It was midnight,' he concluded impressively, 'when they arrived back at the hotel.'

He looked round at the faces of his family. Henry apart, none of them had the faintest idea what he was talking about.

'I once reckoned it up,' he went on. 'I put it at eighteen miles, and eight thousand feet of ascent.'

'I expect it was the porridge,' suggested Giles. 'Though you'd have to be brought up on it from infancy.'

There was no suppressing him that evening. Watching him teasing the little maid Morag about her 'young man', Richard Fleming felt a stab of envy for his cousin's carefree charm. His own sunlit days were now long gone.

He was overshadowed then. A dark shade, it might have been, passing across a window. Or else Richard, looking round the drawing room at his family, saw with other eyes. God, how Adam would have curled his lip at all this.

Then he was back at Trinity, taking his seat in Hall, feeling that sudden tug on his gown, hearing again that keen-eyed rebuke. *Don't sit with the other comrades. Scatter. Remember, you're an agitator. Never waste a chance for a little propaganda…*

Ah, Adam, you were one of the lucky ones. You died in good time.

It was one of those flashes of light that seemed only to deepen the darkness.

— CHAPTER FIVE —

Looking back over those years Richard saw him everywhere. A big, raw-boned man, with a shock of dark unruly hair, deep eyes and a deep, slow Yorkshire voice. At a Socialist Sunday tea, arguing endlessly, sheer stamina grinding down the opposition. In the Market Place, preparing his troops for a clash with Moseley's Blackshirts. At Parker's Piece, addressing a demonstration, bent arm, clenched fist, hammer and sickle rolled into one, nailing down each point. *Merely putting the case, comrade... merely putting the case...*

At Trinity he was thought odd. Scruffy. Usually in need of a shave or a haircut. The ragged gown, half the regulation size, from which he was forever pulling another tatter. And too serious by half. A square peg in a place like Cambridge. And that was true. He had no small talk. The movement was all that mattered. It was more than a faith, it was the air he breathed. It was all in all.

It was the year of the King and Country controversy. You'd been in Cambridge scarcely a month. You were going along the Chesterton Road, minding your own business, when you heard a brass band, and a boozy chorus of *Rule, Britannia*. A large crowd with Union Jacks had gathered outside the Tivoli cinema. You found yourself next to an undergraduate wearing a rugby shirt. *What's going on?* First mistake. You should have kept walking. *Some of those conchie cranks are in there planning to bust up the film show,* he yelled in your ear. *We're going to bust them up.* The film was a patriotic piece entitled 'Our Fighting Ships'. There was a sudden surge at the front of the crowd... a burst of cheering... then a sudden *mêlée* into which you were swept willy-nilly. There was no telling who was who. Trying to struggle free from the press of bodies, you were clobbered suddenly on the head. Found yourself on the pavement. Dazed, you were hauled to your feet by a big fist attaching itself to your arm. *I know you*, said a deep voice. *You're at Trinity. My name's Stone, Adam Stone.*

That night after Hall he invited you back to his room. A bare, ramshackle den above New Court. Naked bulbs. Nothing in the way of adornment other than a potted palm left by the previous tenant. Chairs, tables littered with open books, pamphlets, sheets of scribbled notes, half-empty milk bottles, unwashed pots. Stone refused to allow his gyp to wash up for him.

'How can you live in such chaos?'

'It's not chaos until things get lost. And I know where things are if I want them.'

That night, over horribly strong tea, you received your first political lesson.

'Here in Cambridge there is a culture of indifference. What we have to do is shock, provoke clashes, make a stir. We want to put politics on the map, to bounce people into the real world.'

Stone poured himself another mug of the revolting tea. You tipped yours into the potted palm while his back was turned.

'Look, tomorrow's Armistice Day. There'll be another demonstration at the War Memorial. Why not come with us?' All the while that keen-eyed gaze, as if to fathom what you were made of. Then a sudden grin. 'Even the Christians are coming...'

Richard smiled at Morag, who was handing him a cup of coffee.

If not a first taste of battle, he reflected, it was certainly a baptism of fire. All along the way the rowdies had bought eggs and tomatoes to hurl at the march. Water-bombs, bags of flour, showers of white feathers. You stuck one in your coat, he remembered. Trumpington Street. That's where the real trouble started. Just where the road narrows outside Peterhouse. That's where they used cars to try to cut the column in half. Where the police drew their batons...

Why did you go, he wondered as he sipped his coffee. Like most people you'd been vaguely anti-war. Hated the kind of jingoism forced down one's throat at school. But you'd never agitated about anything. Never made an exhibition of yourself. Too self-effacing by half. No, it was because of Stone. He made you feel it would be a kind of running away if you didn't. Besides, you'd objected to being hit on the head by some rugger thug. Deep down, that was probably it. Shades of Hammersley. That big, red-faced oaf who'd terrorised you at school.

Ah, you never dreamt then that the Hammersleys would one day rise in their hundred thousand, perfect evil sweeping across Europe, and all one could hope for, hope against hope, was that one day the pendulum might swing the other way.

Quietly Richard set down his coffee cup on the sideboard, and surveyed the tranquil scene: dear old Henry chuckling over the latest Wodehouse; Vanessa, struggling with the crossword in the *Daily Mail;* grandmother killing time with another game of patience; grandfather teaching the boys to play chess; 'No, I wouldn't move there,' he was advising gently. Hearts at peace under a Scottish heaven. They seemed to him wrapped in a dream. The world they lived in simply petered out at Dover. But of course it would. They were English. The best that was thought and said happened here in England. Literature was *their* literature. Poetry, *their* poetry. To be civilised was to be like them. Ah, but the Hammersleys were coming. The Hammersleys were coming...

Richard had been quartered in a shepherd's cottage on the other side of the cattle grid beside the Banachdich burn. A small room, simply furnished. Bed. Table. Chest of drawers. A simple room for a single man. That was OK with him. *I prefer to be on my own*, he'd told Henry. He often found it necessary to get up at night and go for a walk. It was the only way he knew to shake off the dreams that haunted his sleep.

Bidding good-night to the family he went out from the Lodge, and took a deep breath of cold night air. He stood for a moment looking up at the dark silhouette of the ridge. The Cuillin seemed very high and remote, only a little way below the stars. The frosty air nipped his cheeks, nipped the tip of his nose. A bitter night in Aragón, it struck him then. The cold venomous. The mountain torrents stiff with ice. He thought of the men standing to beside the Ebro. But no, no more of that. He shut his mind to that.

Assailed then by an intense loneliness he set off, walking aimlessly, a lone man on an empty road, a man alone in the world. Family? What was his family? He had no family. A great gulf separated him from them. A gulf that could not be crossed.

A wave of pain and anger swept through him then, a flashback of the ugly scene at dinner the previous night. And with it the despair you have to turn to hatred if you are to carry on being a soldier. Only he wasn't a soldier. Not any more.

He thought then of what grandfather had said, taking him aside that morning. *You mustn't allow Millie to upset you. Try to remember,* the old man had added dryly, *she has not enjoyed our advantages.* It was, he supposed, a laying claim to a kinship of a kind. If you could call surviving a kinship.

Poor grandmother, he thought. And yet what a truly terrifying revolutionary she would make, if she were one of us. Another Madame Defarge, knitting the names of the fascists into her register. Marking them down for death. No, we live in different worlds.

That Lent Term, he remembered, he'd gone round the college taking a collection for the hunger marchers.

To call them 'hunger marchers' is not only sentimental. It's absurdly exaggerated.'

'Oh, they're hungry, grandmother. I've seen them. So are their wives and children.'

But no. They were 'red dupes', whose leaders were paid with 'Moscow gold'.

You'd gone out to Girton to welcome them with refreshments. Many of the men were wearing their medals. The same medals grandfather might have worn. And yet they were poles apart. Then you'd all marched back together down the long hill into the town singing *Pie in the Sky*, and *Solidarity for Ever*.

Later, in the Corn Exchange, you'd wandered round with a tray of tea, witnessing at close quarters the gaunt faces, the clothes hanging from bodies, the bad teeth when they smiled their thanks, the broken boots. Stone was tending the feet of an older man. You saw how gently he cut away the rough home-knitted socks. Bathed the blistered feet. *He feels that man's suffering as if it was his own*, it struck you then. *Only he will transform that pain into action. That's what a Communist does.*

Later, crossing the Market Place together as you walked back for Hall, Stone talked about the Calder Valley where he came from.

'Take any labourer. He works long hours. Hard physical graft for a miserable wage. He has no security. He can be put out of work in a moment through no fault of his own. For a few weeks, providing he's kept up his contributions, he'll receive benefit amounting to a third of the average wage. Should he remain unemployed he'll be put on Public Assistance. He'll then get a visit from the Means Test man. Some nosy little clerk will probably instruct him to sell his few sticks of furniture. Or maybe pawn his wedding ring. Oh yes, Richard. These things happen. Meanwhile, his wife will have gone without food herself in order to feed her children. And what brings about this sad state of affairs? An act of God? A law of Nature? No! The capitalist system!'

He wants me to join the Party, you thought.

You halted a moment in Great St Mary's Passage while Stone put a few coins on the tray of a be-medalled hawker. Shook his head at the proffered matches.

'There is no middle way, Richard,' he went on quietly as you turned into Trinity Street. 'Not to take sides is to leave everything as it is.'

Again that keen regard, that searching for a spark. What was it he used to say? *If only a man is honest you can make a revolutionary of him.*

That very night you joined the Party.

To say that the family were shocked would be putting it mildly. If his joining the Socialist Club had been regarded as a youthful indiscretion, this was altogether different. This was at once a stride into another country. Leo couldn't understand it. He simply couldn't comprehend what was happening in the universities. He spoke of a fever in the blood of the younger generation. Grandmother was outraged. Even Hitler was marginally less wicked than the godless Russian Bolsheviks who'd murdered the Tzar and his family.

Yet what it amounted to was unremarkable enough: Marxist study groups in college rooms, the humdrum business of distributing pamphlets, selling copies of the *Daily Worker*, listing names of possible sympathisers, evenings spent street chalking or 'working on the masses'. In all this Stone took the lead. He seemed blessed with extraordinary vigour, never tiring of discussion, never lacking for an argument. He had a gift for the telling detail of a situation, that poignant case from which he would then draw out the political lesson. Yet there was nothing sentimental about his Marxism. Though he would make use of whatever presented itself to win over the sympathy of an audience, at bottom it was the cold, inexorable logic of the dialectic that drove him. And yet at times he could rise to visionary heights.

Richard cherished a lasting memory of him that final summer in Cambridge, in the Market Place addressing a crowd.

'What we believe in, comrades, deceives no one, conceals nothing, knows no discouragement, endures all things, waiting patiently, waiting its time.'

The time, the place, was Spain.

Adam was one of the first to go. There followed a couple of letters from the Aragón front. Very much those of a newcomer. An Englishman in a strange land.

Both sides have something in common. Not surprising, really. Being Spanish they're insanely brave, but also cruel, and quite contemptuous of death. And so perhaps can kill more easily than we can. It's harder for us…'

Then you got a call to say he was back in London. You met up at Lyons Corner House in Oxford Street. He was wearing *aspargatos*, the rope-soled sandals of the Spanish worker. He was still in a state of high excitement. He spoke of his own amazement, seeing what he'd only ever known in theory actually happening on the streets. Of the amazement written on the faces of the people. As if they couldn't quite believe it. What was really needed over there, though, almost as much as arms and ammunition, were disciplined foreign comrades to fight alongside the militias. The Party had brought him back to help recruit more volunteers.

A few days later he went back again with half-a-dozen comrades. You saw them off at Victoria. Hanging out of the carriage windows. Fists clenched. *Viva España...* Your first thought had been to go with them. You even tried it out on Giles. *I'm thinking of going to Spain...* Poor Giles. Hadn't the faintest idea what it was all about. *What on earth do you want to do that for?* He really hadn't a clue. *Oh, boredom, I suppose,* you ad-libbed, as lightly as you could. *Besides, the weather's so much better in Spain. This autumn has been dreadful...*

Why Giles? Because politically he was a child? An innocent? Because you knew what he would say? What you wanted to hear? Sheer incomprehension? You wanted to be shocked out of it. For mother's sake? Or maybe you never really trusted yourself even then.

No, it was Adam's death that finally shamed you into it. He left a pattern of the cause for which he gave his life. All you had left was your Party card.

It was dark in the glen, and silent but for his own footfalls. As he walked the moon was rising imperceptibly above the ridge, picking out the river, and the pale track climbing out of the glen. An owl called from across the river. A desolate cry, trembling in the darkness. It brought back thoughts of his comrades on the Ebro. He was pierced then by a pang of longing. Of longing, and of shame. He walked on sweating with pain. Only when his foot struck a loose plank of the wooden bridge did he realise how far he must have walked. He turned to look back. Saw pinpoints of light, the lights of the farmhouse, and the little crofts further down by the shore. Steady lights that might have spelt welcome for the weary traveller, but not for him. For him they seemed as distant as the stars.

— CHAPTER SIX —

After breakfast, collecting a packed lunch from the hall table, Marlowe went out in search of MacRath. He found the farmer securing a stable door amid a racket of dogs. A couple of the collies, released from confinement, were leaping around him yapping excitedly.

'Jess will be having her pups any time now. So we're having to keep her in.'

Marlowe had been brought up in a Yorkshire rectory, and attended the village school with the children of dalesmen. He was himself at heart a dalesman. He felt at home in the company of farmers and shepherds. So the two men fell to discussing the ways of shepherding, and what was needful in a dog to herd the Blackface sheep of the Cuillin.

'Aye, they're quite choosy about their grazing,' said MacRath. 'And they'll go high. Higher than deer, if need be.'

Marlowe might have lingered to urge the merits of his own native Swaledales, but he had plans for the day ahead.

'This is what I hope to do,' he said casually, handing his host a folded note. 'Better not say anything,' he added.

MacRath, who was used to the ways of climbers, glanced at the note and nodded.

The two men crossed the yard together, the dogs sniffing eagerly wherever their noses led. Through the open door of the dairy came the sound of a girl singing softly in Gaelic. Marlowe glanced enquiringly at his host.

'Oh, that'll be Morag, to be sure.'

The Englishman stopped to listen.

'Will no one tells me what she sings,' he murmured softly. 'Perhaps the plaintive numbers flow for old unhappy far-off things, and battles long ago.'

'Well, there were plenty of those, to be sure. There was a famous one in the corrie where you're heading. *Am Blar Fuathasach*, as it's known. But you having the Gaelic, you will know what that means.'

'Having *some* Gaelic, Gideon,' laughed Marlowe. 'Having *some* Gaelic.'

It was a cold morning, ice in the puddled ruts, frosted grass lining the verges as he set off, tramping along the cart-track that served for a road. He'd told the family he intended to make an early start to Coire na Creiche. Well aware of his preference for solitary expeditions, no one was surprised he should choose to make his mountain walk alone. His darker purpose he'd kept to himself.

Sleepless as usual, he'd lain awake long before dawn going over in his mind the previous day's visit to the climb which bore his name. Despite earlier promptings to the contrary he felt an urge to set foot on it again. He'd actually reached out a hand, wonderingly, to touch the rock. Felt again how much of himself he'd given that day, felt it still *held* there. And what if there were moments when certain emanations stamped on rock surge up again with the old potency? Yes, he was very tempted to have a go. An old man's folly? Well, perhaps as far as the strenuous chimney, he'd told himself. Then, if necessary, they could lower him off. Whether he was actually up to it was another matter. Was he strong enough? Had he got the stamina? He thought he might make a trial of his fitness. A straightforward scramble. Long enough to test him, yet one he could get off easily if he felt too tired.

At the wooden bridge he turned aside from the road, and began to traverse the steep slopes of Sgùrr Thuilm, putting up dozens of dark-winged butterflies as he went. They fluttered slowly ahead of him, dipping and rising between tall tussocks of rank grass. The great bulk of Thuilm cast a long shadow into the heart of Coire na Creiche, where the peaks and ridges of the central Cuillin reared up against the sky. Across the wide, shallow mouth of the corrie, between the forest and the long, north-west ridge of Bruach na Frithe, the green moorland path climbed in sunlight over the Mhaim towards Sligachan. It was a path he'd often travelled, coming and going in those dark days after the war. Now, once again, he was heading into the corrie. He took his time. He was in no hurry. He wanted the sun to get on to the rock before he made a start. At his age the sun made a difference.

He looked across the corrie at the squat pyramid of Sgùrr an Fheadain, thrust out from the main ridge. A narrow blade of sunlight was catching the edge of the slabby buttress left of the Waterpipe. It looked amiable enough that morning. See it on a dark day, though, thrusting sullenly forward, louring at you out of the mist, with its infamous gully a black sword-slash gaping open from top to toe, the very image, it might be, of some unquiet memory imprinted on the rock. *Am Blar Fuathasach*. Well, a desperate battle was the last thing he needed. Was it the MacLeods slaughtering the MacDonalds, or the MacDonalds slaughtering the MacLeods? He couldn't remember. A place of slaughter, anyway. Not difficult on such days to think of landscape as a kind of palimpsest; the past seeping through into the present, the doom of a day long gone-by echoing almost like a doom to come. Small wonder the old tales told round the peat-fire were filled with forebodings: the corpse lights seen on the mountain, the doleful lamentations heard amid the torrent's roar, a testimony of lives lived at the edge of survival. Even modern man was not immune to the nameless dread that haunts the lonely hills. The mist shifting silently. The only sound the clatter of stones under your boots. And when you stop, the silence closing, almost palpably, around you. Even Collie, alone on Ben Macdhui, stumbling blindly among the boulders, once fled in terror down to Rothiemurchus. At such moments even a Fellow of the Royal Society might discover his cloak of rationality to be more permeable than he'd thought.

Today, though, the late September sun was streaming through the glen. Gradually, as it rose above the shoulder of Thuilm, the terraces of Bruach na Frithe began to flood with golden light. Either side of Fheadain the inner corries of Tairneilear and Mhadaidh were still in shadow, but the peaks and ridges of the northern Cuillin stood out blue and hazy against the sky. Threading a path through the boulder field, Marlowe made for a line of grassy margins that offered a corridor below runnels of scree. There he picked up a sketchy trod dropping down towards the mouth of the gorge below Coir' a' Mhadaidh.

He crossed the burn and made his way down towards the broad, slabby front of Fheadain. Wanting to keep to rock as far as possible, he chose a line midway between the Waterpipe and Spur Gully, one that would avoid the grass that broke out further to the left. He chose a pale slab for his starting point. It looked dryer than those a little lower, further to the right, where water had seeped down from a grassy break. As he unlaced his boots to change into *kletterschuhe*, a present from Henry, he felt a flutter of nerves. Was it wise, at his age, to be doing this? What was he letting himself in for? Though he knew very well the answer to that.

At first the easy-angled slabs were interspersed with grassy breaks. These soon gave out as the rock became more continuous, offering little in the way of positive holds. He climbed on his toes, stepping so lightly it felt as if his feet had acquired some strange buoyancy from contact with the rock. Before long, though, it steepened sufficiently for him to recognize that but for the adhesive grip of the gabbro he would certainly have lost his footing. Now he began to flow, recovering an old delight that might have been waiting there for him all these years; delight, coupled with the strange sensation of being held in place, an illusion in which he was not deceived, knowing as he did that Nature has a double face.

At length he came to the first in a series of irregular overlaps running horizontally across the slabs. He pulled over it without difficulty, and continued on his way. There was no trace of the passage of other climbers. Here and there a downy feather caught in a break, or the pellet of some small creature, spoke of a life other than his own. Otherwise, there was no indication of human presence here before him

He had progressed a considerable distance up the buttress before he encountered the first real obstacle, a much steeper overlap rearing up in front of him. He was comfortably placed, the rock beneath his feet not steep, his hands well anchored in the break beneath the overlap, which was no more than a few feet to be sure, but bold, bolder than the others, and offering nothing by which to pull up onto the upper slab. Minutes passed as he cast about for an easier line, edging first left, then right, without success. There was nothing for it but to retreat. The alternative, traversing left below the overlap to easier ground, would have to be made largely on friction, there being the sketchiest of holds. He began to wonder whether getting off this route would be as simple as he'd supposed. He felt the first quiverings of alarm. He was a long way up the buttress. He judged it at two hundred feet at least.

In the end he was forced down to a ramp trending left, then climbed diagonally to approach the overlap at a more broken section. That was the end of the excitement.

Now that he'd reached easier ground he was a little disappointed with himself for having backed off the first real difficulty. He could have tried harder. And the excuse of age was just another capitulation. At the same time, though the angle was amiable enough, an accelerating slide down two hundred feet or more of gabbro was not an outcome he cared to contemplate. He crossed a grassy terrace and followed easy slabs, debouching on to scree. Now the buttress was falling back, narrowing to a broad, rocky spine climbing alongside the Waterpipe. It struck him as very Alpine in character, exposed where it hung over the left edge of the great gully, a dark declivity plunging into unknown depths.

Now, up on the crest of the ridge and out of the shadow of the buttress, he was in full sun.

It was warm work scrambling up the vertebrae of the ever-narrowing ridge. He was soon sweating. He reached the summit, a small rocky pulpit atop the crest, cast off his sac, and sank down into a shady corner. Beyond, the narrow crest continued, falling away to the col immediately below, before climbing again to the south-west summit of Bidein Druim nan Ramh. Down at the col, a tiny green platform, a ewe with its lamb was cropping the grass. On either side steep scree swept down to the corries far below.

Raised up as he was he had an extraordinary feeling of space around him. Far below lay a land of clean colours, of rain-washed earth, stretching across forest and loch to the white cottages of Struan and Bracadale. North-west, on the edge of the ocean off Idrigill Point, he picked out MacLeod's Maidens washed by the sea. Further inland, the Tables, standing proud above Durinish, twenty miles away. In that immensity of space his gaze travelled on through leagues of air and ocean to far-off headlands, and islands held together in a haze of golden light.

Opening his sac he made a start on the sandwiches Mrs MacRath had put up for him that morning. In these high places the old accusing silence had long since given place to a compassionate stillness untouched by the brutalities of war. Maybe it had been there, even on the Somme. A ground of being waiting to be found. So near, and yet so far. Like the larks in that interval when the guns fell silent, and before the blowing of whistles. The songs of larks going up over the scorched, blistered earth, soaring higher and higher in the summer sky, singing of another world. That was the real world, he thought, and somehow we had fallen out of it.

Faintly, there came to him the sound of the Allt Coir' a' Mhadaidh roaring distantly in its rocky gorge. Then the harsh *cronk... cronk...* of a raven somewhere out of sight. Suddenly he realised that he was happy. There was nothing complicated about happiness. It simply was, and he was it, a thing as natural as the flight of the raven, soaring now high over Tairneilear.

That, too, was a kind of ground. He knew then that recovery lay in the resonance he felt with something primal, something beyond the activity of busy minds, which found its echo in the wilderness. No, God was not civilised. He had nothing to do with what Henry, in his Archdeacon's way, thought He could or ought to do. God was wild. Wilder than Henry dreamed of. He was the God of wildness.

But already the moment was fading from him. Or else he was returning to himself, conscious suddenly of other realities: the hardness of rock against his backside, a sudden breath of air cooling the sweat at the back of his neck. From the col came the plaintive call of the ewe seeking its lamb which had wandered off.

It was fading from him. He was returning to himself, and

that great absence, that sense of something gone from his life, something lost on the Somme where, finally, there was nothing of Nature; not a tree, not a bird, not a flower, not a single blade of grass, even. Nothing left alive. Only deadened men floundering in a morass of mud and slime that swallowed friend and foe alike: men, guns, horses, transports, as the fighting slithered in and out of sludgy pits and slimy dug-outs, petering out at last in blizzards and torrential rain.

He might not have bothered with dinner that evening, were it not for the form of the thing. He didn't want to give the impression he was too tired to eat. Though no one would expect him to eat very much. So he sat toying with his food as usual, conscious of Millie's quizzical eye.

She slipped her arm through his as, after dinner, they entered the drawing room.

'Perhaps a rest day tomorrow,' she murmured quietly.

He sank gratefully into his armchair, and closed his eyes. He was dog-tired. Any lasting satisfaction he might have had from his climb had been largely dissipated by the rigours of the descent. Getting down from the col was an ordeal. The big boots clumsy after the *kletterschuhe*. He'd waited too long on the summit. Stiffness and fatigue set in. Then that purgatorial scree. God, what a stony horror. Time was, he thought, when you would have run that scree. Out of the question now. Knees no give in 'em. Legs rubbery. Again and again the toe of a boot catching a stone. It had been a relief to get down at last to the grass of Tairneilear. Then a devious weaving in and out and up and down those stony hummocks to reach the floor of Coire na Creiche and the track back to the road. Should have been a blissful walk-out, water flashing in the falls of the burn, heather filling the air with wafts of honey. Too tired for that, though. All overshadowed by a grim determination to get to the road. A case, he told himself, of just putting one foot in front of another. That's all.

The day was drawing to its close, and the first stars peeping out above the setting sun, as he came up the steep bank to the road. A kindly motorist, who might have been waiting for the purpose, got out of a bull-nosed Morris, and offered him a lift back to the Lodge. My God, he'd been glad of that lift. Good fellow, that motorist. *Aye, that'll be Mr Hart, the botanist. He's staying at Cuillin Cottage.* Trust MacRath to know. He'd tramped wearily up the gravel to find Richard waiting in the porch. *Grandfather! We were just about to organise a search party. Even mother was pulling on her boots...* Then, seeing the state of you, *Are you OK?*

He might have dropped off then, only to be roused by Vanessa's voice, 'Time for bed,' followed by the twins' nightly protests.

'Bed,' said Henry firmly.

Reluctantly the boys bade their goodnights.

Marlowe closed his eye, then opened them again. *This will never do*, he told himself. *Sleep now, you certainly won't sleep tonight.* He surveyed the quiet room, seeing whom he might engage in conversation; Millie at her patience table, Giles and Richard playing chess, Nicko watching. Susannah had picked up *A Date with Death*, Agatha Christie's latest. *A gripping first-rate story*, according to the *Mail*. He hadn't got beyond the first ten pages.

'Did you know, mother,' said Henry suddenly, 'that you have a fellow-enthusiast staying at Cuillin Cottage? A Mr Hart.'

Millie looked up from her cards. 'Not A A Hart?'

'MacRath simply described him as Mr Hart, the botanist.'

'There is an A A Hart who writes botanical notes for *Country Life*. We have exchanged views on a number of occasions. He refers to me as *'my doughty correspondent'*.'

'Exchanged views?' Marlowe raised an eyebrow. 'That's putting it mildly.' Millie's diatribes against the despoiler of wild flowers were a familiar theme.

'Let's say we've had our disagreements. I only wish they had been profitable disagreements. Unfortunately Mr Hart is an avid plant collector. If he's come to Glen Brittle it won't be for the views, believe me.'

Millie turned up a red queen, placed it on a black king.

Miranda was immersed in a book.

'What are you reading,' Marlowe asked her idly.

'*Rebecca.*'

It was all the rage with the Marlowes. Had been round most of the family.

'And do you like the heroine?'

'Absolutely not,' declared Miranda very decidedly. 'She's such a drip! I prefer Mrs Danvers. I fancy she looks like grand-mama.'

Millie raised her eyes from the fall of her cards and fixed them silently on her granddaughter.

'It seems to me,' remarked Henry, 'a very questionable novel in which the hero is allowed to get away with murder.'

'I can't understand,' said Susannah, looking up from her book, 'why de Winter should have found it necessary to kill Rebecca in the first place.'

'Because she was too hot to handle, that's why,' said Miranda. 'Clearly, the man had a castration complex.'

Vanessa shot a sharp look at her daughter.

'One thing's for sure,' continued the young woman calmly. 'That wretched little goose he married wouldn't have chopped the balls off anyone.'

'Miranda! Really!' , said Vanessa, with a shocked glance at her mother-in-law.

But the old lady looked on with benevolent amusement.

'Miranda's an art student, Vanessa,' she said mildly. 'Art students talk like that.'

'Time for the news,' said Henry, clearing his throat. He leant forward, switched on the radio.

A strained silence greeted the announcer's '*Good evening*'. Millie paused in dealing out her cards. The rest looked up from their books. On the Czech-German border fighting had broken out as the Sudeten Germans took over a town. German troops were reported massing near the frontier, while French detachments had also moved to defend Alsace. Meanwhile, the British legation in Prague had instructed all British subjects to leave immediately. As they heard of crowds in the streets of Prague denouncing Britain and France, and calling on the Czech Government to defend their country from aggression, the Marlowes bore the chastened look of people recalled to responsibilities from which they had wilfully absented themselves.

Looking round at the faces of his family, Richard suffered a moment of unholy joy. He advanced his queen, and leant back in his chair.

'Check,' he said to Giles.

Oh yes, he reflected with grim satisfaction. The Hammersleys were coming.

Giles took a long, long look at the board—then, with a rueful smile, toppled his king.

'I'm not much of an opponent, I'm afraid.'

***

Richard took no pleasure in his victory. And his brief moment of *schadenfreude* had left a sour taste. He went out from the Lodge and the talk of war, along the gravel drive and out into the peace of the glen. In the moonlit fields the dim shapes of MacRath's black cattle lay contentedly, each beside its fellow, untroubled by his presence. Across the river the owls were calling to one another in the forestry where the trees concealed nothing but themselves. Here in the dark enclosing refuge of the hills the land remained what it had always been. *Nuestra madre, la tierra...* Yes, he thought, that's what we're fighting for. Only *he* wasn't fighting. Not any more.

He stood for a moment looking up at the ridge, a dark outline under a multitude of stars. The same stars, perhaps, that glittered above the Sierras. The same moon glinting on the steel of bayonets. Another bitter night. He gazed at the long arm of the Cuillin stretched protectively around the glen. No refuge for the men waiting under the stars, waiting with tense, fixed faces, waiting for the attack. The bitter tang of their fires seemed to reach him far away in this untroubled place. He might have reached out then to touch them, the men huddled round their fires.

Qué tal, camarada?
Malo, hombre, malo...

He was filled then with a sudden overwhelming longing for Spain: summer heat... the smell of leather, of olive oil, of garlic... *dobles* of ice-cold beer after the dust of the Valencia road... the blessed shade under the trees... swimming in the Manzanares... *chatos* of *manzanilla* totted up on the table tops of the Cafe Kutz... leaping off the train on that long, slow, haul to Aragón, snatching a few oranges, tossing them through the open door, your comrades hauling you back on board...

Assailed, once again, by an intense loneliness, he turned and went back to his lodging. The room was dark but for the moonlight coming in at the single window. It cast a silvery light over the bed. He groped for the candle lantern on the bedside table.

Lighting the candle, he lay down on the bed and took from his pocket-book a stained and tattered fold of paper, all that remained of a letter that had been his talisman, his New Testament, his Word made flesh. He had carried it through that first bitter baptism of fire at Jarama, through the attack on Mosquito Ridge, the house-to-house fighting at Teruel, the retreat from Caspe, and beyond.

Throwing himself on his bed, he held the page to the candle's flickering light, though he knew almost by heart the faded lines written in Adam's sprawling hand:

'For me this has been my first encounter with the realities of life. With the harsh terms it makes. Its demand for hard, healthy bodies. Its horror of old indulgences. Of surplus flesh. Here you learn to value all vital skills— making and mending—the capacity to endure—to go without. We live now where class difference would be a threat to safety, where any kind of privilege would jeopardise survival. You wouldn't believe the capacity of the masses when they take power into their own hands. You have to see it to understand. That something greater than ourselves we read about in textbooks, or hailed as 'History', it's being realised at last here. in the heat of the day, on the cold, dark

hills at night under the stars. Above all in the faces of our comrades, the men and women of the milicianos. I have come to love them. The Spanish people. They are so amazingly brave and generous...'

A sudden tremor of the candle flame caused the shadow to lurch across the wall. Beyond the window the owls, closer now, were still calling through the darkness. He turned the page, knowing what he would find.

'When first I came out here I was frightened. I thought of just firing the odd shot or two and then go sneaking off home. I'm still frightened, of course. But I know now I have to stick with it. To see it through. Anything less is simply playing at it. So if they ask you in England what we're fighting for, pass on to them this message from a comrade, a miner from Asturia: 'We're fighting for the right to learn to read'.

If chance has it I'm killed, Richard, don't forget me. Above all, don't give up on the cause. Don't give up. I have no doubt, no doubt whatever, who's going to win this war...'

He lay back on the bed. Closed his eyes. He thought of the words he'd once chalked on the walls of Cambridge. Words that had carried him to Spain. Whatever it was he'd sought to analyse had gone now from the end of the dialectical microscope. Maybe it was never there. Never there at all.

But his mind, he thought sleepily, was not reliable. Or else the good words had gone bad. Rotten. Eaten away inside. All that were left were shells. Mere husks. He was himself little more than a husk,

He shivered suddenly and pulled the eiderdown up over his body. For a while he lay dozing, his mind, unreliable he knew, flowing out in the direction words had seemed to point to but never reached.

No, Adam. You were one of the lucky ones. You died before the rot set in.

He fell asleep then, only to find himself lying flat in an olive grove, cowering behind the trunk of a tree. It was just thick enough to provide cover for his head. He knew it was his head he had to worry about. Then a stern voice addressed him. You're too fastidious, comrade. A characteristic bourgeois deformity. You must rid yourself of your dependence. You must liberate yourself. You must change the face of reality.

'I've got to have the words,' he murmured feebly. 'I can't do it without the words…'

Then he was looking around him, searching for the words. Rotten, riddled with holes, they lay among empty cartridge cases amid the olives, or slumped over the burnt-out shells of vehicles, or sprawled among the debris of shattered buildings or, stripped of their valuables, left to swell, stinking beside the road, or stood shivering at the frontier, lacking the necessary papers. You must go the rest of the way, they seemed to gesture, by yourself.

CHAPTER SEVEN

A jolly sea-side holiday. That, at least, was the Archdeacon's intention. There would be outings and activities of sufficient variety to appeal to everyone, with picnics, bathing, boating, fishing, climbing, botanizing for mother among the mountain flora, and plenty of subjects for Miranda's brush. The celebration would culminate in a repetition of father's famous climb. Of course, to the women of the family it meant very little. Why should it? But for the menfolk it was an event written into family history. Marlowe's Variation. They were very proud of it. Young Giles especially so. Indeed, Henry cherished a fond dream that all three generations might be represented in the commemorative ascent. Though whether he was up to it, let alone his father, was not a matter to which he had given sufficient thought. Indeed, whether Giles himself was up to it remained to be seen.

All the young man's climbing had been done in Wales or the Lake District on crags springing from green hillsides, using pocket guides in which the climbs were described pitch by pitch, and where, as like as not, the scratches left by nailed boots left one in no doubt as to the line. Very few had exceeded three or four hundred feet. Climbing in Skye was altogether different. The key to doing a climb in the Cuillin, Giles had decided, was that you made it up as you went along. All you had to go on were the descriptions given in Steeple and Barlow, the unwieldy guide-book published by the SMC. They struck him as rather a sketchy basis for expeditions which might involve many hundreds of feet of virtually unmarked rock. Each night he pored over the Climbing Book kept at the Lodge, attempting to flesh out from visitors' accounts what he found in Steeple and Barlow, collating the information in a little notebook. The result had been less than satisfactory.

I haven't a clue where we are, he would call down breezily, somewhat to his friend's alarm. However won over by Giles' dash and daring, Nicko was rather undermined by these confessions of ignorance. Then Giles would fish in a pocket for his notebook, only to find that whatever bit of rock he was perched on bore little resemblance to what he'd jotted down the previous evening. Well, he would say, it looks OK, so we'll press on.

The previous day had proved particularly problematic.

'We got into rather a pickle, didn't we, Nicko?' he confessed over the toast and marmalade.

'How very surprising,' exclaimed Miranda dryly.

'It was rather gripping for a while,' said Nicko, who'd been frightened out of his wits.

'What were you doing?' asked Marlowe.

They'd set out, on Henry's recommendation, in search of a long climb called Median on the Western Buttress of Sròn na Ciche.

'Hmm. Not a climb I should have chosen for you, 'said the old man. He remembered it as a rambling, not to say confusing line, not easy for its grade.

'I still don't know whether we actually did it,' Giles went on. 'But whether we did or not it was all quite wonderful.'

He reached for another slice of toast.

'We climbed out of this cave,' he went on, 'and we found a deep chimney. But it must have been the wrong chimney.'

'It was the wrong chimney,' said Nicko, with conviction.

'We ended up climbing the most desperate crack. A brute of a thing. It went on for ever.'

'Anyway,' he concluded, buttering his toast. 'we're hoping for an easier day today.'

'What are your plans,' asked his father, while privately resolving it must be Leo and not Giles who led the first rope on Marlowe's Variation.

'The Eastern Buttress,' mumbled Giles, through a mouthful of toast. 'The Direct Route. BB—whoever he was—speaks very highly of it in the Climbing Book.'

'Well, even you should find your way up that,' said Marlowe. 'Straight up the edge of the gully. Just follow your nose.'

They were high on the Eastern Buttress of Sròn na Ciche, overlooking the depths of Eastern Gully, when they heard the plane. They turned to watch it, far below them as it seemed, flying along the bright meanders of the river.

They heard it too in the garden, where Marlowe was resting after his demanding day.

'That'll be Leo and Kitty.' Henry got to his feet. 'I'll go and meet them.'

Marlowe closed his eyes. How very irritating it must be for Leo, he reflected, to have to leave London at a time like this. It breached the first rule of the political careerist: Never go away. Oh, shut it out, he thought. Shut it out.

Still subdued, out of sorts, his exhaustion of the previous evening had deepened into a depression. After that soaring of the spirit on the mountain top he'd been returned to his body with a vengeance. And what a body! Legs no longer quick or flexible enough to react to a rolling stone or larger-than-expected boulder had left him with bruised toes, and a painful ankle where a foot had cockled awkwardly. His left knee in particular was sore and swollen. The blow to his pride was worse. The thought that his children, and his children's children, were on the point of putting boots back on, and setting out to fetch him down from the hill was mortifying in the extreme. He'd tried to pass it off as a simple miscalculation. Misjudged the time... came down in the gloaming... though of course I did know the way... But no one was deceived. He'd bitten off more than he could chew. That's what they were telling one another. Vanessa, he knew, would have been furious. It's so selfish, he could hear her saying, inflicting this on the rest of the family. Even Henry, usually so supportive, had been gently reproachful. Perhaps it's time to think again about these solitary expeditions, father. A foolish, fond old man. That's what they thought. He thought it too.

The twins had been waiting all morning for the plane to arrive. Their father had to hold them back from dashing forward excitedly as the little Rapide taxied to a halt.

First to emerge, graceful even in her disembarking, was a tall, elegant woman of striking appearance. Lady Katherine Marlowe, relict of a Tory grandee recently deceased, had been sculpted by Epstein, painted by Augustus John, and had survived both experiences—so it was rumoured—with honour intact. Certainly she might have been an object of desire for any artist: the strong bones around which the skin had tightened, hollowing the face, the edges of the brow enclosing large, luminous eyes, the long straight nose and full-lipped mouth, the loose, thick locks which, when cast in bronze, resembled nothing so much as a tangle of writhing snakes—oh, and a bust to die for.

She strode now over the Big Meadow, snaky hair flying out behind, as if to take possession of the island. Bounding along beside her, for all the world like an enthusiastic terrier, was her much shorter husband. They were something of a mismatch, she being, in addition to their disparity in height, some years his senior. The more cynical Westminster-watchers had calculated it to be essentially a marriage of convenience: Lady Kitty, the highest of high Tories, and young Marlowe, ambitious to a fault. Certainly, they were political soul-mates. Both thought war more or less inevitable, and believed Winston would become PM. And surely Leo, as one of his most trusted aides, would be offered a seat in his Cabinet? Meanwhile, Leo Marlowe was not popular on the Government front bench. The Home Secretary, who'd been on the receiving end of Leo's witticisms—'a prize specimen in the PM's cabinet of curiosities'—had been overheard to refer to him as 'a bumptious little sod'.

But now the Marlowe brothers each raised an arm in greeting as Henry advanced to meet the new arrivals.

'Good flight?'

'Well, Kit disgraced herself as usual. I actually had to stop her climbing in with the pilot. Frightened the life out of the other passengers.'

He clearly adored her.

'I only wanted him to show me how to drive the thing,' she said huskily in a voice toned, according to Miranda, by a regime of pink gin and small cheroots. She called her 'the merry widow'.

Undoubtedly Lady Kitty had been a great success with her new family, once they'd got over the shock. Millie found her 'most amusing'. The twins, too, thought their new aunt great fun. She played games with them—Marlowe would have it she played games with everyone—and brought them presents. And if Vanessa had been over-awed at first, Henry enjoyed crossing swords with his new sister-in-law, putting the case for negotiation and disarmament as the best hope for Europe.

She would bend her great, luminous eyes upon him, listening with parted lips as if what he had to say was of the utmost importance.

'No, no, Henry,' she would insist, 'you are wrong. You are quite, quite wrong.'

Lady Kitty's conversation incorporated many underlinings.

Such members of the family as were not out and about had gathered in the garden to greet the newcomers.

Leo Marlowe spread wide his arms in generous acknowledgement.

'How very good,' he announced impressively, 'to see you all. '

'I'm sure we're all very grateful you were able to tear yourself away from the crisis,' said his father dryly. 'Can the country spare you?'

'The country,' said Leo cheerfully, 'will have to get along without me.'

Marlowe's sons had long since learnt to ignore their father's uncomfortable ironies.

'I insisted he should come,' said Lady Kitty.

'Oh, absolutely. I'm hoping to climb something. I thought you might take me up the Cioch, father. Collie's Route, of course.'

'Don't patronise me, Leo,' said his father sourly.

'Very well then. I'll take you up it,' said Leo, not in the least put out. 'How about that?'

'God, what these politicians are,' muttered Richard, just audibly, from his deckchair.

'Well,' said Henry, brightly. 'You'll want to get settled in. You're billetted in one of the farm cottages. I'll show you where it is.'

'By the way,' he added, 'you ought to know that the generator is switched off at eleven o'clock. So it's candles to light you to bed.'

On Eastern Buttress the young men had been enjoying themselves with that self-forgetfulness which comes with glad absorption in the mountain day. One delight followed another; up edges, around corners, by cracks and chimneys, with ample leisure on the open stances to gaze out to sea, or wonder at a little tent, not noticed before, pitched in a grassy recess under the Western Buttress of Sgumain, or gaze across Eastern Gully at the huge hanging mass of the Cioch jutting above its giant slab. There was a climb there, Giles remembered. In the angle there. But that must wait for another day. And suddenly the succession of days seemed endless while such delights existed, as if youth and energy should never cease. So engrossed was Giles, so filled with the elation—for the steep, final wall was everything BB had said it was—tiny holds, screaming exposure—he'd scarcely noticed a sudden drop in temperature, a general darkening of the air. Emerging at the top of the buttress he was quite taken aback to find himself enveloped in mist.

His intention was to descend via the Sgumain Stone Shoot, a thousand feet of steep, loose scree and boulders debouching onto the lower floor of Coire Lagan. To reach it involved a short scramble up to the summit of Sròn na Ciche, then the circumventing of a steep drop, before arriving at the Bealach Coir' a' Ghrunnda, and the start of the descent.

'I'm pretty sure this is it,' said Giles uncertainly, staring down at the scree vanishing in the murk below. 'At least, I think it is.'

At the same time he was acutely conscious that it might not be, aware of the habit of scree slopes in the Cuillin to terminate abruptly in a sudden drop.

'I think we'll go back the way we came,' he said suddenly. 'I believe we can get off the shoulder of Sròn na Ciche.'

He summoned up what little he could remember of the topography of Sròn na Ciche. The ridge ran roughly east to west. Beyond the summit, after a short dip, it should flatten out for a while, broadening to a plateau as it descended. That much he knew. Yet these wraiths of vapour, fluctuating, re-forming, seemingly without any agency, had dissolved the familiar world into a wholly different place. Giles had become acquainted with a sense of his own limitation, a troubling burden compounded by the responsibility he felt for the safety of his friend.

The mist had fallen back a little when they found themselves once more on the summit of Sròn na Ciche. The two men stood as if on an island set in a sea of uncertainty. Now and then they caught glimpses of the corrie floor far below, dark and gloomy under a swirling mass of vapour. Already the autumn day was waning, such of it as was left giving up the unequal struggle with the gloom. Though Giles's watch told him half-past two the grim half-light said nothing. It might have been dusk, dawn, or some incalculable hour on the surface of an alien planet. Down the slope, ahead of them, lay the mist, waiting. With, it seemed, an eerie air of expectancy. Giles felt as if the world in which he'd seemed so at home a short while ago had taken on a strange transformation. Then there came into his head a typically gnomic utterance of his grandfather's: Remember, a day may come when the rock will close itself against you.

***

The author of that dark prediction sat in the garden on a bench set against the wall of the drawing room. Seeing Richard sitting alone in the garden, and thinking to keep him company, he had gone out taking an armful of the newspapers Leo had brought with him that morning.

'Have you seen the papers?'

Richard, though, shook his head, a mute signal which seemed to darken the isolation which enclosed him like a cloud.

The old man feared for Richard. And he knew Susannah, too, feared for her son. But since he could think of nothing else to say that wouldn't have sounded contrived, he immersed himself in the *Manchester Guardian*.

It seemed the Czechs had given way. And now the Poles and the Hungarians were feeding on the spoils. A week ago, he reflected, Chamberlain had enjoyed the admiration of the world. Today little of that remained. The *Guardian* was unequivocal in its disillusion. Were the Prime Minister to glance at the newspapers during his flight to Godesberg, it concluded, he would find no trust that he could save any shred of principle from the wreck, no belief even that he could recover the country's honour.

It was peaceful in the garden; silent, but for the distant murmur of the burn. Already the short afternoon was passing. Already the first jackdaws were returning to their roosts in the trees around Glenbrittle House. Did they, he wondered, still build their nests in the limes around the rectory garden? As a boy he used to watch for them at the beginning of March, flying in with twigs for their nests, an untidy jumble of sticks that in winter looked like flotsam stranded in the bare winter branches. He loved to see them, sitting companionably beside their nests, chatting to one another, cocking a speculative eye from the top of a gable, flying down to put a foot on whatever scraps he might throw out for them.

Ah, the trouble with growing old was that so many of your thoughts went backwards, to where you could never go yourself.

The long streamers of mist which had been gathering for some time over Sròn na Ciche had now been absorbed in thicker, darker cloud. Setting aside his paper, the old man began to muse on the unpredictable character of the Cuillin, and the incertitude of one's relationship with rock, the moments of doubt and heart-searching insecurity as the mist swirled and the wind whispered; most treacherous of all, its habit, on occasion, of assuming whatever features a disoriented man might hope to recognize. He thought then of the boys on Eastern Buttress. Though they should be well on their way down the Stone Shoot by now.

'Have you ever given any thought,' said Richard suddenly, 'to the word 'love'? Our headmaster was very fond of it. Love of God, love of country—that kind of thing. We used to hear a lot about love in chapel.'

The edge of bitterness in the voice was unmistakeable. Marlowe realised this was going to be one of those conversations a man has with himself. His part was to listen.

'I believed the Party cared far more for humanity than God. We would clear away the crimes of history, and actually build the kingdom Christ spoke about. Only it would be a classless society.'

Richard lit another cigarette, blew out smoke.

'Harry Pollitt came to visit us after Jarama. Comrade Pollitt. I can see him now, standing on a rock, thumbs stuck in his waistcoat pockets, jaw stuck out. He looked like Mussolini. He spoke about the fallen, just like my old headmaster. Not one of your lives, comrades, is forgotten. The bastard had us in tears. The next day we went back into the line. He went home.'

There was a pause in the voice. The speaker might have been reflecting on the enviable act of going home.

Up on the moor a small heft of sheep had appeared on the horizon. They came cascading down in a woolly stream towards the pens, with the dogs racing back and forth. They must gather them in batches, thought Marlowe. Corrie by corrie.

'We had a Cockney machine-gunner in our section,' Richard went on. 'One of those who covered our retreat at Jarama. A bit of a barrack-room lawyer. But that's all he was. He spoke out about the sort of thing we all moaned about at one time or another—the food, the lousy equipment. By then things were bad. Apart from a bare two weeks in Madrid, we'd spent four months in the trenches. We were seeing the first desertions. You'd hear of a lorry gone missing from the cookhouse. Then it was rumoured that the driver and four of his chums had taken off for Barcelona and a boat to England. And of course Wally had something to say about that too.

You have to have one of these to get leave—that kind of thing.'

Richard had been toying with what appeared to be a piece of pasteboard, turning it over and over between his fingers. Now he held it up. Marlowe picked out the black print on a red ground, The Communist Party of Great Britain.

'Wally was ILP himself. In the eyes of the Party that made him a Trot. The Communists aren't the only ones resisting the Fascists, he said. That was after the rising in Barcelona. There are others in this fight too, you know. Of course, that did it. He was arrested. Accused of spreading rumours, undermining morale. That made him a saboteur. But it was all nonsense.'

A man's shout, mingled with the bawling of lambs, came distantly from the pens.

'So I went to the company commissar. He rebuked me, of course. I shouldn't trust my own judgement in such matters. It was distorted by my bourgeois class-consciousness. Trust the Party line, comrade. Always stick to the line. He was a decent little man. A Jew from Manchester. What will happen to him, I asked. He'll be sent for re-education. I must have looked at him as if to say we both knew what that meant. He hesitated. Then he said, quite kindly, really, A romantic revolutionary's no use to us, lad. You have to have revolutionary discipline.'

The old man's mind had gone back to September gathers in the dale when the lambs were spained and the wethers sorted, back to the autumn fairs and shows, and a youthful vow, sworn in vain, never to leave that land of lost content. Then he cursed himself, and wrenched away from all that, and back to his grandson.

'Well, I wasn't satisfied with that, so I went to see Templeton, the Battalion Commissar. He used to come along the trenches sometimes when the Fascists had stopped firing at us, giving us lectures on the importance of dialectical materialism. I could have him shot, he said, banging his fist on the table when he heard what I'd come about. I knew his type. A typical public-school bully. Surely he has some rights, I protested. Deviation has no rights, he said, and went back to his papers. You're too fastidious, comrade, he shouted after me as I went out. A characteristic bourgeois deformity, he called it. We never saw Wally again.'

Richard lit a fresh cigarette from the stub of the first.

'I began to wonder if I'd ever really known the Party for what it was. Then I remembered something a French comrade had said to me. There's no such thing as a just army. But there are just wars, and this is one of them. Then I told myself I was only seeing part of the picture, not the whole. It was the struggle that mattered, not my personal feelings. Even if Templeton and his kind had become dehumanized in some way, the struggle remained. The cause was still worth fighting for.'

He fell silent then. Nor could the old man find anything to say. He was reflecting on the fellow Templeton who went along the trenches lecturing exhausted men from the frozen heights of the dialectic. That had no life of its own, unless continually warmed and nourished by the human heart. Then it became a consuming passion. As it devoured, the complexities dropped away. You forgot the cruelty, the horror. You forgot... or learnt to accommodate.

'I had a friend, a comrade, who gave his life for the Spanish people. He had complete faith in the Party. If one loses anything of that faith, he used to say, you're done for as a Communist.'

Richard turned to look at his grandfather.

'Now all I have is this.' It might have been a worthless piece of junk he held between his fingers. 'And do you know, I can't throw it away. I can't throw it away.'

Flinging down his cigarette he got up suddenly as if unable to sit still any longer and wandered off to the far end of the garden.

Marlowe gazed after his grandson. He and his contemporaries had been swept into the Great War on a tidal wave of illusion. What was the line? Yes, 'like swimmers into cleanness leaping'. Richard, though, had made an authentic choice. Richard had broken open the closed circle of English life, and what had he encountered? Irreparable loss. What would he do now? And what was required of him, his grandfather? How was he to embrace and redeem that loss, that helplessness?

Slowly the old man got to his feet and went in search of his wife, with that cry of bitter destitution still lodged in his mind: Now all I have is this…

As the afternoon drew towards its close the family gathered for tea in the drawing room. Vanessa, though, was watching the mist beginning to roll down over the moor.

'Shouldn't they be back by now?'

'One can never predict the length of a mountain day,' said Henry. 'They'll be back soon.' He seemed quite unconcerned.

But on Sròn na Ciche the mist had thickened appreciably. Weird figures, knuckles of rock, shapes that were simply shapes, forming, dissipating, came and went in the gloom. Now and then a black mass, looming suddenly through the vapour, seemed to raise a giant fist in threat or warning. Giles was acutely conscious of the mouth of Eastern Gully lurking somewhere on their right. Recognizing it for what it was was another matter. There were other re-entrants cutting into the plateau. It was not so much the thought of straying into one of them, as of simply walking over the edge that unnerved him. On either side of this, the narrowest part of the plateau, the great cliffs falling into Coire Lagan and Coire a' Ghrunnda presented a constant anxiety. He had become so disoriented he simply didn't know whether they were heading directly along the plateau, or straight for the huge drop which lay in wait on either hand. Blindly they went on, casting about in the mist over greasy blocks and loose scree, with no track, no visible cairns, nothing to serve for a line.

But now the ground sloping away in front of them, fading into the gloom, persuaded him they were heading south-west. He thought of his grand-father's instructions for getting off the summit of Ben Nevis in a white-out. How to avoid the yawning man-trap of Five Finger Gully. So many yards on such-and-such a bearing, so many more on another. But here in the Cuillin the compass, he knew, was not reliable. From time to time he glanced at the needle in its housing swinging stubbornly to the north. He hoped it was north. There was nothing else to fasten on. No sound. No landmark. There was only his own breath rasping in and out, The crunch of boots. And the mist retreating eerily as they advanced. Keeping its distance. Closing in behind.

Vanessa became increasingly anxious as the evening drew in. Several times she went out into the garden to see if she could see them. But the Cuillin were now veiled in heavy cloud. A fine drenching rain was falling in the glen. Richard, who knew all too well the shapes that fear could take, saw them forming in the woman gazing anxiously across the darkening moor. She'd no idea what they were embarked on, or where they might be now, or how long it might take them to return.

He slipped out to join her.

'Surely they should be back by now?' She turned to look at him.

He could see she had them lost, or badly hurt, or worse.

'Don't worry,' he said gently. 'They've quite a way to come. In this weather it's bound to take a while.'

'Why must he do it, Richard?' She was peering anxiously, straining to see into the mist that was drawing ever closer, drawing in about the Lodge. 'It frightens me.'

Then he was himself peering through a misty wood, eyes straining for the first glimpse of a white turban. He could hear the Moors advancing. The beating of their drums. Bullets slashing through the branches rained fragments all around.

He put his arm around her shoulder.

'You'll get wet standing here,' he said. 'Let's go back inside. If it'll make you feel any better, I'll go out and look for them. But I'm sure they'll be back soon.'

Then, with the light all but gone, he had a quiet word with Henry.

'Perhaps we should take a look. They might have gone astray. Even so, there's only two ways they could have come down. If you and Leo go over to the flank of Sròn na Ciche, I'll make for the Stone Shoot.'

It was Miranda, peering through the window into the darkened garden, who brought relief.

'They're back.'

That evening after dinner, notwithstanding a marked lack of enthusiasm among the majority of the party, Henry had drummed up an entertainment in the drawing room.

'Your father is quite inexorable when it comes to organising others,' sighed Millie, as she settled on the sofa beside her granddaughter. 'It comes of being an Archdeacon.'

Each of the twins had been required to learn a poem which, standing in the middle of the room, hands behind their backs, they duly recited, aided by promptings from their mother. Their discomfort at this humiliation, though, was as nothing compared to their mortification as their father, affecting an excruciating northern accent, performed a comic monologue after the manner of Stanley Holloway.

The adults, though, clapping politely at the conclusion, seemed to accept it with a good grace.

'And now,' announced Henry, 'I've managed to persuade father to give us a short reading from his magnum opus.'

Glances were exchanged around the family. Everybody knew it would have taken little persuasion. Professor Marlowe's translation of *The Odyssey* had been long in preparation, and was still far from finished. It was one of his little vanities, however, whenever an opportunity arose, to try out his work-in-progress on a live audience.

'This passage,' he began to explain, 'is from Book Five, in which we first meet Odysseus himself, imprisoned by the nymph Calypso on the island of Ogygia. I'm afraid the authentic verse form has proved rather beyond me. But at least I've avoided the barbarous practice of rendering the poet's dactyllic hexameters into prose.'

Clearing his throat, Marlowe began to recite in a reedy sing-song:
'On Calypso's isle in exile groaning,
Once more beside the sea-shore weeping,
Staring out across the barren ocean
Odysseus shed bitter tears... '

Succeeding verses went on to tell how that unhappy man, after shattering experiences in war and on the stormy seas, had been cast ashore on the isle of an enchantress; and how, in hardship, and with neither gods nor men to help him, and with a heart inured to suffering, the outcast wanderer had set out once more across the unending waves in search of his lost home.

Giles had been unusually subdued since his return from the hill. Now, as polite applause greeted the conclusion of the recital, he turned to his friend.

'Grandfather has the heretical notion that it wasn't Homer who wrote The Odyssey. Apparently it was some unknown woman poet. Isn't that right, grandfather?'

'So Samuel Butler believed, and so do I,' said Marlowe good-humouredly. 'She was probably a Sicilian noblewoman. My colleagues, however, take a different view. On that subject I'm in a minority of one.'

Meanwhile Miranda, sensing some discomfort in her grandmother, pressed her hand consolingly.

'And now Morag is going to sing for us.'

Hugh, who had been about to pull a face, was transfixed suddenly by his grandmother's eye.

Smiling, Henry beckoned towards the door where the girl stood with Mrs MacRath. She came forward shyly. Then, standing in the middle of the room, without preliminaries of any kind, she began to sing. It was a voice entirely without artifice. A voice that was simply a vehicle, yet with a plangent quality that had much to do with its soft vibrancy, the notes issuing without any apparent effort of breath, soft as rain, a melodic line rising, falling, pure as spring water, the grace-notes fluted forth as effortlessly as from the throat of a bird.

The effect upon the English visitors was startling. Having composed themselves to listen indulgently to a servant girl's singing, they found themselves, as if under an enchantment, driven apart from one other, each into a deeper part of the wood. For some, at least, of the rapt faces looking up at her, overshadowed by bitter memories of an earlier war coupled with the fear of a war to come, her song might have told of some longed-for destination, a place apart. Entranced, Marlowe's face reflected, if not what she sang, then what he heard. Long ago, at the height of his passionate love affair with the Highlands he'd taught himself some Gaelic. He'd long since forgotten much of it. Yet what greater bliss, the song seemed to be saying, than to be young and happy here in those days before the war? Rising early on a May morning, shafts of sun on the hill, sorrow a stranger, heart leaping the height of joy. For Henry, eyes closed, it might have been a glimpse of hearts at peace under an English heaven. Richard Fleming, though, was carried back to a taverna sweating in the heat, a baked, hawk-like face upturned, and the harsh voice of a woman keening a grief that had echoed down the centuries, a grief that told of exile and betrayal, and the young man's heart wept again for Spain.

As the last, soft notes sank finally into silence it might have been a song without end that continued to echo in the rapt attention of the listeners.

'What was the song about?' enquired Lady Kitty suddenly, in her brisk English voice. And the spell was broken.

Miranda, though, saw that her grandmother's eyes were filled with tears.

Sometimes, when Millie looked back to those first months of the Great War it was as if to a bygone age, a picture gallery of shaven heads and waxed moustaches: plumed, helmeted, blank-eyed in the grip of grand designs, or glaring in demented pride, the crowned heads, the arch-dukes, the generals and field-marshals at whose behest so many husbands, fathers, brothers, sons, had marched away.

And whenever she was caught unawares, as she sometimes was, by John McCormack singing on the wireless:

'There's a long, long trail a-winding
Into the land of... my dreams,
Where the night-in-gale is singing,
And a white moon beams...'

What she heard, beyond the high, reedy tenor, was an ancient tramp of boots, and the deep, sad voices of an endless line of marching men, winding back to a catastrophe she'd never come to terms with, remembering it was said to be for women like her, the wives and sweethearts, but knowing only that he never should have gone. I expect he wanted to have an adventure, exclaimed little Miranda, clasping her hands. For the story of how their grandfather had dyed his hair to fool the Army into taking him had been a favourite with the children. Oh no, said the grandmother. Your grandfather wanted to kill a German.

No, he never should have gone. But the heroes marched away. And the young girls pelted them with flowers. Girls with pure closed faces pronouncing a doom on those, ah, they should have clung to.

When he came home after those first weeks on the Somme he might have been struck dumb. Slumped in a chair, staring wordlessly. From time to time covering his head with his arms, as if trying to obliterate some bleak point of consciousness, to pull down closeness, darkness. What is it? What's wrong? She put her arms around him. It was no use. She couldn't reach him. Nothing she could do would bring him back.

That night, she remembered, he'd lain next to her, inert, frozen. She woke to find him sitting up in bed, shaking. Oh Millie, the wounded... the wounded... he'd suddenly blurted. And clung, sobbing, while she held him.

Sometimes, in those years after the war, she would go up to her sewing room at the top of the house and weep for what had been done to Stephen. It was as if there was some darkness locked up inside him. And he couldn't let it out. And she hadn't been able to get at it. What is it, she used to ask. What's the matter? Though not expecting to be told. And would reach out a hand towards his shoulder. Where it lay unregarded. Until at length she had to fetch it back. Sometimes, when the darkness had been more than usually perplexing, she would take out his letters and go through them again, letters trying so hard to be bright and cheerful, but favouring always a green envelope from which would slip a dried-up scrap of crimson (picked, he wrote, from the sandbag in front of him). Supposedly an uncensored letter, in which he'd told her how much he loved her. Don't you believe it, someone else had written in red ink.

Yes, those years at the front had left their mark. His face strained, unsmiling, with a flinty, narrow-eyed way of looking about him. It was as if a shutter had come down, closing off great parts of him, leaving her to live on what was left.

Somehow they had found their way to a kind of co-existence, he in his teaching, she in the routine of her daily life, discovering a middle way that somehow kept at bay the darkness. Yes, things might have gone differently but for the war. But she never held him responsible for that. She would never have done that. What hurt her so was that, instead of turning to her, he should have chosen a stony refuge where love could find no purchase.

But now Mrs MacRath and her daughter were coming in with trays of fresh coffee.

'That was beautiful, Morag,' continued the Archdeacon. 'Quite beautiful.' Looking meaningfully around the family, he led the applause.

Miranda, though, had laid a hand upon her grandmother's arm.

'When my own Odysseus came back after the war,' Millie was

saying softly, amid the clapping, 'there was a space around him. A kind of 'No Man's Land'. She smiled her thanks at Andrew who was handing her a cup of coffee. 'You see, your grandfather was one of those men who never quite climbed out of the trenches. I don't think he ever has, really. To me he is still listed as missing.'

Then her grand-daughter, with a sudden stroke of insight, asked gently, 'Is that why you wear black?'

The old woman smiled. 'Perhaps it is, my dear. Perhaps it is'

And so, because one confidence will often invite another, or else because the young woman was longing to tell someone, Miranda yielded to impulse.

'You know I told you I was in love with someone? It's Charles Bartrum.'

Instantly she realised her own miscalculation.

'Oh dear,' said Millie, after a pause.

'Well, I did tell you he was unsuitable,' said Miranda lightly, with a nervous laugh.

'And do you wish to marry Charles?'

'Yes.'

'Because you believe you can change him?' It was an assumption, not a question.

Miranda said nothing. Because no. That was not what she wanted at all.

Her grandmother sighed. 'It's never wise to marry someone in the belief you can change them. Far better marry the right man in the first place.'

— CHAPTER EIGHT —

Henry was up early the next morning. As usual he had the day's events all arranged. He'd organised a boat trip to Canna for the twins. Their mother, though, had made her usual fuss about it.

'They'll be perfectly safe,' Henry assured her. 'MacDonald is an expert boatman. He's spent all his life fishing these waters.'

'You're too protective of those children, Vanessa,' said Millie. 'You always have been. That's the way to lose them.'

But no. Vanessa was not prepared to entrust her sons to some island peasant. Some responsible person must go with them. Fortunately, Richard had been good enough to volunteer.

Henry had just seen them off, and was returning to the Lodge when he encountered his father chatting to MacRath outside the barn.

'Giles seemed rather subdued last night,' said Marlowe abruptly. 'I take it he'd bitten off rather more than he could chew.'

'Well, we've all done that, father,' said Henry, who'd thought the same. Once again he resolved Leo and not Giles would have to lead the first rope on Marlowe's Variation.

Richard and the twins had already left for their boat trip by the time the rest of the family began to appear at the breakfast table.

'Kit will be down shortly,' announced Leo, as if they were all attending her arrival. 'As you know she's rather a night bird. It takes her a while to get going in the morning.'

Lady Kitty had proposed to lead a cliff-top walk for the ladies.

'Well, who's for Collie's Route?' Leo asked, helping himself to eggs and bacon. 'Henry? Father? I dare say Giles will want to lead his rope up something harder. '

As usual Miranda was late for breakfast. And since she wanted to climb with the men they took their time over the meal in enjoyable anticipation of what promised to be an exciting day.

'Do you know, I'm really looking forward to this,' Leo went on. 'It's years since I climbed in the Cuillin.'

'I do hope this will not result in our names appearing in the papers,' remarked his father dryly.

Leo's guided ascent the previous summer of the huge east face of the Watzmann had found its way into the gossip columns.

'A politician has to keep his name before the public eye. It's part of the job, father.'

'When is Charles arriving?' asked Giles suddenly. He rather admired Bartrum. The worldly good looks, the raffish reputation. That dramatic dash to the Pyrenees to rescue Richard had seemed to him especially daring.

'Oh really, Henry,' said Vanessa. 'You haven't invited Charles Bartrum, surely!'

'I merely mentioned it to him,' said her husband evasively. 'I don't suppose he'll turn up.'

'I don't dislike Charles Bartrum,' said Millie, rather surprisingly.

Miranda flashed her grandmother a grateful smile.

'Millie! He's an absolute Italian. The worst kind of philanderer.'

'We have to accept Charles for what he is, with all his imperfections on his head,' said the Archdeacon. 'He's unique.'

'He's a rogue,' said his wife tartly.

'Oh, that's a bit strong,' protested the Archdeacon. 'Besides, I don't suppose he'll turn up.'

'Well, I for one will be very glad to welcome him,' said Susannah firmly. 'He brought me back my son.'

***

It was now a pleasant morning, warm, with a hazy sun, though a cap of cloud hung over the Coire Lagan summits as the climbing party set out across the moor. They traversed the north side of Loch an Fhir-Bhaillach before crossing the mouth of the corrie, pausing at the burn flowing down from Coire Lagan to fill water bottles. Their way now lay up the Sgumain Stone Shoot, skirting the great buttresses and gullies of Sròn na Ciche. Nicko pointed out the little tent pitched in a grassy recess under the Western Buttress of Sgumain.

As they drew level with the Cioch Buttress a faint sound of voices, a confused shouting it might have been, drifted down from somewhere high overhead. Retreating further out into the corrie, they gazed upwards at the gigantic hanging nose of the Cioch. High above, on the Upper Cioch buttress, amid an irregular fretwork of cracked seams and jutting shadows, gleams of September sunlight fell across pale terracotta slabs.

It was the sharp-eyed Nicko, though, who was the first to spot a human presence.

'There they are,' he cried, pointing. 'No, there! There!' Jabbing a finger at a conspicuous dark smudge shaped vaguely like a question mark—the depth of shadow suggested an overhanging crack or chimney—beneath which a tiny figure was just visible, attempting to communicate, as it seemed, with some unseen companion. What was being said exactly it wasn't possible to make out. But a heated discussion appeared to be in full swing.

'I wonder if it's their tent,' said Nicko.

Giles, though, was gazing up at the climbers seven hundred feet above the floor of the corrie where he stood.

'What are they on?'

'It looks like the Crack of Doom,' said Marlowe.

'It's supposed to be the hardest climb in Skye,' added Henry.

'What is the 'crack of doom'?' asked Miranda curiously.

'It's a quotation from Macbeth. It means 'a very long way'.'

'It doesn't look all that long.'

'I expect it just feels like that,' said Marlowe dryly.

'Well, you should ask Richard,' said Henry. 'He's done it.'

'That was in the days before mountaineering became a frivolous bourgeois pastime,' Leo couldn't resist adding.

Toiling further up the stones at length they reached a break in the rocks which marked their next objective, the start of the Terrace, a well-defined rake climbing steeply across the face of Sròn na Ciche.

'Does anyone want a rope on this?' asked Leo, gazing at the

initial mauvais pas.

But they managed without, edging round a rib on thin footholds, before crossing the gap of Eastern Gully and arriving at the grassy continuation of the terrace.

Now, rising at their feet, was a great, pock-marked slab, glittering where the sun caught crystal facets in the gabbro. And far overhead, though hanging, as it seemed, directly above them, the Cioch Upper Buttress, a huge mass of shadowy grooves and overhangs. Slanting up the left edge of the slab was a deep crack, the line taken by Collie's first ascent forty years before.

'This is where we start,' announced Leo. 'You're over there, Giles.' He pointed into the shadows where the far end of the slab abutted against the massive pillar forming the base of the Cioch itself. 'You go up the corner, then out on to the left wall.'

'Good God,' said Nicko, who'd read in Steeple and Barlowe of a rough slab sparsely provided with holds, but was not expecting this. It looked intimidating. Not so much the angle as the sheer size of the thing, the towering blankness.

'The grippiest gabbro in the Cuillin,' said Leo stoutly. For Miranda was looking dubious, to say the least. 'You'll be fine,' he reassured her. 'You'll see. Your kletterschuhe will stick like glue.'

Collie's Route began in the trench-like crack set at an easy angle, following the edge of Eastern Gully. Marlowe, climbing comfortably in the crack, found he was able to savour in perfect safety the considerable drop on his left. After two rope-lengths, where the slab began to steepen, Leo led his party down to a ledge on the wall of the gully, traversing across the wall to reach the gully floor. A short distance further up, a rather wet scramble brought them up to the shelf, a secure recess under the over-hanging Upper Buttress that ran parallel with the top of the great slab.

Here they climbed up onto the sloping crest of the shelf, narrower, more exposed than Marlowe remembered, and descended to a surprising grassy belvedere behind the neck of the Cioch. Here they found Miranda munching a chocolate bar, while Nicko belayed Giles as he prepared to descend from the Cioch itself.

'Have you done it?'

'Not as bad as it looks,' she called out. 'Giles is on the scariest bit now.'

The three older men had gathered behind the low parapet which formed the top of the great slab, from which the huge protuberance known as the Cioch jutted like a gigantic prow, and to which it was connected by the neck, a sloping arête that narrowed as it descended, and up which Giles was now edging gingerly. It really was extremely exposed, with a long drop down the Cioch Slab on one side, and an even steeper, longer plunge into the Cioch Gully on the other.

'What an amazing place', Giles called out as he joined the rest of the party.

'Well, father,' said Leo, 'if you'll just watch the rope.'

Without more ado he set off down the narrow arête with, it struck the onlookers, a certain swagger. No inching à cheval for him. Now followed the option of a short traverse out across the gully wall to gain a chimney which led, within a few feet, to the top of the Cioch. I bet he won't take it, thought Marlowe. Sure enough, scorning the traverse and the comforting chimney, Leo stepped boldly up the exposed, slabby corner of the Cioch, and was soon on the summit platform.

'Trust you to choose the easy option,' shouted his brother gaily.

'It's the proper way to do it.'

Marlowe, though, was reflecting that any way was proper which would get him up and down again in one piece. He stepped down the neck as far as he thought prudent and finished the last few feet à cheval.

Shorter than his sons, he found it more convenient to use the lower traverse line for his hands, with his feet on the gully wall, and was soon pulling up into the chimney, any apprehensions he might have had soon dissolving in its close embrace.

A few moments later he emerged onto the roof, a spoon-shaped, sloping platform some twenty feet in extent hanging over the great bowl of Coire Lagan.

'Would you believe it,' he gasped, 'I once drank champagne on this very spot.'

'Aha,' said his son, who had not forgotten that oft-repeated story. 'I have a surprise. Though it might be a bit fizzy after all this bouncing about.'

Reaching into his rucksac he produced a half bottle of Pol Roger.

'If you want a glass, Henry,' he shouted down, 'you'll have to come up here.'

'Climbing,' shouted the Archdeacon.

'I thought that would bring him,' said Leo as his father took in the rope. Delving into the sac he brought out three glasses, each muffled in a sock wrapped around with a towel.

'Technically very easy,' remarked Leo, as his brother emerged from the chimney, 'but still a real expedition, don't you think?'

'I formed the impression our line was probably a touch harder than yours,' said Henry. 'If less exposed.'

But all agreed, as they sipped champagne, that it was indeed a real expedition. On such a day as this, the further world swallowed up in misty distances, it had a real, old-fashioned mountain atmosphere.

'Do you know,' said Leo, 'I don't know why a man should want to bother with politics when he can do this sort of thing.'

'Don't we get any champagne?' came a voice from below.

'Certainly not,' Leo called back. 'Champagne is a pleasure best reserved for one's maturity. I'm sure Mrs MacRae will have included some oranges in your packed lunch.'

So, laughing, chaffing one another, they made their way, a merry party, back along the shelf to Eastern Gully, and the final obstacle, an enormous boulder blocking further progress.

Giles began casting around for some alternative.

'It can't possibly go up here,' he cried, horrified. Though it seemed all too probable. Here being a vertical side wall, dripping with water, with one discernable hold, and what looked like an appalling finish.

'You'll find the key under the boulder,' quipped Marlowe. 'Well, not so much the key as the key-hole,' he added. And so it proved, a narrow slot in a cave-like recess which offered a passage through to the top of the wet wall.

Giles was the first to pull up, slither, and squeeze through.

What followed provoked much hilarity, the top halves of bodies emerging painfully, like corks from a bottle, providing as funny a sight for those who'd already made the transition as the wriggling bottom halves provided for those waiting their turn, Leo, who'd remained behind to pass up the rucksacs, being the last to follow.

Within a minute or two they'd arrived on the stony, summit plateau of Sròn na Ciche.

Now, with the mist rolling away, they ate their sandwiches, watching Canna, Rhum and Eigg coming into view across the Minch. They searched the sea for the tiny boat carrying Richard and the twins, but all surfaces were shimmering as one in that multi-faceted expanse of ocean.

It had been a day of mountain happiness. Of much laughter. And there was more laughter too, at the memory of Giles's face contemplating that wet wall, or Henry's bottom-half as, puffing and blowing, legs kicking, he'd squeezed through the hole in Eastern Gully.

All agreed that the Cioch was indeed unique.

'I didn't dare look down.'

'I did,' said Miranda. 'I lay on my stomach and peered over the edge. Those great boulders in the Stone Shoot looked no bigger than pebbles.'

'How far is it?'

'To the scree?' said Leo. 'About 600 feet.'

'I was hoping to see the Crack of Doom,' said Giles.

'I don't think it's visible from the Cioch.'

'I do wish Richard could have been with us,' said Miranda suddenly. 'It's all been so wonderful.'

If no one spoke it might have been because they, too, were registering, perhaps with a sense too quick for the mind to hold, that same resonance with a larger reality to which they felt somehow akin. As if something had broken through the carefully erected boundaries which divide mind from nature. As if it were all alive; mountain, moorland, sea and river and sky. For a moment they were turned outwards; might have felt, with a rush of relief and thankfulness, that they were not yet quite lost to the wonder and strangeness of things. Marlowe, looking round at the party assembled in this place of fullness, saw them united in a simple happiness unsullied by anything other than itself.

He'd first climbed up here with Millie's brother thirty years before. Robert it was who'd brought champagne to celebrate, as they'd believed, the first direct ascent to the Cioch. Before they drank, Robert held up a hand. First, he said, a libation… pouring a generous measure onto the rock. To the mountain gods.

As he looked back over the years, that far-off day seemed to have come alive again, renewed in the joy of this day, not simply as a memory of something gone forever, but as the return of what was undying in his life.

Looking now at his family, he hoped they might remember this time and place of fullness, and cling to it as a promise. That it might be to them, even amid the wretchedness and dereliction of a war which he firmly believed was coming, an irruption of joy. The affirmation of a world that remained a gift.

After a vigorous day on the cliff-top, much blown about by the sea breeze, the ladies were ready for tea. Vanessa, though, not finding the twins on her return, walked up by the burn to meet her husband as he came down from the hill.

'Have you seen the boys?' she called out anxiously. 'They're not in the Lodge. I thought they might have walked up to meet you.'

'They must be back,' said Henry. 'That's MacDonald's boat out on the loch. I expect Mrs Chisholm is giving them tea.'

At that moment, though, they were surprised by the sound of a low, throbbing engine note. Marlowe took it for one of MacRath's machines.

'That sounds like Charles,' said Miranda suddenly.

If no one remarked the brightness of her face it was because the rest of them had turned to gaze where a distant cloud of dust was approaching noisily down the glen.

'It is Charles,' announced Giles, for whom the throaty growl of the six cylinder engine was unmistakeable. He set off down to the road immediately with Nicko and Miranda to await the new arrival.

'And whose idea was this?' hissed Vanessa furiously. 'What did he say to talk you into it?'

'The suggestion was entirely mine, Vanessa,' said Henry firmly. 'All Charles said was that he'd never been to Skye. That's all.'

'And so of course you had to invite him,' retorted his wife scornfully. 'How easily duped you are, Henry!'

Marlowe, tactfully declaring his need for tea, took Vanessa back to the Lodge. Henry followed the track down to the road to greet his guest.

'Where's Charles going to sleep?' Miranda asked her father.

'I've put him in one of the farm cottages. I must remember to let him know that the electric lights go out at eleven o'clock. '

'Gosh, it really *is* a Lagonda,' exclaimed Nicko, as the rakish red two-seater drew to a halt beside the sheep-pens.

No one knew how Bartrum had come by such a princely possession. Some said he'd inherited it from a rich uncle. Rumour had it he'd won it in a card-game from the same used-car dealer in Warren Street who used to take it back in pawn whenever Charles was on his uppers. Whatever the truth of it, the great scarlet motor car was its owner's pride and joy.

'It's very demanding to drive,' a deep voice was explaining. 'You need the leg of an elephant to step on the clutch, but it keeps me in shape,'

The speaker was a tall, handsome man of striking appearance, broad-shouldered, with a neat beard and dark, abundant hair, tumbling into curls. Charles Bartrum had the look of a man very much at ease among other men. Though in fact it tended to be women with whom he achieved the more success. Miranda loved the grey eyes set deep under the broad brow, and the way the skin wrinkled around his eyes when he smiled. She loved his quite unconscious habit of stroking the edge of his moustache absently with a finger, when considering. Her mother, though, had observed that Charles Bartrum invariably glanced in any mirror he might happen to come across.

Something of a leech, though generous when in funds, he was also 'a splendid, incomparable talker' according to Henry, who'd once bought him dinner at Schmidt's.

'He talked for three hours,' the Archdeacon told his father. 'A brilliant extemporization on everything under the sun. For the most part I did nothing but listen. I might have done better to have remained silent altogether. My disposition to argue a particular point cost me an extra bottle, most of which went the same way as the first.'

Bartrum, though, had paid for his dinner with the only currency he had.

His powers as a *raconteur* were firmly established among the *habitués* of the pubs, the out-of hours drinking clubs and jazz dives of Fitzrovia, men and women of whom it might be said that talking while drinking was a way of life. A spirited account of his Pyrenean adventure, suitably embellished, had made its way from the Fitzroy Tavern to The Black Horse in Rathbone Place, to the Bricklayer's Arms just round the corner, to The Wheatsheaf, then across the road to The Marquess of Granby, then further up the street to The Duke of York.

That night it was heard again with evident enjoyment in the dining room at Glenbrittle Lodge, for Bartrum was one of those storytellers so exhilarated by his own narrative that the passion of the thing invariably engaged even the most sceptical of listeners.

'What you have to realise,' he began, 'is that the frontier means very little for the people who live there. You quite often have members of the same family living either side of the border. And of course it's a lawless region. They've been smuggling back and forth for centuries. '

Miranda sat gazing down the table, her eyes fixed on him as he went on to tell how he'd made his way to the *Bar Cathar* in the village of San Vicente, and found the man Primitivo in a bar 'full of dark, grizzly brigands', as he put it.

'I tell you, every voice fell silent. Every eye in the place was fixed on me. Well, I thought, I've seen the last of the Lagonda.'

Bartrum laughed aloud at the memory. And when he laughed, it struck Miranda, his whole face leapt into life.

'Who was Primitivo?' she asked...

'A smuggler. A man of few words. Those mostly unrepeatable in present company.'

He laughed again.

'I began to fear we might have to pay a ransom to get Richard back,' he went on. 'Indeed, I was by no means convinced I wouldn't have to wire Henry for more funds,' he added teasingly, with a glance at Vanessa. 'But it seemed Primitivo had already been well paid for his services. Either that, or he was mortally afraid of whoever it was had given him his instructions.'

So it was that they learnt how, setting off with his guide by little-known mule tracks, the speaker was led at last to his quarry, delivered as promised to a squalid *cabane* on the side of a mountain, a dramatic narrative in which, in a mixture of English, French and Spanish, punctuated with guttural bursts of *patois*, Bartrum played all the parts himself. Sometimes leering, sometimes frowning hideously, brows drawn together, sometimes affecting a nervous twitching of an eye, he was by turns innkeeper, smuggler, muleteer, goatherd all in one.

'But if the Fascists had caught you you might both have been *shot.*'

Miranda was looking at him with shining eyes.

'Oh, no.' The speaker affected a careless nonchalance. 'I would have talked them out of it.'

There was a burst of laughter around the table. There were some there who almost believed him.

Weren't they stopped on their way back through France?

'Oh yes, we were stopped,' he said. 'We were stopped several times. But it was as I expected.' Bartrum demonstrated, with eloquent hand gestures and Gallic shrugs of the shoulders, how he'd dealt with the *gendarmes*. 'They were far more interested in the car than the English *milord* and his passenger.'

'But the *real* story,' he concluded, 'belongs to Richard.' He turned deferentially to the man sitting at his side.

Richard, though, only shook his head. He looked thoroughly alarmed.

As they were crossing the hall after dinner Leo took Henry by the arm.

'When are we going to climb father's route?'

'Well, it should be the climax of the holiday, don't you think? One day next week?'

'Well, don't leave it too late. Though the weather seems settled now it could change at any time.'

'True. How about Monday? Though I think I'd prefer you to lead the first rope, Leo. Giles is a good climber, but he has little experience of tackling these longer routes on unfamiliar rock.'

Tired after the day's exertions Marlowe sank gratefully into his armchair. He'd enjoyed his day and, like most if not all of those present, had found Bartrum's narrative richly entertaining. The fellow certainly had a talent to amuse. Meanwhile, the younger members of the family prepared to pass the evening with the customary diversions. As well as the previous day's papers offering a variety of crossword puzzles, they had Agatha Christie, not to mention Wodehouse, Priestly, Louis Golding and A J Cronin, besides the usual games.

Lady Kitty played *Snakes and Ladders* with the twins.

'I've never been beaten at *Snakes and Ladders*,' she announced impressively.

'Be warned, she cheats,' said Leo.

And so she did. Aunt Kitty, it seemed, went *up* the Snakes as well as up the Ladders.

'No self-respecting snake would swallow a lady,' she told them solemnly. And got away with it too.

Miranda found a book to hide behind, while watching anxiously as her mother engaged Bartrum in conversation.

'You had a long drive from London?' enquired Vanessa coldly.

'Very long,' agreed Bartrum politely. He knew better than to turn on the charm.

'Almost as far as the Pyrenees, in fact.' She was convinced the Archdeacon had once again provided funds for his journey.

'Not quite. Very nearly, though,' he added helpfully.

Millie was turning the cards as usual. Watching her, Marlowe reflected how much of her life now was given over to the practice of patience. Watching, waiting, *'until the white-rob'd Reapers come'*.

As Aunt Kitty's bending of the rules began to pall, and good-humoured protests seemed more and more likely to end in rudeness and bad manners, the twins were whisked away to bed.

Kitty fell to perusing the Climbers' Book.

'Why, some of the entries here go back well before the war.'

'Ah, the Golden Age,' said Leo playfully, looking up from *The Times*. 'Father would very much prefer to return to things just as they were in 1914.'

Was that so very far from the truth, thought Marlowe, remembering those joyful days of old. 'Joy' was the first source in which his life then had been grounded. He frowned, and shook his head.

'On the contrary, Leo. I'm well aware those days are gone forever. I fear that what fell upon us in 1914 may only have been a prelude to a far greater horror that awaits us now.'

An uncomfortable silence descended on the family. Once again the old man had cast his shadow over their bright day.

'Does that radio work?' asked Leo suddenly. 'It's nearly time for the news.'

Henry reached across and, fiddling with the knob, located a succession of crackles and hisses from which a faint voice eventually emerged.

Earlier today the Prime Minister flew to Bad Godesberg for his second meeting with Herr Hitler. 'European peace,' Mr Chamberlain declared, 'is what I am aiming at…'

'What he's aiming at,' said Leo grimly, 'and what he's going to get, are entirely different.'

'Absolutely! Poor Debbo was actually present at that ghastly demonstration in Nuremberg.'

Lady Kitty's daughter, boarding with an aristocratic family near Nuremberg, had been taken to a Nazi rally by a Wehrmacht officer. *I think you should come,* he told her. *It would be educational for you.* For the young English girl it had proved too much of an education—the goose-stepping boots cracking onto the metalled road—the raving, maniacal voice—the frenzied baying of the crowd…

'Debbo sent us the most frightful account of it,' continued Lady Kitty. '*Why did you take me to that awful display?* she asked him. *Because I want you to go home and tell everyone about it.* Doesn't that say it all?'

The crackly voice of the announcer, which had faded briefly, now returned more strongly.

This evening the Ministry of Health issued the following statement. Thirty-four hospitals in the London area have been allotted as clearing stations for air raid casualties. Detailed plans have been prepared for removing between three and four thousand patients by ambulance trains to towns over fifty miles from London. Casualties would be taken to the railway stations in motor coaches converted to carry stretcher…'

A sombre silence followed the conclusion of the bulletin. Millie thought of the Zeppelin hanging over the Houses of Parliament the night of the 'Theatreland' raid, the huge air-ship lit up by the searchlights in Whitehall. She thought of her cousin, Henry Daintrey. Hearing the roar of explosions in the Strand he'd left his chambers behind the Law Courts moments before they were destroyed, only to run directly into the path of the following bomb falling in Chancery Lane. Henry remembered the report in *The Times* of Baldwin's aerial warfare speech; that the bomber would always get through. Leo, who'd been in the House to hear that speech, thought of the interminable delays in getting the new interceptor fighter into production, though the factory was already working at full capacity.

'They're as good as telling us no power on earth can protect us,' whispered Vanessa.

She had been clinging to Lord Beaverbrook's assurance, repeated over and over again that summer, that there would be no war. Yet war seemed closer than ever.

'Well, we can only hope,' said Marlowe quietly, 'that Chamberlain may yet pull something out of the fire.'

Bartrum caught Miranda's eye, and the anxious look directed at him. He smiled at her reassuringly, as if to say '*Of course he will*'. Though he didn't think it very likely.

— CHAPTER NINE —

He'd first met her in Coldstream's studio in Fitzroy Street. She sat on a cushion on a low, wide window seat, her slight, slim torso naked to the waist, the lower half of her body draped in a sheet. Her head was turned to one side, eyes modestly cast down, presumably as Coldstream had instructed. Sunlight, streaming in at an angle behind one shoulder, fell on the curve of a breast. She glanced up, startled by the stranger. He'd had no more than a glimpse of her before she snatched up the sheet to cover herself. He saw then that her eyes were almond shaped, and of an olive green.

'This is Charles Bartrum, Miranda,' said Coldstream. 'A local ne'er-do-well. You should steer clear of him. '

'Hello Miranda,' said Bartrum. He smiled at her. Lit from behind, her corn-coloured hair seemed all a-flame.

She stared uncertainly. Then she, too, smiled shyly. Her mouth, it struck him, quite likely sulky or sensual by turns, hinted at capacities of which the young woman was perhaps not yet aware. *For Christ's sake*, he told himself. *She's little more than a child.* He wondered sometimes if it was the predator in him that found vulnerability so very attractive.

'OK, sweetie, that'll do for now.'

The girl slipped out of the chair, enveloped in the sheet, and went behind a screen to dress.

Bartrum, meanwhile, studied the work in progress. Covering the surface of the canvas was a grid on which were arranged a great many small ticks and crosses aligned vertically over or under, or horizontally opposite one another, visual co-ordinates representing a kind of scaffolding for the intended portrait.

'Doesn't look much like her.'

'First you have to assemble the data,' explained Coldstream patiently, while rinsing his brush. 'It has to be exact, which is necessarily laborious. Individuality comes later.'

Bartrum, though, had moved on to another canvas of a seated

nude propped against the wall. He studied the bleached colour, the meagre dole of paint, and the woman's body, drained of life.

'How long did this take you?'

'Oh, a couple of years, I suppose.'

How could a man have spent two years painting that, thought Bartrum, and not noticed that the head was obviously too big for the rest of the body? It was quite beyond him. It was obviously beyond Bill Coldstream, too.

Then the girl re-emerged from behind the screen. She had changed into a short-sleeved dress of cornflower blue.

'Same time tomorrow,' said Coldstream. 'Don't be late.'

Bartrum's eyes followed her as she left the studio. He couldn't help but think of the contrast between the canvas with its washed-out colours, and the living body he had glimpsed all too briefly.

'Hands off, Charles. She's a clergyman's daughter.'

'How every enticing,' he said dryly.

'An Archdeacon, no less.'

Bartrum glanced sharply at his friend.

'Not Henry Marlowe, by any chance?'

'The very same. Why? Do you know him?'

'I do indeed. He once hauled me out of the gutter.'

'Only once?'

'Well, perhaps once or twice,' laughed Bartrum.

The Archdeacon's sympathy for lame dogs had long been a sore point with his wife.

'You're far too inclined to see redeeming features where none exist.'

Where Bartrum was concerned, the truth was Henry didn't know the half of it. He'd first come across him on a pastoral visit to Wormwood Scrubs, Bartrum having been caught out filching one too many volumes of *Gray's Anatomy* to sell cheap to impecunious medical students. Described in court by his barrister, a guinea-a-time dock-brief, as '*part of the sad flotsam and jetsam of humanity that fetches up in London's Bohemian Quarter*', he supplemented a small annuity with such income as he could pick up on the fringes of the literary world, reviewing for the weeklies, collaborating on film scripts, or devilling for editors at the BBC. Henry, who had literary leanings himself, had done what he could to put further work his way, introducing him to Graham Greene who, captivated by Bartrum's talk, had commissioned some pieces for *Night & Day*. Bartrum, though, despite repeated promises and reminders, had failed to send in any copy.

His principal earnings, such as they were, came from pieces of the reportage (*Notes from the Underground*) with which he had first made a small reputation in the weekly journals as the pseudonymous '*An observer of the London scene*'. Though his territory was that rough square mile between Portland Place and Tottenham Court Road, and bounded by Oxford Street and the Euston Road, an area for which he was the first to coin the name (though subsequently stolen by a gossip columnist in the *Daily Express*) 'Fitzrovia'; 'a rogue republic', as he called it, 'flourishing in the very heart of royal London', where virtue was the abnormality and every kind of vice traded to the great profit of some and the ruin of many more.

The demands of his calling carried him into the clubs, the after-hours drinking and gambling dens patronised by pimps, crooks, dealers in pornography, thieves, dope-pedlars and the gangsters spilling over from Soho. Here he uncovered a world as old as mankind, an anarchic *demi-monde* which both attracted and repelled, and which provided a testimony to his own dual nature. Whatever a man's mood or taste in prohibited desires and inclinations it could be accommodated in Fitzrovia. Indeed, if you wanted a banned book, or had a friend who needed an illegal operation Charles would know someone who could find you a man for the job. He'd become an *habitué* of pubs frequented by tarts of both sexes who, for the price of a drink, would complain to him about the hardships of their trade, the difficulty of making ends meet, what with grasping landlords and unpredictable clients, and the constant persecution by the police, not to mention competition from younger boys or girls who'd only been five minutes in the business and thought they knew it all. And he would listen and drink and talk himself, and afterwards write up the copy for his *Notes from the Underground*. And as the drinking and the talk increased so his work had fallen off, a fate which, as he was well aware, had overtaken many another literary aspirant camping out in Fitzrovia.

Only too conscious of the contradictions of his own character he took comfort from some words of Henry James: '*So armed you are not really helpless, not without your resources, even before mysteries abysmal.*'

For several days after that first meeting he could think of nothing but Miranda. It was warm for early March, and the London streets seemed filled with that sense of restless expectancy which signalled the approach of Spring. For Bartrum though, haunting Fitzroy Street, that restlessness was tinged with a sense of weary self-disgust. What was he doing here? Up to his old tricks? Lying in wait for yet another woman? If he sought them out much as a shipwrecked sailor thirsts for a sail it was, he told himself, because they offered a refuge from the constant burden of discouragement, of self-reproach, plans framed and torn up, and resumed only to be again abandoned. And if each affair invariably fizzled out, each fresh liaison brought with it the buoyancy of a new beginning.

Then, one afternoon, he came face to face with her coming down from Coldstream's studio. She was wearing the same short-sleeved dress of cornflower blue. He couldn't think what to say. Awkwardly, he asked if she would like some tea. It was the first thing that came into his head.

She looked at him uncertainly for a moment. Then smiled, nodded.

'Yes. That would be nice.'

He was at a loss to know what to do next. His own rooms suddenly seemed unutterably squalid for such a genteel thing as drinking tea. He wasn't even sure he had any tea.

'There's a Lyon's teashop in Euston Road,' she suggested tactfully, coming to his rescue. 'We go there sometimes after school.'

'School?'

'The school of Painting and Drawing. William's school.'

'William? Oh, Coldstream. Everyone calls him 'Bill'.'

'I call him William.'

They both laughed.

She was obviously familiar with the tea-shop, and led the way to a table in a discreet corner well away from the window. He ordered a pot of English Breakfast tea.

'Shall we have biscuits?' she asked hopefully. 'They are a penny extra.'

Usually at his ease with women he was as tongue-tied as a boy. So they sat in silence, nibbling their biscuits. At length she hit on a topic of conversation in the shape of the black-clad waitresses darting between the tables.

'Why are they called 'nippies'?'

'I don't know. I suppose it's the speed with which they work.'

'William said I should steer clear of you,' she said suddenly. 'Why is that?'

Bartrum was taken aback. 'Oh, it was just his joke.'

'I don't think so. He always means what he says, even when he jokes.'

That was true, Bartrum reflected. Coldstream had the most acerbic tongue in London. He changed the subject.

'What's it like, sitting for him?'

'Well, I'm not allowed to look at the painting. And if I make the slightest movement I get shouted at.'

'Don't you get bored?'

'Oh no. He has lots of stories. Some of them are quite outrageous.'

A waitress passed with a tray of pastries.

'I say. Shall we have something else to eat.' She chose a toasted sultana tea-cake. 'They're thruppence.'

'I think I might manage thruppence,' he said.

'Posing always makes me terribly hungry,' she explained. 'I think it's the way William looks at me. It's quite different from the way he looks when he's telling one of his stories. And the way he suddenly switches from one to the other. It's like looking suddenly down the barrel of a gun. You know he's got you in his sights.'

'The hunter and the hunted?'

'That's right.'

'And do you find that exciting?'

'Yes, in a way I suppose I do.'

'And that makes you hungry?'

'Oh yes.'

Like sex, he thought. He was always hungry after sex. He was assailed then by a memory of her naked breasts.

'Why on earth do you want to let him paint you?' The question sprung on her so suddenly, with such vehemence, she was taken aback. 'He's no good.'

She stared at him. He cursed himself for his frankness.

'I'm sorry. I shouldn't have said that. It's just that I don't like his work very much. But lots of others do, of course.'

Then, humorously, 'You'll probably be a middle-aged matron with children tugging at your skirts before he finishes it. *If* he finishes it.'

'I know. He takes ages over a painting. He says he can't do anything in under sixty hours.'

'And you'll be covered with ticks, you know. '

She giggled.

'I know. But that's just the way William works. He calls them 'visual correspondences'. He says it's the equivalent of not having tucked one's shirt in properly.'

She sat with one slim arm resting on the table. He longed to rest his own arm there, flesh to flesh.

'Why did you choose to go to an art school?'

'Why? Because I want to be an artist.' It might have been the silliest question.

'And do your parents approve?' asked Bartrum, amused. Really, he thought, she's no more than a schoolgirl.

'Oh yes. My father is really quite progressive. But he wanted me to attend a school whose principles he approved of. He's a socialist, you know. And William is a member of the Artists' International. Most of his friends are socialists. Poets and writers, that sort of thing.'

'I don't suppose there's too much poetry in his teaching.'

'Heavens, no! William says that for the artist there's no substitute for prose. Anyone can get away with poetry.'

'I wonder,' said Bartrum dryly, 'what his friend Auden would say to that.'

Again that uncertain smile. She'd no idea who Auden was.

'He's a poet,' he said. 'He used to lodge with Bill and Nancy. Bill painted his portrait.'

She, though, was mopping up butter from her plate with the last of the tea-cake.

'But you haven't answered my question,' she said, licking the butter from her fingers. '*Why* should I steer clear of you? Are you really mad, bad and dangerous to know?'

She looked directly at him across the table.

He couldn't make up his mind then if she really understood what kind of man she was dealing with, or whether she was merely flirting with him. But there was nothing flirtatious in the green eyes fixed candidly on his.

'Whatever I may be,' he assured her gravely, 'I'm not dangerous to you.'

He meant what he said. He couldn't bring himself to harm her. And it *would* be harm, he knew that very well. He couldn't rid his mind of that first glimpse of her in Coldstream's studio, turned to one side, her slim shoulder catching the light, her naked breasts. And that first impression, true if only because untainted then by desire, of vulnerability. And his self-administered rebuke: *She's little more than a child.* What was it she said? *'We go there sometimes after school'.*

Socially adroit, like most young woman of her class, yet he recalled how much of uncertainty and diffidence there was lurking beneath that superficial self-assurance. Yet she'd gone off, alone, with a man who'd lain in wait for her and struck up a conversation with only one thing in mind. Young as she was, she must have known that, surely? She was, after all, an art student. He'd had brief liasons with more than one girl from the Slade. *Are you really mad, bad and dangerous to know?* Such a question coming from one of those girls would have been pure coquettishness. God knows he was weary enough of that.

But there was nothing of that in the gaze with which she'd surveyed him. Simply curiosity, as about some strange beast with which she'd come face to face.

Did her father know that she posed for Coldstream? Then it struck him that he'd concealed from her the fact that he knew her father. Why had he done that? But then concealment was so much a part of his treatment of women it had become second nature. And he was very drawn to her.

What was he to do? His usual way to resolve an uncertain situation was to act on impulse, and let the consequences carry him where they would.

He decided that for once in his life he would do the decent thing, and not pursue her. No, he would leave her alone.

It was entirely by chance that he ran into her again, heading for Warren Street tube station. 'Hello,' he said, surprised. 'Where are you off to?'

Startled, she looked up. Her eyes brightened. She flushed slightly.

That women found him attractive he was well aware. Why, exactly, he couldn't say. But he had capitalised on it for years, acquiring in the process an easy charm, knowing instinctively what note to strike, a facility which he'd exploited many times, often with women he scarcely knew. So it should have come as no surprise that this young woman responded like all the rest. And yet he saw it with a sinking heart.

She was on her way to Victoria to catch the train to Herne Bay. A sea-side project for her art class.

'I'll drive you there,' he said impulsively. The offer was out before he knew it. 'Much quicker than the train. We'll be there in no time.'

Though he'd no idea how far it was, or how long it would take to drive there.

She hesitated.

'The car's just round the corner,' he added, though it was rather more than that. 'I keep it at Jackson's in Rathbone Place.'

He led the way to the yard at the back of the garage where, pulling off a tarpaulin, he uncovered a long, low machine in pillar-box red, with gleaming twin exhausts snaking out from under the bonnet.

She gazed in amazement.

'How on earth do you come to have a car like this?'

'Ah, well, that's rather a long story,' he said mysteriously. And left it at that.

'Why Herne Bay?' he asked, as they drove over Westminster Bridge.

'Oh, it could be anywhere, really. But I chose Herne Bay because we used to go there on holiday. Can it really go as fast as that?' she added, peering at the speedometer.

'Well, a car quite like this one covered over a hundred miles in exactly one hour at Brooklands last October.'

He slowed to make room for a taxi pulling out from Waterloo.

'But we shan't be going quite as fast as that,' he added with a smile.

'Oh, I'd really love to go fast.'

He laughed, and shook his head.

'We shall be observing the new speed limit,' he said reprovingly.

And so they did, driving sedately through the dreary thoroughfares of south London, through Camberwell and Blackheath and on to

Dartford and Gravesend.

'It's rather like having to keep a dangerous animal chained and muzzled,' he said as they emerged at last from the suburban sprawl.

But once unleashed, on the old Roman road towards Rochester, the great red beast leapt forward with such a sudden rush and roar that the girl was thrust back against her seat.

It was sunny and warm for April. Not a cloud in the sky. Just the day for a spin in an open two-seater tourer, and she was enjoying the thrill of it.

'What have you been doing at school?' he shouted, above the drumming engine note.

'We've been painting posters for Spain.'

'*Viva la República*, eh?'

Something flippant in his tone repelled her slightly. She told him, rather stiffly, that her cousin Richard was fighting with the International Brigade.

'Good for him,' said Bartrum firmly.

He drove through Sittingbourne and Faversham, finally following the twisty road from Whitstable into Sea Street and along the Central Parade.

'All this is new,' she said, as he drew up outside the entrance to the pier, pointing out where Mazzoleni's café had stood that was burnt down in the fire. But the original curved stone balustrade that was taken from London Bridge was still in place.

'Let's go down to the beach to watch the Punch and Judy. It was always the first thing we did. Giles loved the crocodile.'

'What about your painting?'

'Oh, never mind that.'

They stood laughing and applauding as Punch laid about him with an enormous club, disposing of his foes one by one, finally flattening the Devil with a triumphant squawk: *That's the way to do it... that's the way to do it...*

'Daddy used to give us a little lecture about the different characters,' she said as they came away at last.

The Gay Companions were appearing at the Grand Pier Pavilion, and as they set off along the pier she began to speculate as to what the concert party might be performing.

'Oh,' he said, '*Rose Marie*, for sure.' And launched instantly into the famous duet, first in an improbable falsetto masquerading as Jeanette MacDonald, '*I am calling yooo… ooo-ooo-ooo… ooo-ooo-ooo…*', then responding with Nelson Eddy's manly baritone, '*With a love that's trooo… ooo-ooo-ooo… ooo-ooo-ooo…*'

'Do you know,' he continued, 'I think I should have been a Mountie.' And began trotting rhythmically, cock-horse fashion, along the pier, his hands rising, falling on the reins:'*Dead or alive… we are out to get you dead or alive…* 'until she was in fits of laughter, and the fishermen along the railings of the pier were turning in astonishment.

Still laughing, they strolled together along the pier. It was, she said, the second longest pier in England. Three-quarters of a mile.

'We used to walk right to the end, though Mummy always insisted we took the tram back.'

Bartrum said he thought that might be a good idea.

She prattled on, pausing to point out the landmarks along the shore; the hotel where they used to stay, the children's roundabout, the clock tower, the copper domes of the bandstand… And did he know Herne Bay was the scene of a notorious murder? Oh, yes. One of the brides-in-the-bath.

And all these, he realised with sudden tenderness, were the memories of a child. Yes, he thought, she really *is* still a child.

The thought then that she, with her life all before her, had yet to be embraced by its wonder and excitement filled him with longing. He saw in her a state of grace he had long since lost. Oh, to embrace the joy of life again, joy freely given, still with the wonder of a child.

When at last they arrived at the pier head they found quite a number of people gathered on the landing stage. A distant siren, accompanied by a rhythmic churning of engines, signalled the imminent arrival of the paddle steamer.

'Oh, do let's stay and watch.'

It used to be the highlight of her holiday, the trip on the *Medway*

Queen.

'We had to catch a very early train to meet her at Chatham,' she said as they watched the passengers disembarking. The breeze was tumbling her hair about her cheeks, to which the bright sea air had brought a rosy glow.

'Daddy's mad about trains,' she added inconsequentially. 'He never goes anywhere without his Bradshaw. Then we used to steam back to Herne Bay.'

As the passengers began to disembark, flooding onto the landing stage, he put his arm around her to draw her in from the path of a man lugging a bulky suitcase, and it was impossible to resist brushing with his lips the golden hair, the flushed cheek. She lifted her face towards his. He looked at her intently for a moment, then kissed her on the mouth.

For a moment she clung to him, then disengaged herself. As she did so, he saw her fearful look. She's terrified, he thought. Did she fear she might be seen by someone who recognised her? Knew her parents? But no, it was much more than that.

'Shall we catch the tram?' he suggested gently.

Silently they stepped aboard, sitting alone together in the last car.

'You know all about me, don't you?' he said at last, breaking the silence.

'No.'

'You must do.'

'I know what William said about you. That's not the same thing.'

He stared at her. It was as if a door had opened suddenly in front of him, a door he thought could never open again. Oh, he knew it was an illusion. He was gazing at a mirage. Even so, he knew he must stay close to her. In her presence lay newness of life.

— CHAPTER TEN —

Saturday dawned fine and bright. It was the day of the planned boat trip to Coruisk. Marlowe had been looking forward to it. He had once spent a memorable day in Coruisk, and longed to see it again for what would probably be the last time. The rest of the family, though, were in sombre mood as they gathered for breakfast. The sense of a worsening crisis, augmented by the news bulletin the previous evening, had brought home the possibility that the worst might indeed be visited upon them. Marlowe apart, no one seemed in much of a mood for an excursion, Vanessa least of all. Though she had reasons of her own.

'I shall never, *ever*, again put to sea in another small boat,' she said firmly.

'Oh, it's hardly putting to sea,' protested the Archdeacon. 'It's simply a trip round the headland, from one loch into another. And to a very wonderful place,' he added meaningfully.

The twins were all for it. Their trip to Canna had been rounded off with a splendid tea at the Post Office, and they were looking forward to another voyage. They loved catching things as long as they weren't expected to eat them.

'I hope we see some sharks,' said Andrew.

'Sharks!' Vanessa looked alarmed.

'There were two or three sharks breaking and slashing about close round the boat yesterday,' Richard explained. 'MacDonald was angry because you can't fish when they're about.'

'Ronnie says they're nasty enough,' chorused the twins, who'd learnt from their older siblings the game of baiting their mother.

'But they don't eat boys,' added Hugh, relenting.

'What a pity,' observed Miranda.

'When are we going?' asked Andrew, for the second time in five minutes.

To the twins, who had wolfed down their eggs and bacon in double quick time, breakfast seemed to be taking the grown-ups an unconscionable age.

It was agreed that Vanessa would accompany Millie, who'd arranged to go botanizing with Mr Hart.

'I hope you won't allow him to lead you into anything reckless, mother,' said Henry. 'Lachlan saw him the other day in Eas Mor. 'A spry wee gentleman,' Lachlan called him. He was coming up very nimbly from the ravine, where he'd obviously been rootling for specimens.'

'I couldn't have put it better myself, Henry. "Rootling" describes Mr Hart's activities exactly.'

'Botanists can be dangerous companions in the mountains,' Henry continued. 'Charley Montague once met a botanist who talked him into taking him up Hanging Garden Gully in search of a rare plant. The fellow hadn't the faintest idea how to go about things. Whenever he saw a plant that interested him he scuttled after it, darting about in the most alarming manner. He paid no heed to Montague on the other end of the rope. He might have killed them both.'

'You need have no worries on that score. I know Mr Hart of old. We shall try to prevent him from vandalizing the rarer plants, won't we Vanessa?'

'When are we going?' wailed Hugh.

His protest was given urgency by Morag's shy announcement that Mr Campbell was waiting in the kitchen. Campbell was skipper of the Loch Eynort lugger which would be taking them to Coruisk. The dinghy by means of which they would board the *Minerva* lay beached on the north shore of the loch. They set off in a party, accompanied by Millie and Vanessa to speed them on their way.

It took a while to get them all aboard since the tiny dinghy could accommodate no more than four at a time. This embarkation took place under the eagle eye of Millie, who called out a peremptory instruction.

'Andrew! You will *not* fall into the loch again.'

The *Minerva* was a traditional Loch Fyne skiff built at Tarbet, wide in the beam and likely to roll, thought Marlowe, in a swell.

The lugsail was hard and hazardous to work. Today, however, with the mast lowered and the sail furled to accommodate passengers amidships, the *Minerva* would be powered by its Kelvin engine. Once aboard, Henry opted to sit in the stern with the skipper. He hoped to be allowed to take a hand with the tiller.

They rounded the point, Rubha' an Dunain, and immediately met with a heavy swell which, as Marlowe had expected, tossed them about until they entered the Sound of Soay. The sun shone brilliantly, and the wide waters towards the Small Isles glittered with white horses.

'There's Canna,' shouted Hugh, pointing. 'It *is* Canna, isn't it, Mr Campbell?'

'Aye, that's Canna right enough.'

Once clear of Soay, with Eigg on the starboard bow, and the low blue hills of Ardnamurchan in the distance, they entered the sea-loch of Scavaig. Now the mountains were drawing close again. As they neared the rocky promontory of Eilean Reamhar they gazed at the sea breaking over a black skerry on which, Campbell assured them, they would not wish to run aground.

Marlowe stared up at the steep flanks of Garsbheinn towering to the left. Across the bay little Sgùrr na Stri looked no less steep. There were the three peaks of the Dubhs, in full view as the *Minerva* turned towards the shore. It was forty years since he'd first sailed into this place. He'd been a young man then. Now, his life seemed to have gone by in a flash. Yet here nothing had changed, the waterfalls of the Mad Burn still plunging into the sea, and the little Scavaig river cascading down from Coruisk over the same vast boiler plates of slabs. And so it would be, forty years from now, when other young men sailed into Loch Scavaig to rejoice in what had rejoiced him so many years before.

So, in bright sun under a blue sky, they sailed on into the green waters of little Loch na Cuilce, where a dozen or more blue-black heads rose from the waves to stare in whiskery astonishment -'Oh, wonderful,' cried Miranda. 'Look, seals... *seals*!'—and made a landfall in the lee of Eilean Glas.

As Campbell busied himself with his mooring Henry read them an account of the dark and dreadful place to which he'd brought them, as described by earlier travellers; of profound and perpendicular precipices enclosing a sombre lake on whose waters never since the Creation had the sun shone. So, having mounted an iron ladder fixed to the slabby rock and following a rough, twisting path towards the loch, they were mightily relieved to find the entire length of the glen was filled with sunlight; sunlight picking out the long slope of the Dubhs' ridge climbing up from the waters of Loch Coruisk, and picking out the slanting gullies of long Druim nan Ramh running north to meet the central peaks of the Cuillin whose southern flanks rose almost golden brown from the great bowl of Coir'uisg at the head of the loch.

'You wouldn't believe, would you, that Sir Walter Scott ever set foot here?' declared the Archdeacon. *'For rarely human eye has known,* 'he declaimed, *'a scene so stern as that dread lake, with its dark edge of barren stone...* Absolute nonsense, as you can see.'

For their picnic site they chose some glaciated slabs looking down where the loch ran into the river, the party spreading out in twos and threes among the grassy bays. Marlowe, sitting alone, munching his ham sandwich, gazed up at the Dubhs' ridge, lost in memories of the expedition he made with Millie's brother, slogging up Coire na Banachdich on an afternoon of baking heat, and the sudden chill as they crossed into the shadows of Coireachan Ruadha *en route* for the Dubh slabs. Another world, it might have been. Another century certainly. And the stag, as they reached the flats of Coir'uisg, crossing the burn above them, scenting man, stopping, staring a moment, then off in a flash, bounding over the rock-strewn fell with enviable ease. Then the bivouac under the stars on a summer's night. And the day that followed: over half a mile of immaculate gabbro climbing up to the summit of Sgùrr Dubh Beag.

Then the blistering sun as they toiled over Dubh Mòr and Dubh an Dà Bheinn, and the terrible thirst, and the longing looks cast at the green lochan in Coir' a Ghrunnda a thousand feet below. It all came back to him with extraordinary presence, one of those spots of time returning with re-vivifying power, as sharp as the rasp of gabbro against the finger-tips.

He wondered if that was all that was left to a life so reduced, so much less than what it was.

Remembrance of things past. And might it not be better that way for an old man? Retreat to some inner room and shut the door on a world that seemed to be falling apart? Well, at least Proust had his book to write. All he had were memories. And what, in any case, could he communicate of the fullness of that day. No, that time is past, he thought, *'and all its aching joys are now no more, and all its dizzy raptures…'*

He thought of Wordsworth in old age when his gift had failed, a Victorian patriarch reading morning prayers to the assembled household, going through the motions of being a poet until the very end. He thought of that last autograph, shakily inscribed in a young girl's album: *To me the meanest flower that blows can give thoughts that do often lie too deep for tears…*

Wasn't that true of every old man's life? Thoughts too deep for tears?

But he was getting mawkish. Thank God for the young, he thought, as he heard Giles's voice.

'Grandfather! Which is the ridge where you and Uncle Robert had such a wonderful day?'

'The Dubhs ridge?' Marlowe pointed it out. 'It starts in a grassy gully to the left of the ridge proper. The only hard bit, as I remember, was getting established on the slabs.'

First, though, he told of the long slog up the corrie from Glen Brittle to cross over the main ridge, and the baking sun that afternoon; of shirts, wrung out in the icy burn, pulled on again to give some respite from the heat, and the abrupt drop in temperature as they stepped into shadow at the *bealach*. Then, tired, sweating, eaten alive by midges, toiling down to the Coruisk river, then the welcome breeze and the crash of falling water, and the bivouac in a grassy hollow, lying there in the dark night gazing up at the Plough and the North Star high over Druim nan Ramh. Then waking in full sunlight, sun flooding the central peaks of the Cuillin beyond Coir'uisg, oh, and the day of fullness that followed.

After lunch the party went their various ways. Bartrum and Miranda wandered off together, she to paint, he pressed into service to carry her equipment. Marlowe smoked a pipe with Donald Campbell, who spoke of the perils of his living, of the arduous labour of hand-lining, and of men he'd known whipped over-board by a dipping lug sail.

Richard, opening his sack, produced a rope, much to the twins' delight.

'Who wants to go climbing?'

They set off in search of suitable rock, with the rest of the family strolling along behind. Further along the loch Richard came across an area of glaciated rock set at an agreeable angle. He tied on to his rope, and set off up the slab. Leo remained below to see that the boys were properly roped.

Henry stood with Susannah watching as Richard, now belayed at the top of the slab, shouted instructions to Hugh who was struggling rather.

'Stand up straight, Hugh. Remember, weight on your toes. Don't lean in to the rock.'

'He seems to have turned the corner, don't you think?' said Henry.

'Let's hope so. I was praying Skye might make the difference. I think the twins have been the catalyst. He seems to have made firm friends of them.'

Giles and Nicko, after watching proceedings for a while, set off to inspect the Dubhs ridge further down the loch. There was really no mistaking it, a long sweep of slabs rising, as it seemed, from the water's edge, and climbing diagonally to the summit of Sgùrr Dubh Beag.

'We might just look at the start,' said Giles

Occasional bursts of hilarity followed in their wake: Lady Kitty's fluting voice -'I don't need a rope, do I?'—followed by Leo's firm rejoinder -'You need a rope.'

Giles had already marked a grassy gully immediately to the right of a toe of steep slabs. As usual, he strode on ahead, always anxious to get quickly to any objective, and to get there first.

He entered the gully, only to retreat abruptly.

'No, that's not it,' he said hastily. 'It must be further on.'

He set off smartly, with his mystified friend in tow.

Bartrum and Miranda, though, folded in each other's arms, were conscious only of one another.

They'd met whenever they could that summer, and always in secret, for she was terrified that someone might see her, and the news get back to her parents, her father being so well known in the parishes of Bloomsbury and St Pancras. For his part, Bartrum no more wanted to be seen with her than she did with him. Hopeless though it seemed, he wanted her to remain uncontaminated by his earlier life. But to do that she had to be kept apart, especially from those who knew him for what he was. So she would catch a tube, he would meet her somewhere south of the river, she would climb into the car and they would vanish into Kent or Sussex, seeking out some lonely coombe or hollow among the downs.

She never asked if these were the places where he'd brought his women. Nor did he tell her that they weren't. All they wanted, desperately, was to be together in a place where no one knew them, somewhere out beyond the *status quo*, a space where each might freely become what had been revealed to the other.

Yet these moments of happiness were, for him, never more than fleeting, since he would become conscious again of the difference between them. He feared this love affair was bound to fail like all the rest. Most of all he feared that she saw in him something that wasn't true. That she saw him as he was *not*. He longed for authenticity, yet couldn't bring himself to believe it could ever be recovered, such scepticism being in the very air he breathed.

They'd made love once on the edge of a chalk escarpment above the Medway. He'd raised himself to look down intently at her as she lay, eyes closed, on the rug laid over the cropped grass. Asked again the question that was always uppermost in his mind.

'You *do* know all about me, don't you?'

'No.'

'You *must* do.'

'No.'

'I'm sure Coldstream hasn't spared you the grisly details.'

She opened her eyes and looked tenderly at him.

'My grandfather never left any record of what he and his climbing friends had done in the Highlands,' she said, lifting a finger to stroke his cheek. 'They didn't want to spoil the adventure for those who came afterwards. They thought they should find out for themselves what was involved.'

'Is that how you see this? An adventure?'

'Of course. Isn't love always an adventure?'

It was with a sinking heart he heard, for the first time on her lips, a word he'd counterfeited many times before.

'I'm ravenous,' she said suddenly. 'Let's find something to eat.'

Their meetings were irregular and occasional, snatched when the opportunity offered, since she would not cut any of her classes. As her father was paying for her tuition she felt honour bound to attend. In any case, she wanted to learn.

In the intervals between, Bartrum continued to earn a sketchy living from such literary scraps as came his way. He drank his morning coffee at Madame Buhler's in Charlotte St, ate at Bertorelli's or from the *plat du jour* at the Tour Eiffel, picking up notes and messages left for him in his usual haunts, pursuing his contacts wherever they led, whether in bars and cafes, or illicit afternoon drinking dens, or the steam room of the Russell Square public baths, or the Harem night club.

At six o'clock each evening, as soon as the Fitzroy Tavern opened, he would take his notebook and sit in his usual corner next to the barometer and begin drafting a review or putting together the latest *Notes from the Underground*. Then, as the bar gradually filled and the noise grew louder, he would surrender himself to the fug of smoke and beer, and the clink of glasses and the tinkling piano, above all to the never-ending flow of contumacious wit and laughter, eventually leaving perhaps to buttonhole an editor someone had seen in the Wheatsheaf, or the Black Horse, or the Burglar's Rest, then at 10.30 dashing across the street into Marylebone where licensing laws were kinder, fetching up at the Duke of York or the Marquis of Granby. Yet he was only too aware that this was no longer a satisfying life. At the mercy of his own destructive impulses, he couldn't bear to contemplate what he couldn't deny was true. He felt an anguish of desire for some further life so that he might at last do the real thing that he had it in him to achieve. Yet the years had passed, and still he'd failed to find it. The real thing. Sometimes, as he sat at the bar in the Fitzroy, he would look up at the a row of recruiting posters, mementos of the war to end all wars, and fear that only a similar apocalyptic disruption might offer any hope.

Yet he only had to think of Miranda to be lifted instantly out of all that. It was as if she released him from the self in which he'd been imprisoned for so many years. Everything that mattered most to him, everything that was best and dearest, everything which now made life worthwhile, went on in secret. And in that he differed in no respect from the writers, the painters and composers for whom the Fitzroy Tavern was also home from home, since all that was most precious to them also went on in secret. For them, too, the inner life was what mattered most. Yet here they were, men with far more talent than he ever had, pissing it away against a wall.

That row of recruiting posters might perhaps have alerted them to what was looming just over the horizon. Yet the famous Tavern clock set in half a beer barrel, which had stopped at the eleventh hour of the eleventh day of the eleventh month and never been rewound, seemed to decree that in this place time should stand still; that the boozing and the talking might go on indefinitely, an illusion to which all who drank in the Fitzroy Tavern eventually succumbed, until the company, the pyrotechnic conversation and the drink all but absolved one of the urge to work.

He was seized then with a sudden dread. Of gifts wasted, of waning powers. Already his hair was beginning to turn grey. Whenever he looked in a mirror he could detect the signs of aging. In a few years from now he would have lost his looks. He had only to look around the bar of the Fitzroy to see women he'd slept with, two or three of them once very beautiful women who'd modelled for Epstein and Gaudier-Brzeska, for Sickert and Augustus John, none of them now as young as when they first climbed into bed with him. Capricious, predatory, undiscriminating, they seemed doomed to follow the older regulars who might themselves have been beauties a decade earlier. Shabby, rarely sober, smelling of drink, red mouths beginning to wilt, still with the same hungry faces, bloodshot eyes looking each newcomer up and down…

Lines sprang to mind then, lines that would have been greeted with shouts of laughter in the Fitzroy.

'As hags hold Sabbaths, less for joy than spite,
So these their merry, miserable night.
So round and round the ghosts of beauty glide,
And haunt the places where their honour died.'

Cruel? Well, Pope was cruel. Not so cruel, though, as life. No, of one thing he was sure. Fitzrovia was not a place in which to grow old.

It was one of these same women, three-sheets to the wind as usual, though sitting erect on her bar stool, who greeted him one evening,

'Charles, my dear. A little bird tells me you're in love again. How wonderful! It's not that little straw blonde I've seen you with, is it?

Bill Coldstream's model?'

Instantly he saw it as Nina herself saw it. Just another of his *amours*. One of those hungry, loveless adventures that ran hot for a short while, only to cool and fizzle out like all the rest. And would it? Was that all it amounted to? He was always conscious of the differences between them. He was so much older than her. Once, in a wooded coombe on the North Downs, he sat up suddenly and turned on her a despairing look.

'This can't lead anywhere?'

Puzzled, she smiled up at him uncertainly.

'Why must it lead somewhere? Why can't it just be what it is?'

He saw then that for her love was an eternal present.

'Because time won't stand still, my love. Not even for us.'

She seemed to him so trusting, so transparent. Yet already she was learning to deceive her family. And he was leading her into this deception. Then he was appalled by the thought that he was, in fact, corrupting her.

As summer drew towards its close she told him she'd be away from London for a while.

'We're all going to Skye,' she said. She explained about *Marlowe's Variation*.

Bartrum had vague memories of the mountain photographs covering the walls of the family house in Russell Square.

'What will you do with yourself?'

'Oh, I expect I'll paint some of the time. And of course I'll climb.'

'Climb?'

'Of course. I must do some climbing.'

'Aren't you frightened?'

'Oh yes. That's half the fun of it. '

'What? Being frightened?' Bartrum laughed. 'You're an extraordinary girl.'

Sometimes he wondered if he was idealizing her. Then he felt like a man staring across an abyss he knew he could never cross, and yet he longed with all his heart to stand on the far side.

She, though, had grown bolder, hungrier.

'I say,' she said suddenly. 'Why don't you come too? I can't very well ask you myself, but you could wangle an invite. Your credit's pretty good at the moment. '

Though Miranda believed it was for her sake that Charles had agreed to rescue Richard from the Fascists.

He was taken aback.

'Is that wise?'

'At least we'd be under the same roof,' she added. 'Besides, you're very much *persona grata* with the family at the moment. Well, with most of them.'

'No,' said Bartrum dryly, 'I haven't exactly clicked with your mother, have I?'

In the event it was Henry who, on hearing Bartrum remark that he'd never been to Skye, replied in all innocence, 'You'd be very welcome to join us.'

The little waves of Loch na Cuilce, clear sea-green water washing over sand, flashed from sky blue to aquamarine as the *Minerva* slipped her mooring and headed south towards Loch Scavaig.

It was a boatload of contented passengers, Marlowe reflected, that Donald Campbell was ferrying back to Loch Brittle. Susannah sat chatting happily with Miranda, Bartrum with Nicko. Only Giles, the old man noticed, sat silent, seemingly a stranger to himself.

As they entered Loch Scavaig they began to attract a noisy following of gulls swooping and circling over the boat. The wind, too, was getting up, so that the passengers were having to shout to make themselves heard. The twins, who'd had a lovely day, were full of themselves, and had to be restrained from hanging over the gunwhales looking for 'tysties' which, Campbell had told them, might sometimes be seen flying *under* the boat.

'What are 'tysties'?', shouted Susannah.

'It's the local name for the black guillemot,' Marlowe shouted back. He knew about such things. 'Like all the auks they use their wings to swim under water.'

He and Bartrum then fell to speculating on the likely derivation of the word 'bonxie', another local name for the great skua. Nicko thought it was probably Norse.

Lady Kitty was engaged in earnest discussion with her brother-in-law.

'As for those volunteers fighting for the Reds,' she was declaring, 'believe me, it has more to do with pathology than politics. After all, most of them belong to the very class they choose to hate. Not politics, Henry—pathology!'

In that same moment the wind dropped momentarily, so that the brisk English voice carried quite clearly above the screaming of the gulls. Richard, sitting not six feet away across the well of the boat, couldn't fail to hear.

'If you had any idea,' began Richard fiercely, 'any idea at all… what you are talking about… ' He seemed to struggle for words. 'Each one of those men is worth a dozen of you,' he burst out at last.

The anguish in his voice was plain for all to hear.

Leo, it was, who broke the silence.

'Well,' he said, looking round, 'when are we going to do father's climb? Tomorrow? I don't think Henry would be quite up to it, so I suggest two ropes of two. Giles and his friend, and myself and Richard. What about it, Richard? Shall we call a truce? Sink our political differences for the sake of the climb? What do you say?'

It was a genuine olive branch. Everyone could see that.

'Do say yes, Richard,' said Miranda eagerly.

For a moment Richard hesitated. The whole family might have been hanging on his answer.

'Tomorrow's the Sabbath,' he said eventually. 'I don't think local susceptibilities would quite approve.'

All in all, Marlowe reflected, it had been a good day, in spite of Kitty's unfortunate remark.

Leo's olive branch had been well judged. Richard might almost have been on the point of accepting it. He'd been climbing, if only a scramble with the boys, and seemed to be making some sort of return to the family. Yet how close to the surface his anguish remained.

Millie, too, seemed to have enjoyed her day out with Mr Hart.

'Oh, we've found out what he's up to, haven't we Vanessa? It's as I thought. He's on the track of a rarity. '

One of the rarest of all British alpine plants, *Arabis alpinus* was not known anywhere else but in the Cuillin. Since it was to be found in rocky places, stream sides, damp ledges and the like, Mr.Hart had been following the burns one by one up into the corries.

'And did you find your rarity?' asked Marlowe.

'No, I'm happy to say. Had we done so I wouldn't put it past Mr Hart to go back tomorrow to dig it up.'

For all that, the day ended much as it had begun, the sombre mood of crisis deepened by the evening news. Talks with Hitler had broken down. Czech and Hungarian forces had been mobilised. France and Germany was also said to be massing troops. Moreover, Hitler had now set a deadline. If he didn't get what he wanted by the following Saturday the implication was that he would take it by force.

Chamberlain, though, remained tight-lipped. Speaking at the airport on returning from Bad Godesberg he told waiting reporters,

'My first duty, now that I am back, is to report to the French and British Governments on the result of my mission, and until I have done so, it would be difficult for me to say anything more.

I will say just this: I am confident that all interested parties will continue their efforts to find a peaceful solution to the problem of Czechoslovakia, because thereby hangs the peace of Europe in our time.'

'Czechoslovakia?' snorted Leo. 'It's not the problem of

Czechoslovakia, it's the problem of Hitler!'

'But it *is* the problem of Czechoslovakia, Leo,' said Henry. 'You know it as well as I do. Czechoslovakia was created expressly for the purpose of destroying German hegemony in Eastern Europe.'

'Wasn't it Lloyd-George's fault?' asked Vanessa. She had a vague idea it was.

'L G is a *Welshman*,' said Lady Kitty. She might have been pointing out some mitigating disability. 'He's bound to favour small nations.'

'But the Czechoslovaks are not a 'nation'',said Henry patiently. 'How can they be when they are comprised of so many Gemans, Poles, Slovaks and Hungarians?'

'The frontiers should have been revised long before Hitler came to power.'

'If German grievances had been properly addressed, father, he might never have *come* to power.'

'We are where we are, Henry,' said Leo quietly.

That was so depressingly true there was really nothing more to be said.

'Neville really does believe,' sighed Lady Kitty, 'that somehow or other he can persuade a frightful little bounder into doing the decent thing. He's quite wrong, of course. It should have been made plain to Hitler months ago we would not stand for any dismemberment of Czechoslovakia.'

'I fail to see the value of issuing threats unless one is prepared to carry them out. We are neither equipped to do so, nor is the country prepared for such a step.'

'All the same, if only we could have given some indication that if Hitler marched into Czechoslovakia we would act, we might all be out of the wood by now.'

'That's easy to say. '

'It's true,' said Leo quietly.

They all stared at him.

'Just take my word for it.' Leo was being mysterious as usual.

'Believe me,' he went on, 'there are people in Germany just waiting for the signal to remove Hitler from power.'

It was not the tale so much as the manner of telling that compelled attention.

'Last month,' he couldn't resist adding, 'Winston received a contact from Berlin. I can't say any more than that.'

The swift glance which passed then between man and wife radiated a barely suppressed gleam of excitement. Leo and Kitty simply *had* to be in the swim of things, thought Marlowe, never mind if they got out of their depth. For them the crisis was first and foremost an enormously thrilling game.

'As it is,' Leo went on, 'the country has to rely for its safety on the feeble-minded baronet whom Baldwin appointed Minister for the Coordination of Defence, a man whose only experience of war lies in waging it against the revision of the Prayer Book.' He paused, looked round the table. 'The most extraordinary appointment, if I may say so, since Caligula made his horse a consul.'

'You might as well say so, Leo,' remarked his father dryly, 'since others have already done so.'

A sudden blast of martial music from the radio had Henry reaching for the switch.

'No, don't turn it off. It's Ivor Novello. Don't you remember, Henry? We all went together to see it at Drury Lane last year. '

'Yes, and what stupendous nonsense it was,' said Henry.

'I remember staggering out afterwards,' said Leo, 'feeling as if I'd had rather too much Christmas pud.'

'And I *especially* remember,' said Lady Kitty, 'Miss Gilbert' s manly contralto issuing from the side of her mouth.'

It was a wavery tenor voice, though, that launched into the refrain: *'Rose of England, thou shalt fade not here, Proud and bright from rolling year to year. Red shall thy petals be as rich wine untold. Shed by thy warriors who served thee of old.'*

'Oh for God's sake,' exclaimed Marlowe. 'Turn it off! *Turn it off!*'

Shortly before eleven that night, a few moments before the

generator switched off, Giles confronted Charles Bartrum outside the porch of the Lodge.

'Bartrum! I want a word with you.'

He'd been lying in wait for that very purpose. He stepped forward into the yellow light spilling out through the open door.

'I don't much care for my sister as another notch on your bedpost. '

There was a tightness, verging on the shaky, in the young man's usually cheerful manner. For all his dash and daring on rock, Giles was all at sea in this kind of thing.

Bartram was too taken aback to notice.

'I can't blame you for thinking that,' he began hurriedly. 'Believe me, Giles, I wouldn't do anything to harm her. I swear it. I wouldn't hurt a hair of her head.'

Giles, though, seemed not to have heard.

'It's disgusting.' Indeed, disgust was written in his face. It took on a queasy hue from the light now flickering in the hall. 'For God's sake, you're old enough to be her father.'

At that moment all the lights went out, leaving them in pitch darkness.

'So lay off her.' The voice seemed to gather conviction from the speaker being all but invisible.

'You understand? Just lay off!'

With that, he pushed past the older man, and stumbled into the porch, colliding with an umbrella stand, leaving Bartrum to blunder as best he could back to his lodging.

— CHAPTER ELEVEN —

With the Lodge now in darkness there was nothing for it but to go to bed. And if it was still too early for some to sleep they might have read by candle-light, or else sat by the bedroom window as Marlowe was sitting now, wrapped in a blanket, with Novello's trite refrain running through his head.

Rose of England...

And was it all to start again? That bankrupt patriotism. The flag-waving? The same old jingoism? He felt sick at the thought. What did it mean to him, England? *Really* mean. He thought of the dale where he was born, and the little boy who grew up there, gazing in awe at the rusty bill preserved in Arncliffe church, and the parchment inscribed with the names of those who'd fought at Flodden; names as fresh in memory as if just entered; *John Knowle—able horse and harness; Richard Atkinson—a bow; William Firth—a bow; Ralph Knowl—a bill...* Four hundred years later dalesmen bearing those same names had gone to war with him. And no doubt would again. And must his grandsons go with them? Richard, fighting again? And Giles?

No doubt hundreds and thousands of others all over the country would feel the same about their little patch of earth. So, too, would the Czechs. Ground was what you were rooted in.

He shifted in his chair, drawing the blanket more closely about him.

The moon cast a cold eye over the topmost buttresses of Sgumain and Alasdair. Spectral in the moonlight, they seemed to have receded beyond the darkened world of men. Or else they were like emanations from a further world. The frontier, it might have been, of a country he had never visited.

He became aware of a faint glow moving below his window. *Phos*, the Greek word. Light, that shineth in darkness. And from the same root, he mused, *apophansis*. Winged words. That are the light of men. For Richard, though, all the good words had gone bad.

Then he saw that the light was accompanied by a dark figure, difficult to make out, moving out of vision. One of the maids, he wondered, going back to her quarters? Gideon, more likely. They work hard, he thought. But that was the life. A sick beast... a difficult calving... That was the life.

A westerly wind had begun to trouble the trees around the house. Rain, he reflected. Rain on the way.

———

Sure enough they woke to rain. Heavy rain, falling in stair-rods. It came flooding down from the roof eaves. In the glen the rain fell white as milk. The Cuillin had vanished.

Well, if it had to rain, thought Leo, watching it streaming down the window, it might as well rain on the Sabbath. It was always a wash-out of a day up here, anyway, for climbing purposes. He might have borrowed a rod, he reflected gloomily, and tried for some sea-trout but, according to MacRath, even the fish wouldn't bite. Not on the Sabbath.

In the dining room Friday's papers, brought back from Portree the previous evening, had been laid out neatly on the huge Victorian sideboard. Marlowe, who had already noted their presence, saw with what urgency Richard seized hold of them. He guessed what he would be looking for, and his heart went out once more to his grandson.

In the months since Richard's return things had gone from bad to worse. Franco's forces had broken through and reached the sea at Vinaroz. Republican Spain had been cut in two. Now the River Ebro had become the effective boundary with Catalonia. The Government, wanting to relieve the pressure on that front, had launched an offensive across the wide, fast-flowing river. The British Battalion, its depleted ranks heavily reinforced with Spanish troops, crossed the river in boats, and pushed inland towards Corbera and Gandesa. The Nationalists, seeing the threat, brought up artillery and men while their planes bombed the river crossings incessantly.

For six days, pounded by artillery, the Battalion stormed a heavily fortified hill, key to the important road junction of Gandesa. By the end of the week the Republican advance had been contained. The relentless counter-attack which followed began to roll back the Government forces. After six weeks of fighting they had lost almost all of the ground they had won. Yet the grim battle of the Ebro continued, fought out in relentless heat, and described by the correspondents in all its bloody detail:

'Yesterday, with the Nationalist advance threatening to cut the road to the river, the British Battalion were again sent into action. They endured such an artillery barrage as this correspondent has never before experienced. Franco's tanks and infantry advanced under cover of the bombardment. No 1 company bore the brunt of the attack. Nevertheless, they remained in their positions until the trenches were overrun. 'They were on top of us before we knew it,' said a company commander. 'Our lads were mown down.' He described it as 'the cutting to pieces of our very bravest'. An immense force of German and Italian aircraft dominates the air. Anti-aircraft opposition from the Government side scarcely exists. The wounded are having to be evacuated under cover of darkness, making the hazardous journey across a pontoon bridge to an emergency hospital in a railway tunnel...'

For Richard it made unendurable reading.

'That sounds like Leo,' remarked Marlowe, at the sound of voices descending the stairs. Always an early riser, he'd been entrusted with the task of ensuring that the twins ate their porridge.

The rain had evidently put a dampener on the rest of the family. Neither Giles nor Nicko had as yet put in an appearance. Bartrum, too, was absent, and of course Miranda was always last down for breakfast. Vanessa and Kitty apart, none of the ladies had emerged from their rooms. Indeed, it seemed that Susannah, who was feeling unwell, intended to keep to her bed.

'Since the war broke out,' Leo was saying, as they entered the dining room, 'over fifty British ships have been attacked.'

He lifted a cover and stared, with evident disfavour, at the porridge.

'Nearly half of them in the last two months,' he added, helping

—143—

himself to bacon. 'The Prime Minister seems to think that while it lasts we simply have to put up with it. He's actually said as much.'

Henry joined him at the table.

'And don't you think the Government has an obligation to protect British merchantmen?'

'I quite agree, Henry.' Leo had himself evoked memories of what Palmerston would have done. 'But no doubt you read what the PM said in the House. To bring the British navy into it would mean active intervention in the conflict, and he's not prepared to risk a general European war. The very next day two more of our ships were sunk. '

Leo accepted a cup of coffee from his wife.

'Some fellow on the other side shouted out that he was encouraging Franco to murder British seamen. And he was quite right. When the time came to vote on the censure motion we could scarcely support the Government. What else could we do in conscience but abstain?'

Richard raised his head from his paper.

'You abstained!'

'That's right,' said Leo coolly, cutting up his egg.

'You *abstained*!'

Rattled now, Leo laid down his fork.

'It's a very serious matter,' said Lady Kitty, 'to abstain in a vote of censure against one's own Government.'

Richard ignored this appeal to political *savoir-faire*.

'You *abstained*!' he repeated, with rising fury. 'You sat on your bottom and gazed at the ceiling. Or did you twiddle your thumbs?'

There was an embarrassed silence, a general avoiding of eyes. It was the passion that shocked, the attempt to draw blood. It was as if a family of English gentlefolk had, at a stroke, been pitched into the middle of a Spanish *corrida*. Nevertheless, shocks to systems notwithstanding, they continued with their breakfast.

'Toast,' suggested Lady Kitty, offering the rack to Vanessa.

Richard, though, white with pain, got up and slammed out of

the room.

That weekend war seemed imminent. Anti-aircraft batteries had appeared overnight in Horse Guards Parade and on the Embankment. All vital buildings were being padded with sandbags. In the London parks there was a frantic digging of trenches, continuing through the night by the light of flares and the headlamps of lorries.

Throughout the country ARP stations opened to distribute gas masks. In the capital loud-speaker vans toured the streets urging every citizen to get his gas-mask fitted as soon as possible. *Please do not delay.* Similar announcements appeared on cinema screens. The same urgent plea was read from pulpits and the stages of theatres. Until late that night hundreds of thousands were still flocking to schools, town halls and other public buildings all over London and the Home Counties to be fitted for gas masks. Mothers anxious for their babies were advised to envelop the infant in a blanket and carry it to the nearest gas-proof shelter. There were no gas masks available for babies.

All police leave had been cancelled. Doctors and nurses were being urged to enrol on a central register. The LCC appealed for ARP workers, for auxiliary firemen, for women ambulance drivers and air-raid wardens, while the Government announced emergency measures to freeze the price of certain foodstuffs for fourteen days.

The full extent of the emergency measures were too recent to have found their way into all but the latest papers. Even so, enough was revealed in the Friday editions to make it seem to the Marlowes that the settled world they had left behind them had been overturned. Returning home would be a step into the unknown. Only Millie, who'd lived long amid the *statu corruptionis* of the world, seemed unmoved. Henry, though, was being thoroughly sensible as usual.

'I see they're appealing for able-bodied men to come forward to help with the digging of trenches,' he observed approvingly. 'Giles, we must do that when we get back.'

Vanessa was at a loss to understand why the Underground should want to close many of its tube lines.

'What on earth for?'

'*For urgent structural alterations*, it says here.'

'Actually,' said Leo, 'it's to convert them into air raid shelters.'

'What are the trenches for?' whispered young Hugh.

'For protection,' said Leo reassuringly. 'If there's an air-raid people can take cover in a trench, either in the park or even in their own back-garden, using sand-bags and a corrugated iron roof. That's the idea, anyway.'

Marlowe had been standing at the window watching the rain falling into the garden. Now he turned to look back at Leo.

'You're not serious?' He knew something of bombs and trenches.

'I'm perfectly serious. The Home Office handbook is probably being pushed through every letter-box at this very moment.'

For Miranda it was the plight of the blind children that struck home. They would be the first to be evacuated from London.

'How awful. Can you imagine? Three thousand of them. Trains full of children. And all of them blind.'

Lady Kitty, though, had found an inspiring message from the King.

'*His Majesty*,' she read, '*bids the people of this country be of good cheer, in spite of the dark clouds hanging over them, and indeed over the whole world. He knows well that, as ever before in critical times, they will keep cool heads and brave hearts.*'

'What are we doing here?' murmured Vanessa faintly. 'What are we *doing* here?'

No one had an answer. At last Bartrum broke the silence.

'Oh, I think there should be time to finish our game of bowls,' he asserted stoutly, 'before we take on the Hun.'

As an attempt at humour it fell rather flat.

The rain slackened during the morning. By noon it was no more than a fine penetrating drizzle, only visible against the dark trees surrounding the garden. Beyond the garden, a solitary figure hunched against the rain, Richard plodded up the path along the rim of Eas Mor. There was an air of desperation about the bowed figure, as of a man at war with himself, a man drawn back to a struggle as yet unresolved, a struggle he should never have abandoned.

As Marlowe watched him, trudging over the moor towards Coire na Banachdich, he was profoundly conscious of the loneliness of war. He thought of that appalling scene at dinner that first evening, of Richard's distress, and Millie's cutting rejoinders, and Susannah's anguished cry as she rushed after him. At one point, lifting his eyes from his book, he'd glanced out of the window to see them sitting together in the garden, lit by the light from the drawing room. Saw, with a pang, that his daughter had put an arm around her son. Had drawn him towards her. Marlowe had watched over his family for more than forty years. If, at times, he'd thought himself wiser, more clear-sighted in foreseeing the consequences of their various blunders, it was always with a sense of just how powerless he was to intervene in their lives.

Now, though, he saw that he must go after his grandson.

He slipped out through the porch into the sodden garden. Clambering over the stile he set off over the moor. After twenty minutes, the thunder of falling water growing louder by the second, he reached the rim of the ravine. It was close and oppressively airless on the moor. Though the rain had given over its humid breath hung in the corrie, a steamy blanket of mist. The sweat poured off Marlowe as he plodded up the rising ground above Eas Mor. Several times he had to stop simply to find some air to breathe. The roar of the cascade gradually faded behind him as he followed a faint, squelching path climbing up and away from the burn. As he breasted the rising ground the corrie gradually rose ahead of him, dark and brooding, with long ribbons of mist drifting along the sides of the ridges. He pressed on, and came at last onto the naked scree. There was no sign of Richard.

Marlowe felt a growing uneasiness. He knew how, when darkness was in the hills, earth and sky could sometimes conspire to make a prison for the spirit. It brought back his own tortured ranging about the Cuillin during those first years after the war, aching for mother-earth and rest, only to find the mountains closed against him. Yes, he knew only too well how they could reflect and reinforce the moods of men.

At length he arrived at a meeting of streams, the water dashing out from the stones and flooding over his boots, the scree rising all around. Above, to the right, he could just make out a dark tower enveloped in mist. The tower of Window Buttress. Up ahead the further reaches of the corrie were hung now with streamers of rain.

Still there was no sign of Richard. Then he heard a clatter of stones.

Alarmed, it struck him that Richard might have set off up the wet rock of the buttress, climbing alone, unroped, not caring what became of him. Hadn't he done the same thing himself? Then he was seized with fear for his grandson, remembering what it was to climb alone, indifferent to the danger, not much caring whether one lived or died, remembering the misery of loss, and the darkened hills, and the rain falling, knowing the blinded spirit's degradation, lost, longing for comfort.

A barely discernable trod had appeared in the scree leading, he guessed, up to the crag. The sweat dripped, the legs seemed to have power for no more than a few steps at a time. Each little gust of air brought a blessed coolness as he toiled up the final scree slope to the foot of the buttress.

At first he didn't see Richard. His eye was drawn up to the steep crack set in an angle of the rock, to the rain streaming down the sloping groove above it, rain spurting out of the gutter. Then he noticed the figure huddled in the lee of an overhanging boulder under the crag.

Awkwardly the old man lowered himself on to a rock beside his grandson. They sat in silence for some moments.

'You see so many die,' Richard began abruptly. 'And what you're up against are machines. Tanks... planes... artillery... And eventually it dawns on you that you haven't a chance. Not a dog's chance...'

He fell silent.

Marlowe reached for his pipe. Fumbled for matches.

'In Spain there is a saying: *'A man does not die of love, or of his liver, or even of old age; he dies of being a man.'* Is there any cure, do you think, for that condition?'

Marlowe put his pipe to his lips, then lowered it again unlit.

'We'd moved from Batea,' Richard began tonelessly, 'to take up a position in the line. We were marching through a village called Calceite when we ran straight into a column of Italian tanks and armoured cars. The CO called on us to scatter. Our group made for a ridge above the village. Most of the others were eventually cornered and forced to surrender. We stayed hidden in the trees. We managed to get away after dark.'

For seven or eight days they'd wandered about the hills, dodging Fascist patrols. No food, no water. Eventually, stumbling over the mountain, they came to a ridge overlooking a valley. Far below they saw Republican troops mustering at a road junction. One of the group, who was still carrying his binoculars, recognised the battalion banner. Calling on the rest to follow him he set off down the hillside. *'Come on,'* he cried. All did so. Only Richard remained, unable to move. Still they called to him. *'Come on... come on...'* Frozen, white-faced, he stood rooted to the spot.

'I knew at that moment I didn't give a damn for Spain. Not a damn.'

He paused, his eyes blank, without expression. Richard might have been suffering again the face of that comrade calling on him to follow, an unchanging scrutiny that defined what he was—a deserter, a man who'd turned his back on the struggle.

Then, with shattering force, there burst upon Marlowe the

recognition that a man was forever what he had been at any time for others. And might, at any time, be called upon to answer for it.

Richard, though, had begun to speak again. He paused, his eyes blank, without expression 'Eventually, I turned and ran down into the forest. I don't know how long I wandered there. Days? A week? In the end some shepherds found me. But I remember nothing of that. All I remember is coming round to find myself lying in a strange, high-ceilinged room. An old man with a white beard was studying me intently. '

There was a distance in his voice. He might have been speaking about someone else.

'Well, Mr Richard Fleming,' he said, in excellent English. He must have found out my name from my *carnet*. My *carnet militar*. Every brigader carries a *carnet*. *'You will have to remain here with us for a while yet. Then we must see what we can do to get you home.'*

So that was it, thought Marlowe. The solution to the mystery of the telegram sent to Susannah.

'The old man was the local *patrón*. Don Antonio Salazar. A scholar. The Spain he cared about was Cervantes' Spain. He didn't care much for the Fascists. *Cabrónes,* he called them. Not a very elegant expression for a scholar. Eventually I was smuggled north. They dressed me as a man-servant. I sat next to the chauffeur in Don Antonio's Hispano Suiza. The fall of the valleys—they run north to south—made for a swift flight to the foothills of the Pyrenees. It's where the nobility of Aragón have their summer estates.'

So, by such fits and starts, the old man lifting his pipe to his lips and putting it down again, was Marlowe carried back to the first battle of Ypres and the men he'd seen, no more than lads some of them, coming down the Menin road having thrown everything away, packs, rifles, everything. And with such a look of absolute horror as he'd never seen, and would never, ever forget.

He would have stopped it there if he could. But the reel continued to run, so that Captain Marlowe was forced again to suffer how it came to pass that to honour King and Country, or to keep faith with the fallen, or for whatever expedient illusion their deaths were designed to foster, a number of terrified young men were strapped to chairs, and rifles levelled shakily at them by half-a-dozen of their comrades.

Oh, yes. One a lad from your own company. When the smoke cleared you could see he was only winged. Even tried to make a stumbling run for it, strapped to the chair as he was. You had to go after him, fumbling to get the Webley out from its holster to give him the *coup de grace*...

Oh, yes. If you suffer long enough some place you never leave it.

Then Marlowe saw that his grandson had begun to sob. So they clung to one another, victims alike of a catastrophe of which each might have been the sole survivor

— CHAPTER TWELVE —

It had been a wild night of wind and rain. Throughout the hours of darkness, sleepers awakened by fierce squalls rattling the windows were made to feel thankful for their beds. Then followed a fiery dawn against which the outline of the Cuillin showed black and menacing. Heaving wind and rain then swept in again with a passion, thunder rolling round the corries as white snakes of lightning struck suddenly and vanished over the ridge.

Miranda was entranced by the storm. She sat on a stool just inside the porch, making notes of its colour and form on a sketching block, until dragged away by the family.

There seemed little prospect of attempting the planned ascent of *Marlowe's Variation*. In the drawing room of the Lodge a disconsolate Leo stood regarding the dismal scene as another furious squall struck the glass.

'It might not last. I don't suppose…' he began hopefully, glancing at his brother.

'Absolutely not,' said Henry firmly. 'Father, you may remember, went astray during the first ascent. And they had perfect weather.'

Really, though, he was thinking of Giles.

'And it can't be tomorrow,' he went on. 'I've organised an outing to the fairy pools. There's a taxi coming over from Carbost.'

Leo groaned. 'Then it'll have to be Wednesday.'

Neither Susannah nor Richard were present at breakfast. They had sat together as usual the previous evening, Richard silent, withdrawn, his mother looking tense and pale. Both had retired immediately after dinner. Marlowe, reflecting on the tragedy of men driven to breaking point, recalled a phrase from Conrad: *'the acute consciousness of lost honour'*. How does one survive that? What would suffice? Confession, Millie would say, threw open the windows of the soul. Let in air and light. But who would absolve Richard? His former comrades? Marlowe thought of the man Templeton. No, no forgiveness there. Besides, who could forgive a man who couldn't forgive himself? It struck him that maybe the capacity to receive came slowly, given time and the right nourishment. What came to mind then was the ordinary, flawed, unspectacular solidarity of a family with all its ups and downs, its rows and reconciliations, its estrangements and returns. Would Richard return to the family? It had seemed possible just a little while before. Now he looked to be further off than ever.

Marlowe feared for his grandson. A man, Richard had said, dies of being a man. Could a man die of shame? Well, guilt fed upon itself. Perhaps only love could make a space for the guilty man to come to terms with himself. But how could he trust a love which remained in ignorance of the truth? Yet how could they comprehend what he had been through, who were never there themselves? Besides, what would be the point? Richard had come back from a place so terrible it was impossible to talk about. And pointless, even if he could. Nor would they have understood it, the darkness of men's hearts.

He had himself shot dead a helpless prisoner strapped to a chair. How do you come to terms with that? No, what a man was in his own eyes, he was for ever.

What was he to do about Richard? For a moment he considered asking Millie. But Millie was not receptive where Richard was concerned. Besides, he felt he already knew what she would say. Richard had brought it on himself. Should he speak to Susannah? Did she perhaps already know? He very much doubted it. What might Richard say to that? But were Richard's wishes even relevant? Hadn't his mother a right to know? She'd had a hard life. She'd married in the teeth of her mother's opposition. Hugh Fleming had been Robert's friend. It was Robert's death at Ypres that had precipitated Millie's bitter prophecy. *He'll be killed and you'll be left a widow.* And of course it proved to be true. Hugh was killed leading his men at Loos. A widow at twenty, Susannah was left to bring up her son alone, a son who'd never known a father. Shouldn't she know what it was Richard had suffered, and was suffering now? Didn't she *need* to know?

Marlowe was at a loss to know what to do for the best.

It was his habit, rain or shine, to go out every day, if only to stretch his legs. Taking his waterproofs from the stand in the porch he went out to encounter MacRath by the sheep pens. The two men stood together amid the bleating of lambs, MacRath leaning on his crook, the wind heaving at them, with the burn roaring past, a torrent of unrest.

'A wild night, Gideon. And more to come by the look of it.'

'Aye. Ye can never be sure what's brewing up there in the mountains.'

MacRath stood four-square to the weather, seemingly indifferent to wind and rain. He went on to tell the story of the great flood that had swept through the house in the time of the MacAskills.

'They do say one of the women here foresaw it coming. '

'*Foresaw* it ?'

'So they say. '*The black storm on the mountain... the shroud upon the corrie... ah, the bitter grief in the glen.*' That was what she said. So they'd been watching for it, d'you see, and got warning enough to escape.' MacRath looked thoughtful. 'Aye, they just had time to fly for their lives before the water was on them. Otherwise all in the lower part of the house must have perished.'

He spoke with authority, as of a familiar thing. It wasn't difficult to imagine him a witness to what he spoke about. And yet it had happened almost a hundred years before.

Well, what were years here? An illusion. The blink of an eye. MacRath's life was grounded in this place. His eyes opened in the morning and there it was, spread out all around him. He saw it in the silent growth of trees and plants, the hay harvest, the swelling ears of corn, the fat lambs gathered in for market, the burn in spate, the running of the sea trout, the beasts grazing in the water meadow, the night sky filled with stars. Small wonder the glen served as a repository of ancient memories, moments of recall cherished in their unexplained distinctness.

'Aye,' he concluded. 'I sometimes feel we live on sufferance here in the glen.'

He might have spoken for all those who'd toiled here before him, men schooled in the same service, fashioned by the same laborious struggle, prudent men who knew, if they used such powers as they possessed of shrewdness and patience, how they might catch at fullness in a harsh, intractable land.

Yes, thought Marlowe, a man in accord with his life. As I am not with mine.

'I hear Professor Collie is back at Sligachan just now,' MacRath went on. 'Will ye be going to visit him? They do say he's much diminished since John MacKenzie died.'

Marlowe hesitated, aware of the keen glance fixed on him. 'No, Gideon,' he said finally, 'those days are gone. Besides, he wouldn't welcome it.'

The wind and rain continued throughout the morning. One or two braver spirits ventured out for a walk on the beach. For the most part, though, the Marlowes were awaiting events. Alarmed by the dramatic revelations in the Friday editions, the BBC bulletins the previous evening had served only to increase their disquiet, and they were waiting anxiously for the latest news. If, that is, the papers ever reached them. For there was some speculation as to whether, in such conditions, the plane would get to Glen Brittle. The thick cloud which had invested the Cuillin earlier that morning had separated into layers, long striations, flat at the bottom with undulating tops, hanging over the corries.

'It'll get here,' said Leo. 'If necessary it will fly below the cloud. The Rapide has a trailing aerial which can be let down over the sea in bad visibility so the radio operator can let the pilot know when it's touching water. Our chap was telling me he once flew all the way from Barra to Tiree and then on to Renfrew without ever having been higher than a hundred feet.'

Sure enough, the little bi-plane touched down later that morning in the Big Meadow. A little delayed to be sure, and in such a wind that Euan MacRath and three of the men had to hold it down while it was taxiing.

That things had gone badly for Chamberlain in Godesberg had been made clear enough over the weekend. Just how far the crisis had escalated was placed beyond doubt by *The Times* which carried a résumé—unofficial but sufficiently chilling to be plausible—of Hitler's demands.

Marlowe, whose seniority claimed first perusal of the paper, gave out the gist.

'The transfer of the Sudetenland is to take place without further delay. It's to be handed over to Germany in its present state. That's to say there's to be no attempt made to destroy or render unusable any military, economic or utility installations or equipment. Nothing is to be removed. No food-stuffs, goods, cattle or raw material. In short, the Czechs are to clear out within four days, taking with them not so much as a single cow.'

'And if they don't?' asked Leo.

'He doesn't say. But I think we all know the answer to that.'

The Czechs, though, seemed determined to defend themselves come what may. The *Daily Express* carried a dramatic account of the scenes in Prague as mobilization got under way. *'They will face the onslaught,'* reported their correspondent, *'with indescribable enthusiasm. With over thirty divisions to call on they are thought likely to give a good account of themselves.'* A more sober military estimate considered Czech resistance likely to be of extremely brief duration.

'Where does that leave us?' asked Vanessa faintly.

'Well, France has given certain guarantees to Czechoslovakia,' said Leo. 'If the Czechs become the victims of German aggression then the French would be obliged to fulfil their commitments.'

'And would they?' asked Bartrum sceptically. 'And if they did, what would be our position?'

'What do you suppose it should be?' demanded Lady Kitty hotly. 'Are we to throw the Czechs to the wolves in order to save our own skin? Or are the British people still capable of standing up to a bully?'

'This is madness,' cried Henry. 'Madness!'

'I quite agree,' said his brother soberly. 'What's more, if October first really is to be the day of reckoning, then the first raids on London will probably be launched shortly after midnight on Saturday.'

'Doubtless we may learn our fate tonight,' said Marlowe. 'It seems Hitler is due to speak in Berlin.'

It was a sombre gathering that assembled to listen to the Second News at 7.30. After the German ultimatum published in *The Times* they feared the worst. So it was no surprise to hear of the immediate mobilization of all anti-aircraft and coastal defence territorial units. All RAF personnel had been recalled from leave. Parliament too had been recalled, and would reconvene on Wednesday. The financial markets were in turmoil, the pound slumping on the foreign exchanges. Meanwhile, people who wished to leave London by the special arrangements should go to the main line stations. Refugees should take their respirators and should wear their warmest clothes. They could take only small hand luggage and they should have with them some food for the journey, and a rug or a blanket. They would not be able to take domestic animals. It would not be possible to allow anyone to choose his destination.

The Archbishop of York had issued a call to prayer. In his statement Dr Temple said it should as always be a prayer for the doing of God's will. Therefore they must pray first for justice and good-will, not first for the avoiding of suffering. Their prayer for peace must spring from their desire for the rule of love in the world, not from their fear of what war might bring to themselves, and they must pray that if they were called to suffer in a just war they might be brave and constant.

A prolonged silence followed the Archbishop's words, a silence broken suddenly by Leo's voice.

'We must go back, of course,' he said urgently to his wife.

'If the House is reconvening,' Leo added, for the benefit of the rest of the family, 'I have to be there.'

'And how will you do that?' enquired his father. 'There isn't a plane until Thursday.'

'I'd gladly take you to the ferry,' put in Bartrum, 'but the Lagonda is essentially a two-seater.'

'In any case,' Marlowe pointed out, putting another damper on things, 'whether or not the ferry is passable depends on the tide. In certain conditions it simply can't operate.'

'I suppose young Euan might agree to take them,' suggested Millie.

'We should be able to get a train from Kyle to Glasgow.'

'I don't think so,' said Henry, who knew about trains.

'Why not?'

'The fact that there isn't a railway line going from the Kyle to Glasgow might have something to do with it. No, you'll have to go north.'

'*North?*'

'That's right.' The Archdeacon had begun leafing through his Bradshaw. 'To Dingwall. '

'*Dingwall?*' It was clearly a place which didn't figure in Lady Kitty's gazeteer.

'Change at Dingwall for Inverness,' said Henry, who was beginning to enjoy this. 'There's a Through Carriage to Glasgow. It is rather slow, though. Doesn't get into Buchanan Street until after nine tomorrow night. There's a train from Glasgow Central at 9.25, but you'll probably miss that. You could catch the 10.45. The Night Scot. No Restaurant Car, though. It *does* have a Sleeping Car. If, that is, you can find a berth. I dare say a great many of your colleagues will be returning from the grouse moors.'

'No,' said Marlowe. 'Sleepers have to be booked in advance.'

'Perhaps we could hire a car at Kyle,' said Lady Kitty uncertainly.

'There are two hundred miles of very bad roads from the Kyle to

Glasgow,' said Bartrum, entering into the spirit of things. 'If I were you I'd stick to the train.'

'You should arrive at Euston at 7.15 on Wednesday morning,' Henry went on remorselessly. 'Rather a gruelling journey, but it will leave you with plenty of time to get to the House.'

But it was time for dinner. As the Marlowes moved across the hall to the dining room Millie took her grand-daughter's arm.

'Miranda,' she murmured quietly, 'I would like to speak to you. Would you come to my room, please, before bed.'

That night the hopes and fears of all of Europe were turned towards Berlin. In towns and cities, in church halls and village halls, in bars, hotels and private houses, folk gathered in tense anticipation of Herr Hitler's speech. Something momentous was about to happen. France had followed Czechoslovakia in mobilizing her forces, and now had a million men in arms along the frontier. Russia, too, had indicated that it would defend Czechoslovakia against German or Polish aggression. Everywhere, it seemed, preparations for war were under way.

Immediately after dinner the Marlowes hurried to the drawing room. Leo immediately began fiddling with the set which whistled and buzzed as he sent the needle trawling through the dial: Berlin... Hamburg... Stuttgart... Vienna... Paris... Hilversum... Prague...

'You won't get anything,' said Nicko shyly. 'The Burghead transmitter can only carry the regional programme.'

As if to bear him out the succession of crackles suddenly gave way to a loud burst of fiddles and accordions. Somewhere a caelidh was in full swing.

'Oh God!' groaned Lady Kitty.

Leo switched it off.

'Trust the BBC not to carry the most crucial speech of our time,' he said exasperatedly.

'Perhaps that's because most of its listeners don't speak German,' said Millie acidly.

'We'll just have to wait for the late bulletin,' said his father.

So they settled down as best they could to the usual pastimes and distractions, Millie turning the cards, Miranda working up the sketch she'd started earlier in the day, others passing the time with a book, or a crossword, or playing chess, though concentration was all but impossible. No one spoke. No one needed to speak. All were troubled by the same thoughts, the same apprehensions. Nor could Wodehouse, nor Agatha Christie, serve to divert sombre fears. Only Richard remained apart, seemingly sunk in his own imaginings, *The Times* disregarded in his lap. Marlowe had no doubt as to what was on his mind. Earlier in the day he had seen the brief paragraph in which the Spanish Government had announced the withdrawal of the International Brigades. The volunteers were to be sent home. Though many of them, the old man reflected, would most likely no longer have a home to go to. Only a prison cell, or the execution yard. The brutal fact was that the Republic had been defeated. All it could hope for now was to search for a formula that might allow a negotiated peace. No peace, though, for such as Richard.

At 10.30 Leo switched on the wireless. The measured tones of the BBC announcer came almost as an anti-climax:

'Earlier this evening Herr Hitler delivered his expected speech to the German people in Berlin. He said that he was grateful to Mr Chamberlain for his efforts, and had assured him that the German people wanted nothing but peace. But his patience was exhausted. He had made sufficient sacrifices and renunciations. There was a limit beyond which it was not possible to yield...'

The familiar voice continued, its level tones wholly at odds with the ultimatum it delivered. Herr Hitler was quite determined. Germany's rights could be ignored no longer. The territory to which the German people were entitled must be his. If it was not delivered to him by the first day of October, his troops would cross the border and take it by force.

Meanwhile, the Czechoslovak Government has declared its determination to resist any aggression mounted across its borders and has called on its allies for assistance...

Leo leant across and switched off the radio.

'It must be fairly unique,' he remarked, 'for a cut-throat to announce in advance the time and place of his crime.'

His remark was received in sombre silence, as the Marlowes took in the implications of what they had just heard, a silence broken by the sudden rustle of a newspaper.

'Well, today's the 26th,' remarked Richard sardonically, looking up from *The Times*. 'You've got four days of peace left. Enjoy them.'

The lights faded momentarily, flickered into life, faded again, and went out. The generator had switched off.

Millie's bedroom was on the southern side of the Lodge directly above the dining room. Miranda, candlestick in hand, tapped on the door. The room was dimly lit by a single candle burning on the beside table. Millie was sitting in the bedside chair, her hands folded in her lap. Her face, thrown into relief by the candle-light, looked worn and strained. She had evidently been waiting.

She looked up as Miranda entered, indicating with a silent gesture that she should take a seat on the bed. Then she looked silently at her grand-daughter. A long, level look. It was a look Miranda knew of old, and her heart quailed before it. She sat as directed, still clutching her candle. She hated these silences. Hated them. They yawned before one, and she always felt that at any moment she would topple forward into empty space.

Somewhere out in the glen an owl's cry, *kee-wick... kee-wick,* stood out harsh and clear against the silence of the night. But Millie's voice, when at last she spoke, was gentle enough.

'Have you told your parents about Charles?'

'You know I have not.'

'Do you intend to tell them?'

Silence.

'Yes, I think I know the answer to that, too.'

There was another, more painful silence. Miranda shifted

uncomfortably. She leant forward and put her candlestick on the table. It was something to do.

'It won't lead anywhere, Miranda,' said her grandmother eventually.

'Why must it lead somewhere? Why can't it just be what it is? Love!' There was more than a hint of desperation in that reply.

'Because time won't stand still, not even for lovers. '

Another silence.

'Oh, I can see the attraction,' Millie went on gently. 'He's handsome, and bold and kind and charming. No doubt he strikes you as gallant and splendid.'

'No. That's how *you* see him. He's not really like that at all. He's quite different underneath.'

Millie sighed.

'And you believe you've discovered the real Charles.'

'I know I have.'

Miranda flinched under the old woman's sceptical gaze. She tried another tack.

'Charles says,' she went on brightly, 'that if we were living in a novel by E M Forster there would be someone, usually an older woman, who possesses the wisdom the rest of the characters are sadly in need of.'

'And you are hoping that I will be your Ruth Wilcox, your Mrs Moore?'

Miranda looked uncertain. She'd never heard of Ruth Wilcox or Mrs Moore.

'But this is not a novel, Miranda. You are children lost in a wood, and there is no one here to rescue you.'

The wind was getting up again, prowling around the house, tapping the sash windows, searching for an entry.

'No doubt Charles is telling himself that what he feels for you is unlike anything he's ever felt before. And do you know why? Because you might be his last chance. You have something he's desperately in search of.'

'Yes, love!' Miranda threw back the word defiantly.

'Innocence. A fresh start with a young woman who still radiates that state of grace which he once had, and lost long ago.'

There was a sudden rattle at the window as another gust struck the pane. The candle flames jumped abruptly, sending the shadows lurching across the chimney breast.

'The other night, very late indeed, your grandfather saw what he thought was a young woman crossing the garden in the direction of the guest cottages. He assumed it was one of the maids. You have always told me the truth, I know. So I am not going to ask if it was you, because I would prefer to continue to believe that it wasn't.'

Miranda, picking at the counterpane, said nothing.

'You know,' her grandmother continued, 'poor Charles is one of those pitiable men who has found no fulfilment in the rackety life he leads. And perhaps is never likely to. He might very well be a man in search of salvation. But you are not destined to be his saviour. Indeed, it's far more likely you may contribute to his damnation. '

Miranda looked up, white-faced. She was shaken to the core.

'I have nothing more to say,' Millie concluded wearily. 'Now you may go to bed. '

— CHAPTER THIRTEEN —

For several days the international crisis had cast a lengthening shadow over the holiday. Now the absence from the breakfast table that morning of Leo and Kitty seemed to bring the gravity of the situation into the very heart of the family. Like thousands of others the Marlowes had gone away in search of rest and recreation. In this they were no different from those whom Henry was wont to refer to ironically as 'the great and the good'. Vanessa had been much comforted, barely a month before, to read that the Home Secretary himself was to be seen strolling on the beach at Southwold in canvas shoes and an open-necked shirt. While the nation's legislators saw fit to relax so informally, nothing very serious seemed likely to happen. But now they had been recalled, and were hurrying back from the grouse moors, from seaside holidays, from Deauville and Le Touquet, from the leafy shires of Shakespeare's England, from grimy northern towns of mean streets and factory hooters, all making their way to the House of Commons prepared to witness the final act of what had proved to be a personal tragedy for the Prime Minister.

So it seemed to the Marlowes who, like everyone else, were steeling themselves for the worst. When war seemed likely to be declared in a few hours time no one was in much of a mood for an outing to the fairy pools.

'What are they, anyway?' enquired Vanessa without enthusiasm.

'An unfortunate name, I agree,' said her husband. 'But they're well worth seeing. A remarkable series of waterfalls, cascades and pools set in a gorge of the Allt Coir' a' Mhadaidh.'

The Archdeacon insisted on the Gaelic names.

'The boys will love it,' he added, beaming at the twins. 'And we've got just the day for it.'

It was indeed a spectacular morning, as different from the previous day as could be imagined. A blue haze blurring all but the silhouette of the Cuillin cutting the blue sky. But here and there, where the sun struck a facet of a ridge there was a glint of wet rock.

Marlowe reflected, not for the first time, what an extraordinary difference sunlight made to the colours of things in Skye. What could seem so drab under grey skies sparkled with life when the sun shone.

The men were to walk to Coire na Creiche, Henry insisting that his knee was perfectedly up to it. Besides, it would be good for the twins. Richard, though, was absent, having offered to go with Lachlan, MacRath's shepherd, to search for a ewe reportedly cragfast in Coir' a' Ghrunnda. Giles, too, was up and away before first light. Chafing after two days of confinement, he had been itching to get out. He and Nicko were to attempt the traverse of the four peaks of Sgùrr a' Mhadaidh, an expedition judged by his father to be quite demanding enough for Giles. It involved a great deal of climbing, the gaps between its four summits being among the deepest along the ridge, and was quite complex to negotiate, even on a clear day.

The taxi from Carbost was due to arrive at eleven for the ladies.

'I could give someone a lift,' offered Bartrum, angling for Miranda.

'Oh, I'd love a ride in a Lagonda,' said Millie unexpectedly.

Henry was most surprised. Bartrum looked concerned.

'It's a very bumpy road, you know,' he said warningly. 'Little more than a cart-track.'

It was no more than the truth.

'I think I can put up with a few bumps,' said Millie cheerfully.

So it was agreed that Miranda, who was in any case equipped with a small collapsible easel as well as her painting satchel, should travel with her mother and Susannah, while Millie had her outing in the Lagonda.

They set off a little in advance of the Carbost taxi which passed them on its way to the Lodge. Bartrum drove with care. Even so, the timbers of the old wooden bridge trembled as the great car rumbled over them. They overtook the walking party a few hundred yards short of the corrie. Millie waved to them as they passed.

The twins, as usual, covered twice as much ground as their elders, dashing off ahead only to return to report on some marvel they'd come across, then dashing off again...

Henry, though, was glad of the opportunity to speak to his father. A staunch supporter of Mr Chamberlain's resolute pursuit of peace, he had further reason to be grateful to the Prime Minister for his recall of Parliament, and with it the return of Leo to London. It was not without a sense of relief that he'd contemplated the two empty chairs left vacant at the breakfast table.

'Well, that's put paid to *Marlowe's Variation*, I'm afraid,' he remarked as they tramped over the wooden bridge.

Privately he'd been racking his brains to think of ways of calling the whole thing off.

'I can't say I'm not relieved. Giles will be disappointed, of course. But to tell the truth, I'm not at all confident of his route-finding ability. It's a long, complicated climb, as I'm sure you'll agree, and he would have been more than likely to have got himself in a pickle.'

Marlowe grunted. He considered the whole idea had been an exercise in futility anyway, an attempt to conjure up some Golden Age none of them had ever known.

At the top of the moor Bartrum drew up beside the corrie and switched off the engine. For some moments they sat in silence.

'Don't you think, Charles,' said Millie suddenly, 'it's rather dishonourable to be carrying on an intrigue with Miranda behind Henry's back?'

So that was it. He was startled, certainly. He'd no idea she knew. Though it took him only a moment or so to recover.

'You must be shocked,' he sighed ruefully, opting for whimsical self-deprecation. 'Here we are on Prospero's enchanted isle, and instead of choosing young Ferdinand your granddaughter has fallen in love with Caliban.'

Millie, though, was not to be charmed. Perceiving his miscalculation, Charles emerged from behind his mask.

'I'm sorry,' he said. 'That was rather silly of me.'

'But look,' he went on earnestly, 'what if those whom love unites have access to regions they could never reach left to themselves? Surely love can be an agent of redemption? It can, can't it? Look at Shakespeare's last plays. Sickness healed, old enemies reconciled, all the mess and muddle of fractured lives put right. And by what? By love.'

'But those lovers are all much the same age, as you well know,' she pointed out ruthlessly. 'There's not an old roué among them.'

'Ouch!' Bartrum winced. 'That's a bit below the belt.'

'You know it has no future. This affair.'

He was reminded, then, of what he'd said himself despairingly to Miranda. *It won't lead anywhere.* And her reply: *Why must it lead somewhere? Why can't it just be what it is?'*

'It's bound to end badly. You know it will.'

His eyes wandered to the rear-view mirror. He could see Henry and his father trudging up the hill towards them.

'Yes, it may fail,' he said soberly. 'Love is always precarious. There's never a guarantee of success. But it's the only hope for a ruined world,' he added, with more than a hint of desperation.

Millie, though, was relentless.

'You must drop her, Charles. She won't abandon you, so you must abandon her.'

'I can't do that.'

'You *must*. If you care for her you *must* do that.'

He was staring fixedly ahead.

'It would come as no surprise to anyone,' she added cruelly. 'And she will eventually come to see it was only to be expected.'

'The first step in her disenchantment, is that it?' he said bitterly.

'Her first lesson in growing up.'

Now reunited on the bank below the road, the party set off in twos and threes to have their picnic. The path led down over the moor to a watersmeet half a mile or so from the road where the Allt a' Mhaim and the Allt a' Mhadaidh joined to form the River Brittle. It was the latter of these two burns that descended in a series of falls, cascading over water-worn rock, and flowing through pools set in the bed of a rocky channel, deepening here and there to a gorge.

Henry walked on ahead with Miranda, carrying her easel. The twins, as was usual with them, ran everywhere. Meanwhile, Bartrum had attached himself to Susannah and Vanessa. Millie, coming on behind with Marlowe, couldn't help but notice him in animated conversation. Charles, who could never resist the challenge of older women, was attempting to charm the ladies.

'You live on the edge of the heath, I believe.'

'That's right,' said Susannah smiling.

'And do you still hear Keats' nightingale in Hampstead?'

'And if she did, it could scarcely be the same bird, could it?' remarked Vanessa cuttingly.

'I'm not sure I'd recognize a nightingale,' said Susannah.

'Ah, now there I can help you. Its song is quite unmistakeable.'

With that he embarked on a series of extraordinary vocalizations.

'*Chuk... chuk... chuk... chirrip... chirrip... wheet... wheet... wheet... woo-it... woo-it...*'

With his longer stride he was continually getting ahead of his companions, so that he had to check himself constantly, shifting from side to side of the path, walking first beside one, and then the other.

How could you trust a man, Vanessa might have ground out between clenched teeth, *who couldn't walk in a straight line?*

Bartrum, though, was warming to his theme.

'*Tseee-ip... tseee-ip... tweedly... tweedly... tweedeldy...*'

But, he went on to explain, should another male nightingale begin to sing, the first bird would seek to superimpose his song on that of its rival, matching it phrase for phrase, only with greater volume and intensity.

Then followed an outpouring of quavers, semiquavers and demisemiquavers: '*Churrr... churrr... chik-chik... chik-chik... chik-chik-chik... chik-chik-chik-chik...*' concluding with a scolding '*tut-tut-tut-tut-tut...*' until Susannah was all but helpless with laughter.

'The object, of course, is to impress the ladies listening in the trees.'

No, thought Millie, watching. He simply can't help himself.

The first waterfall was set among a stand of rowans. At the first glimpse the twins raced on ahead, prompting their father to cry after them'Don't go down go the pools.' But they had already disappeared over the edge of the gully, and were scrambling down the bank even as he hastened after them. His voice could be heard scolding:'I thought I told you not to go down. Some of the pools are much deeper than they look.'

'They're bound to fall in,' called out Miranda to alarm her mother, who hastened after her sons.

The Allt a' Mhadaidh follows a tortuous course in its descent from the corrie, with the path twisting this way and that above the bed of the burn. Every turn afforded the visitors fresh delights. The path climbed the side of the gorge which shortly overlooked a sequence of clear turquoise pools and falls. In the deeper parts of the gorge they were struck by some extraordinary effects; sills seemingly sealing off the main flow of water which, when viewed in the right light and from the right angle, was seen to flow through invisible holes hollowed out under the surface, spurts and jets striking concavities, and rebounding in great gushing arches of water; turbulences where the air, forced down into deep aquamarine pools, billowed up in a froth of bubbles. Some of the pools looked to be fifteen or twenty feet deep.

One pool in particular, filled by a crashing fall, appeared to be cut off from its neighbour by a rocky parapet, though this lower, second pool, serene and placid on the surface, must have been fed through some underwater channel.'

'These,' Henry announced, 'are the fairy pools.'

They descended the bank to water level and were thrilled to see what was in fact a single pool divided by a curtain of rock formed by an arch looming out of the depths. They were able to see past the curve of the arch to the stones lying at the bottom of a pit twenty or thirty feet below.'

'What a super place,' cried Hugh.

It seemed indeed the very spot to eat one's lunch on a sunny afternoon.

Susannah and Vanessa had settled down together in a grassy alcove by the arched pool. Bartrum and Miranda had wandered further off, halting beside a rocky pool below one of the falls where she was setting up her easel.

The twins, once they'd wolfed down Mrs MacRath's cake and sandwiches, embarked excitedly on an engineering project which involved diverting a small tributary stream to flow into a dry watercourse. Henry sat where he could keep an eye on the boys.

'I think I'll go on up to meet Giles and Nicko,' Marlowe told his wife. They'd walked up from the road together, lagging behind the others. 'They'll be coming down from the bealach into Coir' a' Mhadaidh. '

She nodded.

'But you look tired,' he added.

'I'll be all right. I shall sit here for a moment to rest my legs, then I'll join Henry. You go on to meet the boys.'

The interview with Charles had taken it out of her. She hadn't slept well. Long after Miranda had gone she'd remained in her chair, too worn out to undress and get into bed. And when eventually she did she'd lain awake a long time before sleep finally came. No, she hadn't much appetite for these confontations. But it had to be done.

She sat on the bank under some rowans, looking down at the fall of water. Right under her was the stony bed of the gully, with still pools lying like gems between the pavement of the burn. There were blue stones in the pools, light shimmering in the swirling water. Water, sunlight, stone... It was enough.

She looked up to see her husband plodding along the path that now climbed away from the Allt a' Mhadaidh to follow the main burn up into Coir' a' Tairneilear. Did he suspect anything, she wondered? It didn't seem so from what he'd said he'd seen—the figure going between the lodge and the cottages. She didn't think it very likely. Most of the time Stephen was too immersed in his own world to notice anything outside of himself. Henry, of course, was blissfully unaware, as he was of many things. As for Vanessa, such a thing would be so unthinkable she simply couldn't comprehend even the possibility. Should they be told? No, the affair would burn itself out in due course, Millie was sure of that. There would be no point in precipitating a premature conflagration. It could only engulf the whole family. And that would profit no one.

The twins, still engrossed in their engineering, had been joined by their father who was building a dam, infilled with handfuls of silt, under the scornful eyes of his wife and sister. Further off, the two lovers were engaged in urgent conversation. Bartrum, despondent. Miranda, her sketching forgotten, passionate, pleading.

As she watched them the old woman was deeply troubled. What if she was wrong? Miranda had always been headstrong. What if it didn't burn itself out? Passion could sometimes prove an inexhaustible fuel. Besides, the heart had its reasons, against which reason itself was powerless.

Millie sighed. Perhaps, like any wild thing, Miranda must take her chance.

Marlowe crossed the burn, picking up the path slanting below Sgùrr an Fheadain. He was filled with gloom. Hitler's speech had finally extinguished any faint hope he might have had that war with Germany could be averted. *Do you think there'll be a war?* Miranda had asked at breakfast that morning. She had no confidence in her father's belief that reason might prevail. And she was right. War was now inevitable. Only Giles seemed too absorbed in the continuing wonder of his own life to be really conscious of its shadow.

As he passed below Waterpipe Gully he glanced up at the great cleft splitting the mountain above his head. It brought back memories of another time of grief and loss. On that first visit after the war, with the rain hammering down, he'd crept into its dripping depths to mourn the loss of the life that was. Robert dead, Hugh

Fleming dead, and was the wheel now about to turn full circle?

His own war had been fuelled by a longing for some high, redeeming purpose. Something beyond mere day-to-dayness. The restoration of old ideals. Duty, honour, sacrifice. Fine words that were mocked by the reality. By what men did. Its only outcome squalor, misery, horror. *This*, it seemed to say, is what lay behind those words. This is what they pointed to. Richard had fallen prey to the same rhetoric. The tragedy was that he had come to see it too. And were they to go through it all again? It seemed so.

To be born, he thought, was to be thrust into the world in *this* place, at *this* particular time, amid all the apocalyptic goings-on of history. Such was the ground on which to build a life. No, war would overshadow Miranda and Giles just as it had Richard. The die was cast. Hitler wanted the Sudetenland. If it was not handed over to him by the beginning of the month he would take it by force. Again he heard Richard's mocking words: *You've got four days of peace left. Enjoy them!*

Well, Marlowe told himself, there remain the mountains. He raised his eyes to the Cuillin. All before him, from the cleft above his head to the NW face of Mhadaidh, glittered with wet rock. From the base of the Waterpipe he picked a line through a narrow square-cut gully left of the slabs guarding the mouth of Coir' a' Mhadaidh. He wanted to get up into the corrie, to experience for one last time its peace and wildness.

As he climbed up through the gully he could hear the roar of the burn forever cutting its gorge down through the slabs. Rearing up ahead of him now, the steep, dark north-west face of Mhadaidh, for the corrie itself was still largely out of sight, concealed in a fold of Sgùrr an Fheadain. He maintained the same slow, steady rhythmic plod, choosing the good footing supplied by boulders littering the burn, until he stood at last in the very heart of the corrie, a spacious amphitheatre totally enclosed by the rocky terraces of Sgùrr an Fheadain to the north-east, the long spur of Thuilm to the southwest, and the headwall formed by the main ridge of the Cuillin where Bidein Druim nan Ramh was separated from the north peak of Sgùrr a' Mhadaidh by the Bealach na Glaic Moire. Directly ahead, seamed with gullies, were the slabs of the headwall where he'd climbed with Millie's brother so long ago, and above the slabs were the screes of the *bealach*, the pass leading down into Coruisk. The north gully gleamed with running water. There was a small fall gushing out at the bottom.

Settling beside the burn to wait for Giles, he felt a rush of relief and thankfulness. It was still as he remembered it. There was no peace, he thought, like the deep peace of wild places. Yet even here it was not possible to escape the maelstrom of war. Sooner or later it sucked in everyone.

What might suffice to hold their world together? Henry had put his faith in negotiation, compromise, the primacy of reason. '*Here I stand…*' That was his ground. Dear, decent Henry, with his naïve belief that when human beings were shown what was best for them they would quite readily agree to it. Except that human beings were not so constructed. Hitler especially not so.

What would suffice?

Millie, of course, would say Authority. The only ground on which to take one's stand. For Millie that ground was Rome. The rock of Peter. Richard, too, had embraced Authority. *Trust the Party line… always stick to the line…* Only Richard's ground was soaked with blood. Now he had lost that faith. A prisoner of his own bitter knowledge, it encompassed him like a cloud, shutting out the sun.

And what of himself? Estranged, like Millie, from the modern world. Marooned on Lemnos with the stench of a wound which would never cease to fester. He too had no settled faith. He saw no basis for it. He could not see how it differed from any other choice to lay hold of this or that particular illusion. How could one ever be sure what it really was that might emerge from the deepest places of the human psyche? And if all our articles of faith amounted to no more than arbitrary declarations, what grounds did we have for choosing one rather than another?

What would suffice?

Then he saw the stag. It was perhaps 300 yards away, maybe less, for he saw it very clearly. A young stag, perhaps three years old. The antlers stood out distinctly above the light golden coat. It bounded effortlessly down under the north-west face of Sgùrr a' Mhadaidh, froze a moment, scenting the man, stood stock-still to gaze, then resumed its lovely bounding motion, effortless, down through the stones and rough heathery tussocks, down towards the moor.

In that same moment he awoke to himself; knew it for what it was, this sudden irruption into the tension of human events, joy breaking through with the gratuity of something given. It was as if the hills all around him had suddenly caught the light in a totally new way. Or else a voice within him was crying *'Look! Look!'* He felt summoned to the same joy. Joy, amid the radical insecurity of life. Joy, despite the sway of violence and death.

Then, glancing up at the sound of voices, he saw two figures descending the north peak of Sgùrr a' Mhadaidh. He rose stiffly, and walked to meet them as they came clattering down the scree beside the north gully. Still bubbling over with the exhilaration of their day, they threw themselves down on the turf beside the burn to tell, in intervals of scooping up water, of nervy ascents up wet, shattered rock, and Alpine crests, and descents down steep, intimidating slabs, then the circumventing of a daunting *gendarme*, oh, and dizzying precipices everywhere.

'The whole thing was really quite complicated,' said Giles. 'But it was wonderful.'

'Absolutely!' Nicko nodded eagerly.

'Though I'm jolly glad,' added Giles, 'that we did it from west to east. I shouldn't have fancied descending some of those walls.'

Tired as they were, Marlowe saw in their faces the far-away look of men still possessed by joy at the otherness of the world.

Wildness survives, he saw, in the place we have made within ourselves. That these young men had known fullness all one livelong day somehow kept hope alive.

That night, all over the Isle of Skye, in lonely *clachans* and remote communities from Duirinish to Raasay, from Trotternish to Sleat, wherever there was a wireless set, people came together to hear the Prime Minister address the nation. In the kitchen of Glenbrittle House as many of MacRath's household as could be spared from their tasks were gathering to hear the worst that might be laid upon them.

It was an anxious party of guests, too, who collected in the drawing room of the Lodge. For some of them, at least, the day had afforded a brief foray into another world which they might almost have been persuaded was their world too, or could be. But now, as more than one of them reflected, they had returned to the world as it was.

The twins had been packed off to bed early at their mother's insistence.

'I'd rather see them dead than have them bombed,' she exclaimed somewhat hysterically, when they'd gone upstairs.

'No danger of that, surely,' murmured Bartrum, drifting in at that moment. 'At least, not tonight.'

Nicko, hobbling in with the aid of a stick, was the last to enter. He'd turned an ankle returning over the moor, and had to be brought back in the Lagonda.

When they were all assembled Henry switched on the set just as the last details of the weather forecast were being given out.

No one spoke. No one needed to speak; their thoughts were alike, and they were fearful. Everyone sat perfectly still. Only Millie continued turning the cards on her patience table, her face expressionless.

'This is London…'

A hushed expectancy fell over the room, as of something terrible about to happen. Even the calm tones of Stuart Hibberd seemed all but overawed by the gravity of the occasion.

'In a moment you will hear the Prime Minister, the Right Honourable Neville Chamberlain, speaking from Number Ten, Downing Street His speech will be heard all over the Empire, throughout the continent of America and in a large number of foreign countries. Mr Chamberlain... '

It was an old man's voice that addressed them, strained, subdued. It began without preliminaries of any kind, plunging its listeners directly into the crisis by which it seemed itself all but overwhelmed.

'Tomorrow Parliament is going to meet and I shall be making a full statement of the events which have led up to the present anxious and critical situation. An earlier statement would not have been possible when I was flying backwards and forwards across Europe, and the position was changing from hour to hour. But today there is a lull for a brief time and I want to say a few words to you, men and women of Britain and the Empire, and perhaps to others as well.'

'The poor man sounds exhausted,' murmured Susannah softly.

'He's out of his depth,' muttered Bartrum.

First, though, the Prime Minister wished to thank those who had written to himself or his wife during the past few weeks, telling him of their gratitude for his efforts, and assuring him of their prayers for his success. Most of those letters had come from women, mothers or sisters of their own countrymen.

At this Vanessa glanced instinctively at her husband, and reached for his hand.

But there had been countless others besides, Mr Chamberlain continued, from France, from Belgium, from Italy, even from Germany, and it had been heartbreaking to read of the growing anxiety they were feeling, and their intense relief when they thought too soon that the danger of war was passed.

Great though the gravity of what he had to tell them, it was the PM's voice that made the deepest impression. Weary, dispirited, it seemed to cast a shadow over everyone present. It was reflected in the slumped shoulders, the tense faces. For those who had been happy that day that happiness was overturned. For the anxious their troubles seemed to have multiplied a hundred-fold.

'If I felt my responsibility heavy before,' the weary voice resumed, 'to read such letters has made it seem almost overwhelming. How horrible, fantastic, incredible it is that we should be digging trenches and trying on gas-masks here because of a quarrel in a far-away country between people of whom we know nothing. It seems still more impossible that a quarrel which has already been settled in principle should be the subject of war.'

'But Lord Beaverbrook said there would be no war,' whispered Vanessa, bewildered. That celebrated reassurance, proclaimed repeatedly in the *Daily Express* that summer, had served as a rock to which many had clung.

'It's not really up to Lord Beaverbrook,' Henry explained patiently.

Meanwhile, said Mr Chamberlain, there were certain things that they could and should do at home. Volunteers were still wanted for air raid precautions, for fire brigade and for police services and for the territorial units. All of them, he knew, men and women alike, were ready to play their part in the defence of the country. He called on them to offer their services, if they had not already done so, to the local authorities who would tell them if they were wanted and in what capacity. They should not be alarmed, he went on, if they heard of men being called up to man anti-aircraft defences or ships. These were only precautionary measures such as a Government must take in such times as these, but they did not necessarily mean that war was imminent.

'However much we may sympathise with a small nation confronted by a big and powerful neighbour we cannot in all circumstances undertake to involve the whole British Empire in war simply on her account. If we have to fight it must be on larger issues than that.'

'He's preparing to scuttle,' said Richard grimly.

'I am myself a man of peace,' Mr Chamberlain insisted, 'to the depths...'

Radio reception was particularly weak that evening in the western isles, fading, returning, fading out again. The effect was to make the weary voice seem more forlorn than ever.

'For the present I ask you to await as calmly as you can the events of the next few days. As long as war has not begun there is always hope that it may be prevented. And you know that I am going to work for peace till the last moment. '

A bleak silence followed the Prime Minister's 'Good night'.

Henry switched off the set.

'I suppose while there's hope… ' he began.

No one believed him. Nothing could have off-set what they'd just heard. A man at the end of his tether. A man who could do no more.

If there was to be a war, Marlowe reflected, Chamberlain was not going to win it.

— CHAPTER FOURTEEN —

Marlowe slept better that night than he might have expected. Yet within minutes of waking that sense of imminent disaster had returned as a dull, sour fear which grew within him as he lay staring up into the darkness. It was still some while before dawn.

He got up, wrapping himself in scarf and his heavy dressing gown, and sat staring out at the Cuillin. In the glen it was still night, the nearer clouds vague and dark, though with the approaching dawn the mountains gradually took shape as a jagged black line sharply defined against a wash of blood, it might have been. Or else the glow of fires raging in the east.

ed sky at dawning, he thought to himself. Yes, and perhaps a red night to follow.

Would there never be an end to it? No, wars would come and go, war upon war, stretching out until the end of time. And men like Chamberlain would try in vain to avert them, an endless succession of negotiations contending with the powers of darkness. He felt a sudden surge of sympathy for Chamberlain. A fellow-feeling for a man who also had to make his maiden flight at the age of sixty-nine. Not the best preparation for negotiations with a madman. He might well have been in need of the whisky and ham sandwiches with which, if reports were true, he had been provided during the flight. An old man out of his time. *'The poor man sounds exhausted.'* Dear Susannah. Always kind, solicitous for others.

Suddenly he felt something of Chamberlain's weariness flooding through him. He too was out of his time. He longed then to get back to the world as it was. His dialogue with the past, that attempt to hold it fast and recover it which had been the almost daily accompaniment of his life in the trenches, had only grown stronger with the years, in spite of all his denials. Well, that was hardly surprising. Surely there was never a time in the whole history of the world when it was so good to be alive as it was before the war? In those days we had solid ground beneath our feet. Not so now.

Then he remembered MacRath had said Collie was back at Sligachan. He would ask Millie if she'd like to accompany him there for lunch.

He did so as they were descending the stairs together before breakfast.

'I believe Collie is there,' he went on. 'It would be good to see him for one last time.'

He even added a line from Euripides in an attempt to seem light-hearted. *'To meet again after long absence is a god.'*

'No,' said his wife flatly. 'These nostalgic episodes are not good for you. They're not good for any of us.'

She saw in him a troubled mind struggling to free itself from old allurements, all the while cherishing what it sought to cast away.

That morning, throughout the whole country, all thoughts were turned to the crisis. Those who had gone to bed the previous night in the near-certainty that they would wake to find Britain at war found little to comfort them in their morning papers. The fleet had been mobilized. The King had summoned the Privy Council to sanction various measures deemed necessary for the defence of the country. Many people kept their radios switched on throughout the day to hear whatever special announcements might be made. Amid warnings against the hoarding of food, and assurances with regard to the price of petrol, they learnt that the Government had declared a state of emergency, giving the authorities special war-time powers.

More and more of the population continued to leave London by whatever means presented themselves. They were expecting the bombs to fall within a matter of hours. Meanwhile members of both the Commons and the Lords were arriving back in the capital for the recall of Parliament. Leo Marlowe, during a ten-minute stop at Crewe, had managed to obtain copies of the early editions carrying the text of the Prime Minister's address to the nation. He'd been further infuriated by a letter in *The Times*.

'Listen to this. It's from someone called Ian Fleming. *'There will be no peace, no return to prosperity, and no happiness in Europe until England and France agree to the fulfilment of Herr Hitler's stated programme in exchange for a binding disarmament pact.'* This man

Fleming refers to us as *'the slaughter-house brigade'.'*

Kitty, who'd been trying to sleep, gave vent to some grumpy murmurings about Dawson and *The Times*.

Leo arrived at Euston still in a fever of indignation. He'd gone straight to Churchill's flat in Victoria to urge the overthrow of Chamberlain that very morning.

'We have to have you in post, Winston, before the House meets this afternoon.'

In common with the rest of the population the thoughts of the Marlowes had turned to the House of Commons and the statement Chamberlain was to make later that day. Unlike most of the country they suffered the additional anxiety of knowing nothing of what was taking place. Isolated in their remote glen, there were no newspapers to tell them what was happening, and would be none until the plane arrived the following day. Nor could they expect a bulletin on the BBC until the Second News later that evening. Yet they, too, were asking themselves the question, *What will the war mean for me?* How were they to withstand the Gorgon face now turned towards them? They could give their minds to very little else.

So when Marlowe issued his invitation over the breakfast table it aroused little enthusiasm.

'Euan is going up the glen again this morning. I thought I might go with him, and stop off for lunch at Sligachan. Would anyone like to come?'

'I don't think anyone's in much of a mood, father,' began Henry carefully.

For the Marlowes that morning all thoughts of the holiday were at an end.

'I'll come with you, grandfather,' said Richard.

'So will I,' said Giles, after a pause.

'No one else?' Marlowe looked round the breakfast table. Studied the faces avoiding his eye.

'Then I've got off lightly, haven't I?' he said brightly.

He busied himself again with toast and coffee.

'Can I come?' asked Nicko suddenly.

'Of course, if you feel you can manage it.'

Nicko's ankle was so swollen he could scarcely hobble. Susannah, who knew about such things, had applied a cold compress.

'You should rest,' she said reprovingly.

The Sligachan Inn stands in one of the most desolate spots imaginable, where the lonely road from Carbost meets the road from Broadford crossing the Sligachan river. A path runs south-west, following the Red Burn towards the Bealach a' Mhaim, the pass descending into Glen Brittle. Another path leads south-east into the wilderness of Glen Sligachan. On every side the dreary moors stretch far away. The inn is a substantial building, with tall chimneys and dormer windows set in a steeply pitched roof. Like many smaller habitations in that rain-swept district it has an external covering of cladding which makes it visible for miles around. Visitors descending the Tourist Route from Sgùrr nan Gillean may see the clean white walls gleaming in the westering sun and think it far closer than it is, though weary miles of bog and moorland still separate them from their heart's desire.

From whatever direction one approaches the inn, whether from Portree or Broadford or Carbost, it is always Sgurr nan Gillean that draws the eye. The wind was still in the south-west, and though the southern Cuillin had been draped in cloud when the luncheon party left the Lodge that morning, the northern peaks were clearly visible under a lowering sky.

As they drove along Glen Drynoch they looked across at the Pinnacle Ridge, a jagged *arête* with great lumps bitten out of it, climbing up to the summit.

'Have you climbed it, grandfather?' asked Richard.

'Yes, long ago.'

'So have we,' said Giles eagerly. 'That was a terrific day.'

'It certainly was,' said Nicko.

As they drew closer to the inn, where the pinnacles began to merge one with another, the neighbouring summit of Am Basteir swung into view, the Executioner, its savage axe rearing up beside it, with the shapely pyramid of Sgùrr a' Bhasteir to its right. It was a skyline Marlowe had known all his life. It seemed to him now, at a time of turmoil and uncertainty, a reassuring sight.

'You'll not recognize the place since John Campbell finished the improvements,' said Euan MacRath, as he swung the car past the south windows of the inn, and into the forecourt. 'It's quite the luxurious hotel he has here now.'

As they entered the outer vestibule of the inn they saw a white-haired old man sitting by the window. He wore a thick tweed suit, with a great-coat wrapped around his shoulders. Though still lean and long-limbed, he was evidently of great age. His grave face was profoundly lined, with deep-set eyes fixed at a distance. He was gazing down Glen Sligachan towards the Red Hills, and there was about him a remoteness that discouraged intrusion.

Marlowe hesitated a moment before passing on into the hotel, an indecision that did not pass unnoticed by his sharp-eyed grandson.

'Who was that old man? '

'That, Giles, was Professor Collie.'

'Not he of the seven-league boots?' Despite himself, Giles's voice held a note of awe.

'The very same.'

As they were making for the bar Marlowe heard a Scots voice calling his name.

'You go on,' he said to Richard, 'and find a table. I'll join you in a moment.' Then turned to greet an old friend.

'It's been a long time, John,' he said as they shook hands.

'Too long, Professor, too long.' John Campbell was ever the genial host.

Marlowe asked after Collie.

'Oh, he's not been the same man since John MacKenzie died. Did you know John was dead? Aye, five years now. The Doctor thought highly of John. You will remember them, I dare say, pacing up and down together, smoking their pipes. Aye, it hit him hard. After John died he made a solo ascent of Am Basteir. That was his first climb, you know. Aye, Am Bhasteir. It was John who gave him the guidance for that. John was *ghillie* here then, you know. So when John died he climbed Am Basteir one last time. That would be the end, he said.'

At that moment a party of young men came from the outer vestibule, and went on into the bar.

'Now that young fellow there,' Campbell went on, 'the lean dark one. That's Mr Murray. He completed the traverse last year. Yes, the whole ridge from Garsbeinn to Sgùrr nan Gillean. Eleven hours, it took them.'

As he listened to the bantering Scots voices chaffing one another, talking of climbs they'd done, climbs he'd never heard of, Marlowe knew beyond all doubting that his time had passed. That searching intimacy with the mountains, which had once brought him such fullness, had now passed to others.

Collie too was out of his time. Never a clubbable man, he had always preferred his own company, and that of a few close friends. Most of them must now be dead. Only the hills remained. The hills, and an old man's memories.

He had meant then to go straight into the dining room, but lingered, drawn to the photographs adorning the walls. There was one in particular, a small party grouped outside the hotel. Among them a small, solemn young man in breeches and Norfolk jacket. Yes, it was himself, pictured there among the founding fathers of the SMC. It must have been taken, Marlowe reflected, oh, almost fifty years before. He thought of the young men who, in years to come, might stand where he was standing, gazing at these photographs. What would they make of us, he wondered, in our big boots and moustaches, our antique clothing? In those days the rock was blank, inscrutable, utterly beyond the human realm. We were the first to uncover its concealments. We learnt that the Cuillin were more than they showed, gave more than they had. We learnt too, he reflected, that there could be no conclusive reading of a surface.

Still musing, he went on into the dining room. He found the boys had secured a table by the window, with a view of Gillean and Sgùrr a' Bhasteir. Should he tell them about the photograph? No, better not. What had it to do with them? It was all in the past. Even so, the past so possessed him that he found he had carried it into lunch with him. So he began to speak of the men who'd climbed here fifty years before; of King and Naismith and the rest. He told them of the first ascent of the Bhasteir gorge, of Hastings stripping off his clothes to swim the pool that lay in his path, then climbing the waterfall that lay beyond it, stark naked as he was. They listened politely, respectfully, were amused, even. But they had their own, far more recent, exploits to celebrate. And throughout all this Richard sat, withdrawn. And Marlowe could find no way to draw him.

Just then John Campbell brought word that Euan MacRath had come into the inn, and would wait for them to finish their meal. As they went out through the vestibule to the car they saw Collie still sitting as they had seen him. He might not have moved. Marlowe saw with a pang that the past was an island on which a man must live alone.

'Won't you go back to speak to Dr Collie?' asked Richard. 'It seems a pity not to have a word with your old friend.'

'I thought he was rather fine,' said Nicko quietly.

Marlowe only smiled, shook his head.

'I think we'll leave him in peace.'

'How nice,' said Giles suddenly, 'to think he still comes here on holiday.'

'I rather think,' said Marlowe, 'he has come here to die.'

As they drove back along the Drynoch road towards Glen

Brittle Marlowe thought of his last glimpse of Collie, sitting there, lost in a world that had been, lost to the world that was. Without transcendence the physical world was a prison for the very old. *It seems a pity not to have a word with your old friend...* Should he have done so? No. Collie was engrossed in that internal audit of which the young know nothing. He would not have welcomed interruption. And what if the echo of some deep source had finally drawn him back to the mountain wilderness where it all began so many years before, an inner ground that could hold its own against the march of armies, and might persist in spite of all? For the rock, too, resists, endures, sustains, survives. The rock that men were made from.

In Glen Brittle banks of grey cloud were still mustering along the flanks of the Cuillin as Bartrum and Miranda walked down to the beach. The tide was driving green, translucent breakers on to the strand where a few redshank and ringed plover scurried along ahead of the wave. There were gulls, too, feeding among the weed floating off the rocks. At sea level the wind was less than might have been expected. Across the loch, though, up on the headland where a moorland burn plunged over the edge of the cliff, the fall was blown back in spectacular fashion, sometimes streaming up into the air a hundred feet or more, sometimes creeping a yard or two further down its course, before being chased back again by the wind.

Slowly they made their way among the rocks, though slippery wrack and greasy boulders proved an increasing obstacle. Eventually they were forced to clamber up to a secluded platform between the gorse and heather from where they were able to look down on to the rocky flats below, wondering if those were the rocks MacRath had said were a likely spot for otters hunting crabs. Miranda so wanted to see an otter.

Here, too, were deep ravines cutting into the cliff. They held hands as they stood watching the relentless motion of the sea coursing between narrow walls, swirling into nooks and crannies, rising, falling as the incoming tide surged and receded.

Here, in this wilder world beyond the sway of any human ordering, they found a freedom from what so fretted and constrained them. If only he could believe in it Bartrum felt his heart would break for joy. But the memory of his scene with Millie was still too raw.

'I was completely floored, 'he said again. 'I'd no idea she knew.'

'I told her. It was a mistake, I know. I was right the first time.'

'The first time?'

'I told her I was in love. It was so wonderful I had to tell someone. But I didn't say who with. I just said, 'He's not suitable'. I was still thinking like my parents. But of course you are suitable. The most suitable man in the world. Loving you makes you suitable.'

His heart warmed to her afresh.

'Millie believes it's bound to end sooner or later. She wants me to give you up.'

'She said the same to me. 'It won't lead anywhere.' But it already *is* where it needs to be.'

For a while they stood in silence gazing at the sea. A lone cormorant, tossed up and down on the swell, was fishing out in the loch, lowering its head and neck, sliding repeatedly under the water. It had caught nothing.

'I have to tell you this,' he said suddenly. 'Sometimes I also think it's bound to end badly.'

'Of course you do. That's because it always *has* for you. In the past, I mean.'

She turned to face him, looking up into his eyes.

'I'm not ashamed, you know,' she said. 'Whatever they might say.'

'Must it really be 'us' and 'them'?'

'Yes, of course. Because their lives go backwards into the past they think they already know what will become of us. But there never is a future in the sense they mean. It doesn't actually exist. Because if it did, nothing could change. Don't you see?'

It was all so clear to her.

'There are only these present moments,' she went on, taking his other hand.

Just then a seal's head popped up above the swell, swivelling round to stare.

'Nothing outside of ourselves can come between us, if only we hold fast to one another.'

Bartrum smiled. He hadn't that kind of faith.

"Come the three corners of the world in arms, and we shall shock them', he murmured wryly. *"Naught shall make us rue, if England to herself do rest but true.'* No, I fear it's not as simple as that.'

She stared at him.

'You're wrong, Charles. It *is*. It *is* as simple as that.'

Not for the first time he was amazed at her strength of purpose. She was so much stronger than he was.

'You know Giles confronted me?' he went on. 'No, of course you don't. I didn't tell you. I didn't want you to be worried.'

'What did he say?'

'He warned me off, of course.'

She giggled. 'Poor Giles. He must have been so embarrassed.'

'He was. Embarrassment struggling with indignation.'

She giggled again at the thought

'Giles isn't a sneak. He never was, not even as a child. He won't tell tales. And grandmother certainly won't.'

Even so, they both knew that the private world they had enjoyed together was now at an end. Giles had seen them together. Sooner or later someone else would too. Eventually it would get back to her parents. Should they anticipate that? Make a bold self-declaration that very day in front of the whole family? She would have done so gladly, but she felt instinctively he would believe it to be rash, impetuous.

As it was, she didn't know what to do for the best. And neither did he.

Meanwhile, the preparations for war continued. Two-thirds of the population, claimed the *Daily Mail*, now either had their gas-masks, or had been fitted for one. Black-out instructions had been issued for houses and motor vehicles. In Lincoln's Inn Fields, crowds turned up during the dinner hour to inspect the trenches being dug there to see how the experts constructed a splinter-proof shelter. For some at least the situation seemed to hold out promising opportunities. An advertisement in the *Manchester Guardian* advocated the purchase of cellophane to gas-proof windows, and guard against flying glass. Another urged readers of the *Daily Mail* to line their shelters with rubberoid 'Zylex' which, it was claimed, was cheap, waterproof and untearable. Whether or not it was splinter-proof remained unclear.

Herr Hitler, it was now widely reported, had brought forward his deadline. Unless the Czechs accepted his ultimatum by 2pm that very day Germany would mobilize its forces. The arterial roads around the capital saw a huge increase in trafffic as men ferried their wives and children to relatives living in the country, while Waterloo Station was overrun with Americans hoping to board one of the six special trains laid on to take them to Southampton and the *Queen Mary*. All these developments presented to many Londoners unmistakeable signs of what was to come. Leo Marlowe, making his way down Whitehall to the House of Commons passed through a silent crowd gathered at the Cenotaph. Clearly many Londoners feared that they were about to suffer the same fate as Guernica.

In the House itself the mood was sombre. Members packed the green benches, overflowing onto the steps of the gangways, convinced, like many of their constituents, that hostilities were imminent. As many members of the public as it could hold had packed into the Strangers' Gallery. Present too, Leo saw, were many distinguished visitors not usually seen in the Commons. Queen Mary, the Queen Mother, all in black, had taken her seat in the Speaker's Gallery accompanied by the Duchess of Kent and Mrs Chamberlain. In the Peers' Gallery were the Duke of Kent, Lord Halifax, the Foreign Secretary, the former prime minister, Stanley Baldwin, and the Archbishop of Canterbury. The Diplomatic Corps, too, were there in force: the ambassadors of France, the

Soviet Union, and the United States, together with von Dirksen, the German Ambassador sitting yards away from the Czech, Jan Mazyryk, all awaiting the conclusion of routine business, and the arrival of the Prime Minister.

Shortly before three o'clock Chamberlain entered the chamber to a tremendous ovation from his supporters. The sombre mood, however, was soon restored as, step by step, he described the attempts he had made during the summer to arrive at a resolution of the crisis. He told of the journeys he'd made to Berchtesgaden and Bad Godesberg. He explained the rights and entitlements of the Sudeten Germans. He spoke of sparks which, once lit, might give rise to a general conflagration. The country, he said, would not have followed them if they had led it into a war to prevent a minority from obtaining autonomy…

He's going to rat, thought Leo sourly. He scribbled a quick note —*You must speak out*—and passed it down to where Churchill was sitting in the aisle below the gangway.

Chamberlain had been speaking for just under an hour when the Chancellor of the Exchequer, who was sitting beside him, tugged at his coat and handed him a note. Chamberlain read it, removed his pince-nez, looked up—it might have been to Heaven—and then resumed his patient exposition. But to members sitting opposite across the despatch box it was clear that his mood had changed. Gone the haggard, careworn look of the last few weeks. The Prime Minister seemed almost cock-a-hoop.

'That is not all,' he said, as he concluded his statement. 'I have something further to say to the House yet. I have now been informed by Herr Hitler that he invites me to meet him at Munich tomorrow morning. He has also invited Signor Mussolini and M. Deladier. Signor Mussolini has accepted and I have no doubt that M. Deladier will also accept. I need not say what my answer will be…'

There was a moment of stunned silence. Then a storm of cheering broke out in the chamber.

'Thank God for the Prime Minister,' a voice rang out amid the general hullaballoo.

'We are all patriots,' he continued, when the ovation finally subsided, 'and there can be no honourable member of this House who does not feel his heart leap that the crisis has been postponed to give us once more an opportunity to try what reason and goodwill and discussion will do to settle a problem which is already in sight of settlement. I go now to see what I can make of this last effort.'

The House adjourned to a fresh outburst of cheering, and waving of order papers. Almost to a man the Government benches rose to applaud their Leader. Across the chamber members of the Opposition followed suit. For minutes on end the uproar continued, an eruption of delirious joy. Even the members of the Diplomatic Corps had risen to their feet to applaud the Prime Minister. In the Peers' Gallery the Archbishop of Canterbury was observed pounding the rail in front of him with both hands. Stanley Baldwin thumped the floor with his stick. Queen Mary's eyes, it was reported afterwards, had filled with tears.

Meanwhile, the object of this ovation, motionless, unsmiling, stood aloof from it all. It was his moment, and he could afford to savour it.

There were some though, a mere handful, who could not bring themselves to applaud, but kept to their seats in silence. Leo Marlowe became conscious of someone poking him savagely on the shoulder; an angry voice in his ear: 'Get up, damn you! Get up!'

Marlowe had returned from Sligachan concerned for Richard. Throughout the meal he'd hardly spoken a word. Giles and Nicko, of course, had been re-living their traverse of Mhadaidh. It lived again in their faces. Richard sat, a dark shadow entirely separated from the animal spirits rejoicing at the table. For him that light had gone out. It was as if there was something missing in him, an intolerable deprivation, some cryptic gap through which all that he'd cherished most had leaked away. And yet he was haunted by its memory.

Marlowe himself had never suffered that longing for some imagined end-place. But Richard had. What was it he'd said? *We would clear away the crimes of History, and actually build the kingdom Christ spoke about.* He had seen the Future, and he'd believed in it, and his tragedy was inconsolable because nothing could bear the weight of its loss.

Marlowe resolved then that he must speak to Susannah.

He found her alone, sitting in the garden, the book she'd been reading lying forgotten in her lap. She was lost in thought. To her father she seemed the image of that patient endurance which she'd been called upon to show for so much of her life. And now he was about to inflict further suffering.

She looked up at his approach.

'I'm just going up to Eas Mor,' he said. 'It's not far. Will you come too?'

She saw it was a summons, and rose without a word.

They crossed the stile together and set off along the side of the burn, picking up the path climbing over the moor.

'To tell the truth,' he began awkwardly, 'I want to talk to you about Richard.'

She might have sensed his hesitation, for she slipped her arm through his.

'I don't feel altogether easy in my mind about what I'm going to say, since I haven't spoken to him about it. But I feel that you really need to know what Richard has been through.'

So he began to tell her, much as Richard had told it to him: that encounter with an Italian column, the scattering that followed, days on the run among the hills, the sighting of the battalion, Richard's flight into the forest, finally the intervention of Don Antonio.

'The rest, of course, you know.'

She heard it all in silence.

Now the huge rim of the ravine came into view. He halted a few yards further on at a grassy belvedere within sight of the fall.

'He believes he's a deserter,' he said, amid the crash of water.

'And he can't forgive himself.'

But there was more, much more to be said. It couldn't be left at that.

'I've no doubt he was exhausted. Mentally at his wits' end. He'd given everything he had to give, and there was nothing left.' At the same time he realised how useless it was to explain to someone who'd never been there herself. 'You must understand,' he tried to say.

Then, as he sought to explain about the deserters coming down the Menin road, his voice began to tremble, until he was caught up in his own distress, and was swept along willy-nilly, so that it all came spilling out, what he could never bring himself to confess to his wife now blurted out to his daughter, who put her arms around him.

'Men are not good, Susannah,' he blubbered. 'They never have been good. They never will be good.'

She, though, only held him the tighter, with the noise of the fall roaring in her ears.

'It's over now,' she said gently. 'None of it matters. Hush now, it's over.'

Though she saw it would never be over, the terrible place he'd come from, the place that still held him prisoner. Not for him. Not for Richard.

Shortly before 7.30 that same evening, in remoter regions of the British Isles, people gathered round wireless sets in readiness to hear the Second News. As they waited for valves to warm, and frequencies to be located, they sat in expectation of the worst. Reception, always variable, was possible only after nightfall in these far-flung districts as the D layer dissolved and the sky-waves, travelling further out into the ionosphere, were refracted back to earth. That year sun-spot activity over the northern hemisphere had been particularly high, with the usual consequence of intermittent fading of sky-waves. Even so, the voice of the announcer, teetering on the faltering airwaves, gathered sufficient strength to bring through the falling rain the momentous news to Glen Brittle:

'In a dramatic statement to the House of Commons earlier today Mr Chamberlain announced that he would be flying tomorrow to Munich, where he would meet Herr Hitler, M Daladier and Signor Mussolini. The German Government, in reply to representations from Mr Chamberlain and Signor Mussolini, had already postponed for 24 hours the decision to mobilise the army…'

So it was that the euphoria witnessed that afternoon in the House of Commons, registering itself in every household, spreading like ripples in a pond to the farthest reaches of the kingdom, eventually fetched up in the far north-west, where it was joyfully received in the drawing-room of the Lodge. Only Millie, turning the cards on her patience table, seemed unmoved by the general jubilation.

'Thank God!' said Vanessa devoutly. 'It might indeed have been an answer to prayer. Giles could return to Oxford, the twins would go back to school. Her home, her children, the homes and children of all the country were safe, thank God. They had been spared the test of extremity.'

'Who would have thought Mussolini would come up trumps?'

'Didn't I say that at bottom they were rational men? Brutes they may be, but war is no more in their interest than it is in ours.'

'In Downing Street,' the announcer continued, *'the Prime Minister's car was surrounded by the throng of well-wishers. Mr Chamberlain is reported to have waved his hat, and while saying to the crowd, "It's all right this time."'*

'There's tomorrow's headline,' muttered a sardonic voice.

'This evening the Prime Minister and Lord Halifax will be meeting Mr Masyryk, the Czech Ambassador at the Foreign office…'

What pain and distress must it mean, thought Marlowe, for a man to be told that his country must lay down its life at the behest of its friends?

'And do you suppose the Czechs,' he asked, 'are to have any say in their own dismemberment?'

'I have no doubt,' replied Henry firmly, 'that the Czechs' interests will be more than adequately represented by the Prime Minister.'

'And don't forget,' added Vanessa, 'it was Hitler himself who called this meeting in Munich. It's clear, surely, that he wants a peaceful settlement. Isn't it?' *'Meanwhile relief has been expressed in Paris and Rome at the calling of the Four-Power conference. In Rome it is thought that the crisis has entered a new phase...'*

'Let's hope so.'

'A few days' delay in 1914 would have saved eight million lives. Instead, we all plunged into the crevasse one after the other. The same rope links us together today, but now it will be reason and not blind passion that may prevail over catastrophe.'

'You think so?'

'If there *is* a war,' asked a small, anxious voice, 'we *would* win. Wouldn't we?'

The eager voices were stilled for a moment. They had forgotten the children.

'Of course we would,' ventured Bartrum stoutly. 'We always win.'

'There won't *be* a war,' said Vanessa firmly, shooting a furious look at Charles.

'I believe,' said the Archdeacon firmly, 'that we may have come today as near to a sense of the peace which passeth all understanding as human beings are ever likely to do.'

'I think a prayer might be appropriate, Henry.'

'Oh, for God's sake.'

'No, Richard, for all our sakes. For the sake of the whole world. I do believe September 1938 will go down in history. It has been a great deliverance.'

There followed another awkward silence.

'Henry!'

The Archdeacon sighed, and bowed his head. 'Almighty God,' he intoned, 'whom to serve is perfect freedom...'

The younger Marlowes, for whom religious observance had been from their earliest days an inescapable fact of life, bent their heads submissively. Nicko, out of politeness, followed suit. Even Bartrum, after an uncertain glance around him, did the same. Only

Millie, who had crossed the Tiber many years since, continued to turn the cards.

'...Grant that the representatives of the Great Powers, meeting tomorrow in Munich, may be guided by your Divine Providence to a just and peaceful settlement of the present crisis. We ask this for the sake of your Divine Son, our Lord Jesus Christ...'

There was a subdued muttering of *Amens,* then the Marlowes and their guests rose, and went in to dinner.

Marlowe himself remained in his chair. To Millie's questioning look he returned a mute shake of the head.

The old man was too disturbed by what he had just witnessed to sit at dinner with his family. He wanted to think about it. To think, alone and in silence.

He had watched them, and listened to them, excited, chattering away, setting argument against argument, eyes fixed on one another, alert to each gesture, each inflection, utterly oblivious of what was really happening to them. That what they were experiencing was their own fundamental helplessness. Wasn't that so? And wasn't fear the pervading human emotion? Fear, at the radical insecurity of life?

What little control, he reflected, any of us have over our lives: of the circumstances that surround us; the events that overtake us. Isn't that the reality all of us share?

He thought of Henry. His naïve assumption that 'the representatives of the Great Powers', as he called them, had seen reason. Vanessa's euphoria: *'And don't forget it was Hitler himself who called this meeting...* Well, Hitler might keep faith. He might not. Either way they could do nothing about it. Best not to think about that. Better batten down fear—seek relief in fruitless discussion—cling to Chamberlain, the upright man who would provide the illusion of safety. *'A second,'* Millie might quip, *'and the angels alter that.'* And yet wasn't Millie's bulwark against human folly as illusory as Henry's trust in human reason? It was a despairing thought.

— CHAPTER FIFTEEN —

As he set out from Downing Street the next morning Chamberlain carried with him the hopes of millions. It was already, if only in anticipation, a triumphal progress. Cheering crowds lined the streets of the nine mile route to the airport. Every member of the cabinet, bar one, was waiting there to greet the Prime Minister and speed him on his way.

A large delegation stood ready to board the plane. As well as advisors and officials from the Foreign Office, there was the PM's own physician, his personal detectives, plus the usual secretaries and aides, one of whom had been entrusted with Mr Chamberlain's British Airways flight ticket, inscribed 'London/Munich and Return'. The party had been agreeably provided for with luncheon hampers from the Savoy: caviar, smoked salmon, grouse sandwiches and claret, with beer for the Prime Minister's bodyguards.

Something of the general euphoria was reflected in the BBC's live broadcast from the scene: '*Mr Chamberlain is waving his hat with the great air of nonchalance and gaiety, which he adopted once before on the aeroplane, and which I believe he adopted yesterday when he said 'It's alright now' to people in Downing Street. He doesn't mind in the least being importuned frequently by the photographers, who shout 'Mr Chamberlain, Mr Chamberlain, Mr Chamberlain,' and he beams all over his face, turns back to the Cabinet and says, 'Oh, I can't stand any more.*"

A steady drizzle did nothing to dampen the Prime Minister's spirits. Pausing on the steps of the aircraft, he turned to offer a final word of encouragement into the microphone.

'When I was a little boy I used to repeat, *If at first you don't succeed, try, try, try again.* That is what I am doing. When I come back I hope I may be able to say, as Hotspur said in *Henry IV*, 'Out of this nettle, danger, we pluck this flower, safety.'"

Though the deal, it seemed, was pretty well sewn up.

In Glen Brittle the rain of the night before had given way to a morning unimaginably different from the previous day. Though the main ridge was still deeply shadowed, the glen was filled with sunlight, while the clear sky and the brightness flooding into the corries gave promise of a glorious day.

On such mornings the advice sometimes tendered to the visitor at the hotel seems reassuringly persuasive. '*Oh*,' you may be told, *à propos* of this or that route to a summit, '*it's usually far easier than it looks from below.*' No doubt your informant will go on to extol the extraordinary adhesive qualities of the gabbro, though the ridges abound in much less trustworthy rock, basalt and dolerite, treacherous when wet, to say nothing of the loose debris littering the ledges. Indeed, a certain boldness of spirit is required to go safely in the Cuillin. Much of the main ridge is intimidating. There are many places where a slip would almost certainly prove fatal, and this sudden apprehension of mortality can unsettle the nerve of some who choose to venture there.

That morning, though, the urge to set foot on rock was well-nigh irresistible. It looked like the best day of the holiday. For Giles it was a day made for climbing. There could be no question of that, however, for Nicko's ankle was now giving cause for concern. It really was quite badly swollen, bruised as well, and tender to the touch.

'I don't think you've broken it,' said Susannah. 'You wouldn't be able to stand on it, much less walk, if you had. You really should have rested it yesterday.'

'Perhaps we should get Dr MacKay to take a look,' said Henry. 'We have a long journey before us on Monday. We don't want to run the risk of further damage.'

The Archdeacon felt as responsible for his son's friend as he did for the rest of the party. So it was arranged that Bartrum should drive Nicko to the surgery in Carbost immediately after breakfast.

No one seemed quite sure exactly what happened at breakfast that morning. Of course, not everyone was present. Miranda was always late. Millie, who rarely bothered with breakfast, usually kept to her room until it was over. Richard and Bartrum were only just arriving when it happened.

Henry and Vanessa, helping themselves to eggs and bacon from the sideboard, had their backs to the room and were conscious of nothing apart from the crash of crockery. Though Susannah, who was just taking her seat, thought she saw Morag stumble with the tray, and Giles, she thought it was, reaching across to steady her. Certainly it was Giles's voice she heard saying, 'Steady on', followed by a sudden, startled intake of breath. Marlowe looked up from his plate to see Morag flying from the room. Nicko, hobbling to the table while Giles was collecting his breakfast for him, saw nothing at all. Bartrum bent to help Richard pick up the pieces as Mrs MacRath hastened after the girl. All the guests heard the stammer of Gaelic out in the hall. A few minutes later Mrs MacRath returned with extra plates.

'Is poor Morag all right,' asked Susannah anxiously. 'She looked deathly pale.'

'Oh, she's fine now.' Though Mrs MacRath evidently thought something more was needed in the way of explanation.

'Morag has... ' she went on, then hesitated. 'We say *an dà shealladh*. She thought she saw some harm coming...' For a moment she looked troubled, before brightening. 'Ach, but what would the Chermans want with Angus's few cows?' she added cheerfully.

The English looked at one another across the breakfast table.

'A useful thing to have, second sight,' remarked Bartrum amiably. 'Do you believe in it, Mrs MacRath?'

'Well, I don't have the gift myself, Mr Bartrum, but they do say that those that do have it wish they were without it.'

'All this talk of war has obviously given the girl fancies,' said Henry, buttering a slice of toast.

'What's second sight?' asked Andrew.

'It's seeing two of everything,' said Hugh. 'That's why Morag dropped the tray.'

'Is that true?' asked Andrew.

'I expect so,' said his mother soothingly.

After breakfast they all gathered round to watch Nicko loaded into the Lagonda, an awkward manoeuvre given the confined space.

'Do drive carefully,' instructed Henry. 'We don't want him to suffer any further damage.'

Bartrum assured them that he would exercise the utmost care, an undertaking somewhat undermined by a menacing growl as he opened the throttle. But the great car set off sedately enough along the rutted track.

'I suppose I may as well clean the boots,' said Giles gloomily as he watched them depart. He'd no one to climb with.

'I'll give you a hand,' said Richard.

It was the barbarous nature of the district that most impressed itself on some of the earliest visitors to the Cuillin. *'Mist and rain,'* wrote one English traveller, *'mist and rain. The mist lifts only to uncover scenes of the utmost desolation. Truly, this is an awful place.'*

Yet there were always those in whom the very wildness awoke instinctive responses. Some, hitherto confined to the surface of their lives, discovered in themselves a deep nature they might have overlooked, or lost sight of. These were made aware of something akin to a kinship that overturned the carefully constructed boundaries of their social selves. They'd received permission to be themselves. Since coming to Skye Miranda Marlowe had begun painting with a freedom not granted her before, seeing with an intensity that resonated with her own awakened vitality. She used watercolours because they were portable, painting with the colour, not the water, rendering the shelving rock as planes of light and shade, a faceted pattern on the verge of dissolving into pure abstraction.

Sometimes Bartrum was pressed into service to carry her equipment. In Coruisk she'd astonished him by saturating the paper with washes, then scratching at it with her thumb-nail to create a confusion of boulders beside the loch, before finishing with the brush and strokes of the pen. After two hours she was drained, but satisfied.

He'd gazed at a work miraculously recovered from initial chaos; the play of light on water, light and shadow giving form to the mountains, moss and lichen staining the stones.

'Will you show that to Bill,' he asked incredulously.

It seemed to him filled with the same energizing life-force he found in her.

'What would be the point?'

He saw then that she'd written off Coldstream, just as she'd written off her other instructors.

The sun had already risen above the ridge when she set up her easel in the meadow across the way from the farmhouse. She sat with the sun at her back beside a flat-topped boulder on which she laid out her brushes, pencils, paint, ink, water bottles, together with an old tin baking tray to serve as a palette for mixing colours. The glen was saturated with the gleaming, elegiac light of early autumn, a low, slanting light that made luminous every detail, sending long shadows across the fresh-washed fields, the light catching the hills above the forest as she had not seen them before, an earthly unearthliness emerging from the rising mist, so that it seemed a new-found-land. Miranda longed to re-create it all anew, the white-walled crofts, the clear, pebbly river, the purple coves among the breasts of the hills, pouring over it more and more radiant light until it was consumed by the glow of her own joy.

In the garden of the Lodge Giles was prising stones from between the cleats of a boot.

'Will Chamberlain succeed?' he asked suddenly.

The question was so unexpected Richard was taken aback. Of all the family Giles alone had seemed free of the shadow of war, a youth too absorbed in the continuing wonder of his own life to be really conscious of what war might mean.

'Well, he won't come back empty-handed, even if it means offering up the Czechs on a plate. But it won't end there, believe me.'

At the sheep pens beside the burn Marlowe had joined MacRath who was looking over his wether lambs.

'Fat lambs for market?'

'Aye, these are the last of the batch. Though there may be more on the hill still to come in. We had such a poor gather.'

The two men stood for a while in companionable silence studying the wethers…

'Is Morag all right now,' enquired Marlowe casually. 'She seemed distressed about something.'

'Oh yes. She's fine now.'

'But what was it she said, Gideon?'

MacRath hesitated.

'What Morag said, Professor Marlowe… what she actually said… was *'Dh' fhairich mi bas ann an suathadh a làimh'*.

He didn't offer a translation. That in itself seemed significant. But Marlowe wouldn't embarrass his host by asking for one. It sounded like '*I felt Death in the touch of his hand.*' Something of the sort. But whose hand? Marlowe couldn't make any sense of it. Perhaps he'd got it wrong. Whatever it was it had clearly upset the girl.

In the garden Giles was starting on another boot.

'What will you do? If there's a war, I mean?'

Richard was cleaning his pocket-knife.

'I don't know. Probably join the army. If they'll have an ex-Brigader. I owe it to someone. Someone who died in Spain. Though the real question, Giles, is what will they do with me.'

Richard smiled his bitter smile.

'I'll probably be locked up as a dangerous Red.'

'Why *did* you go to Spain, Richard? I've never really understood.'

Richard hesitated. *What do you say*, he thought, *to a child?* Then he remembered what Adam used to say: *If only a man is honest you can make a revolutionary of him.*

So, sighing, he put the question he had put so many times back at Cambridge.

'Hasn't it ever struck you that we may have been deceived, you and I? That our whole education may have been an elaborate fraud?'

He looked earnestly at his cousin, fixing on him the same keen-eyed look he had fixed on so many others.

'What if everything we were taught to think and feel, all that has been affirmed and celebrated in England for a thousand years, was a lie?'

Giles, though, only looked bemused.

Patiently, Richard tried again. He might have been coaxing a dull pupil.

'Try to imagine a sort of picture history of England. A kind of montage of all the stories we were brought up on—Alfred burning the cakes... King John at Runymede signing Magna Carta... Elizabeth addressing the troops at Tilbury... Drake playing his game of bowls... Nelson at Trafalgar... Wellington at Waterloo... And all of that lit up. Brought to you in glorious technicolour, as they say at the pictures. And in shadow, close to the frame, toiling away at the edges, the masses, the millions for whom History was never splendid or thrilling. For me that picture slipped into its negative. What was lit suddenly became dark—what was dark, lit up. Do you see? '

But Giles only stared at him with the same puzzled look. Then returned to waxing his boot.

'Richard,' he said suddenly, 'will you take me up the *Crack of Doom*?'

Richard shook his head. *What was the point?*

Then he said, not unkindly, 'I'm sure you could manage it without me. It's easier if you keep well out on the left wall.'

Giles looked up from his boot.

'I can't do it on my own now Nicko's out of action. Besides, I'd like to climb it with you.'

He gazed pleadingly at his cousin.

Richard hesitated. What had war, or Fascism, to do with that eagerness, that joy-in-life?

'OK. We'd better let someone know, though.'

Dropping the boot Giles dashed off to break the news.

Miranda had finished her picture. Bartrum found her in the meadow still lost in contemplation.

'It's as we thought,' he began. 'It's not broken. But Nicko will have to rest.'

Engrossed, she seemed not to have heard. She had eyes only for her picture, the glowing vision of which had not yet passed from her mind.

'Will there be a war?' she asked absently. 'Grandfather thinks so.' She turned to look at him.

'What will you do?'

He was taken aback. It was the last thing he was expecting.

'If there's a war? Well,' he said cautiously, 'I expect I shall do my bit, like everyone else. I should want to, anyway. Wouldn't you?

'But why? Why must we do as everyone else does?'

Then, while he was marshalling his arguments about doing the decent thing, sticking by one's country...

'What about Love, the beloved Republic?'

He stared at her uncertainly. Months ago he'd quoted Swinburne's lines at her, never expecting them to be flung back at him like this.

'It *is* a Republic, isn't it? That feeds upon freedom and lives ?'

Something entirely unforeseen had broken through into the life she'd come to recognize as her own, and nothing would be the same ever again.

'Why do we have to stay here? Why can't we go away?'

It was the protest of a desire that saw no likelihood of satisfaction in the world as it had shown itself to be, yet sprang from a fundamental rhythm grounded outside that world's mechanisms.

'Where would we go?'

'Ireland... America... *anywhere.*'

'A funk-hole!'

'What does it matter so long as we're out of this madness?'

'And what would they say of me then?'

Oh, she could see what they'd say reflected in his eyes.

'Do you care?'

But he was struggling to grasp far more than what she was

suggesting.

'But we don't belong in America.'

'That's why we'll be free there. We'll be on our own.'

'And what would we live on?'

'I can paint. You can write.'

There was a desperate unreality about all this. And yet he longed to be persuaded.

'Have you thought what pain that would bring to your family?' God, he was sounding like a schoolmaster.

'Of course. For a while. They would come round in the end.'

'To you, perhaps. To me, never.'

'Then never to me either,' she said, and looked unflinchingly at him.

'What if it all goes horribly wrong?'

He needed her to recognize, to face what, in his own heart, he couldn't bring himself to contemplate alone.

'Then grand-mama will be proved right, won't she? '

She emptied out the water bottles, and began methodically to gather up her equipment, her rags and brushes, storing them in her satchel. Methodical it seemed, and yet he saw there was a dangerous spirit at work in her. She was fired up by her own creative energy.

He bent to fold the easel. Then, silently, they walked back together towards the Lodge. Once again he was reminded that he was so much older than her, so much more schooled in the ways of the world. For a moment, though, she seemed to him possessed of a strength that might carry them through all adversity.

The thought of war overshadowed the Lodge that evening as, in ones and twos, the Marlowes and their guests gathered in the drawing room before dinner. No one had much to say. The euphoria of the previous evening had given way to an uneasy foreboding. All occupied themselves in one way or another, though with the preoccupation of those whose minds were otherwise engaged.

Bartrum's thoughts were anywhere but on *The Times* crossword, while Vanessa's eyes lifted constantly from Agatha Christie to gaze at blankness. The high hopes with which Chamberlain had set off for Munich might prove illusory. He might come back empty-handed. And how swiftly, some of them were wondering, would the bombers follow on his heels?

So it seemed to Marlowe. He could only imagine what poor Susannah must be going through. She, more than anyone, knew what war might mean. She, who had lost her husband, and so nearly lost her son.

Only the youngest and the oldest seemed untroubled by the crisis: Millie, turning the cards with the fatalism of one for whom God alone sufficed; and the twins, who'd joined forces to challenge Nicko at chess, and were squabbling over tactics as they took turns to move their pieces.

Hugh moved his bishop, glancing at Nicko as he did so.

Nicko frowned, and shook his head warningly.

'I told you so,' hissed Andrew.

Hugh moved it back.

So it was that Giles and Richard, returning in triumph just as the light was failing, received no more than a muted welcome.

'Well, we did it,' began Giles excitedly. To anyone who would listen.

'Gosh, it's the hardest thing I've ever done,' he went on, catching Bartrum's eye. 'We ambled up this long groove through the slabs. That was easy enough. Then suddenly the groove rears up into a corner and leans over to the left. And there it is, splitting the wall. *The Crack of Doom.*'

He was clearly still full of it

'The Crack itself is only about fifty feet high. But it's pretty fierce, I can tell you. It's wide enough to get an arm and a leg inside, until you get to the chockstone halfway up. After that it gets really narrow. I was glad to get to the top, I can tell you. I was quite done in.'

'Jolly well done,' said Bartrum agreeably, who hadn't the faintest idea what it was all about.

'We didn't do Pigott's *Direct Finish*,' added Richard quietly to Marlowe. 'Giles would have gone on, I think, but I'd had enough. So we finished up the *glacis*. I'm afraid I'm rather out of condition.' He smiled ruefully.

The old man smiled too.

'It's good to see you climbing again.'

Susannah glanced up from her sewing. *Will it last?* her eyes seemed to ask.

For a while perhaps, he thought. Then he remembered that day on the Cioch. Fullness could not be circumscribed. However fretted men might find themselves, however caged, confined, yet fullness would break through the darkness of the world with the gratuity of something given.

The note of exhilaration, though, was shortlived. No sooner had Giles and Richard gone to wash and change for dinner than the sombre silence reasserted itself. Even Henry was subdued.

The Archdeacon had never forgotten the fearful casualties of the Great War, nor how the land fit for heroes to live in had become a country of three million unemployed. He had canvassed for the anti-rearmament candidate in the East Fulham by-election, and supported the Peace Ballot, one of the millions who, like him, had sworn *Never Again*. And while he had never lost faith in the efficacy of reason, he had begun to consider what to do should the worst come to the worst. They must, of course, have gas masks fitted as soon as they got back. The twins, thank God, should be safe enough at school. But Vanessa and his parents must all be got out from under the bombers. Susannah too couldn't be left on her own. Hampstead would be no safer than Russell Square. She would have to go with Vanessa. There could, of course, be no question of leaving London himself. He intended to offer himself as an ARP warden as soon as he got back. Giles and Miranda would no doubt be called on in some capacity. They would want to do their bit.

'It's almost 7.30,' he said, noticing the time. 'I don't suppose there'll be any news from Munich. I'll switch it on anyway.'

They learnt that immediately upon landing Mr Chamberlain had been driven through streets lined with cheering crowds, a reassuring sign, it was said, of the universal desire for peace shared by the German people. The Prime Minister had gone straight to the *Führerbau,* where the talks were to be held, mounting the steps of that imposing building to the accompaniment of a welcoming drum-roll. It was perhaps just as well that nothing was said of those corridors lined with black-uniformed troopers, to whose menacing shouts of *Heil Hitler* Mr Chamberlain had responded with an amiable nod.

At about the time the Marlowe family went in to dinner the members of a select private dining club were gathering in the Pinafore Room of the Savoy. Churchill, of course, was there. But by no means all of those present were supporters of Churchill. Lord Mottistone, for instance, was so far from agreeing with Winston's alarmist views that he'd laid a bet with other members of the club that no hostile bomb would be dropped on the soil of Great Britain for twenty years. Also present were two members of the Cabinet who, despite their reservations over Chamberlain's policy, had so far resisted strenuous efforts to persuade them to resign.

Though it was to be a night for the settling of differences, dinner—the usual modest affair of just three courses—witnessed no hostilities. The roast ribs of beef, the Irish stew—plenty of small onions, not much broth—were consumed amid an uneasy truce. Pears were peeled, and went the way of the Rocquefort cheese and the mixed ice-cream. Then followed the Loyal Toast, to which Churchill, as was his custom, added under his breath, '*And No War*!'.

Yet passions were running high. Some of the men present that evening could scarcely bring themselves to speak to one another. Churchill himself was in a black mood. He'd spent the afternoon trying in vain to persuade various colleagues to sign an open telegram to Chamberlain warning him against making further concessions. Now he turned savagely on the two Cabinet Ministers present. How could honourable men with fine records in the Great War condone a policy so cowardly, a grovelling capitulation to an Austrian corporal? It was sordid, squalid, sub-human and suicidal, since the consequence would inevitably mean the sacrifice of British lives.

Never a man to stomach an insult, Duff Cooper fought fire with fire. He had, he said, told Chamberlain in Cabinet that he'd foreseen only two possible outcomes of the crisis; the unpleasant alternatives of peace with dishonour, or war. Now they ran the risk of being kicked into war by the boot of public opinion, when those for whom they would be fighting had already been defeated. He'd told Chamberlain so.

'But you're still in place,' jeered a contemptuous voice. 'You're still in place.'

Duff Cooper, of whom it might be said that he rarely missed an opportunity to lose his temper, now did so with spectacular effect. The vein bulged in his forehead as, purple-faced, his voice trembled with rage. Insults flew thick and fast as the exchanges exceeded the bounds of civilized behaviour. Garvin, the editor of the *Observer* was next to be put to the sword. Devastated by the death of his only son on the Somme he'd steadfastly supported Chamberlain's attempts to find a peaceful outcome to the crisis. In a vain effort to defend himself he pointed out that he'd written a stiff article only the previous Sunday.

'Yes, a late tumescence,' observed Leo Marlowe acidly, 'after forty flabby failures.'

White-faced, Garvin pushed back his chair and walked out of the room.

It was by now the early hours of Friday morning. The first editions of the papers were already out on the streets. Leo Marlowe was sent out into the Strand to buy a copy. The huge headline, spread right across the page, confirmed his worst fears. 'PEACE' bellowed the *Express*. It could only mean one thing. Peace, bought at the price of complete capitulation. And so it proved.

Duff Cooper, it was, who read out loud the terms of the agreement reached in Munich. They were every bit as bad as feared. Throwing down the paper in disgust he, too, rose and left the room. In twos and threes the rest followed suit until Churchill alone was left with the faithful Leo. So it was that the members of the Other Club departed the Savoy that night in mutual acrimony and disarray, an outcome entirely in keeping with the Club's golden rule, read aloud at every meeting, that nothing should be allowed to interfere with the asperity of party politics.

Churchill was the last to leave, with Leo at his side. Together they made for the exit, pausing as they passed the restaurant. For the revellers within the Prime Minister had brought closure.

'Poor devils,' said Churchill, observing the rejoicing. 'They little know what they will have to face.'

They were like the audience at a play on which the curtain had apparently fallen. Except that there never can be closure. There is always something more to be projected beyond the illusion of an ending. There always remains a further story to be told.

— CHAPTER SIXTEEN —

It was the Archdeacon's idea that they should stay on over the weekend. Since travel from Skye was impossible on a Sunday, returning to London on the Saturday would have meant losing a day of the holiday. And so it had been agreed.

Henry always said that no holiday in the Cuillin was complete without a visit to the headland known as the Rubh'. Of course, Susannah had already been there with Richard and returned filled with enthusiasm. It was an easy walk, one suitable for the whole family. Even Bartrum, who was sedentary by nature, had agreed to go along.

'It really is a delightful place, Charles,' Henry told him.

There were lots to explore. There were the ruins of the ancient home of the MacAskills, a fortified dun, and the chambered cairn which had been excavated only a year or two before. Henry was especially anxious to examine the chambered cairn. It was, moreover, a splendid place for a picnic, with wonderful views out to sea, rocky coves for the twins to splash about in, wild flowers on the moor for Millie, and excellent material for Miranda's sketching. There would be wonderful opportunities to observe seals and seabirds. Even a whale was possible.

Arrangements had been made with Mrs MacRath for a full complement of packed lunches to be placed on the hall table. The forecast was good. Lachlan, who was rarely wrong about Cuillin weather, had promised them a good day. Clearly Henry had thought of everything.

He came down to breakfast that morning with his usual bustle and enthusiasm, and was pleased to see that almost everyone was present, and ready for an early start. The Rubh' demanded a full day to do it justice. Miranda wasn't down yet, of course, but then she was always late. Charles, too, had yet to make an appearance.

'I think I'll just go and bang on his door,' said Henry, finishing his porridge. 'He's probably overslept.'

With that he hurried out of the lodge, and round to Bartrum's quarters in one of the farm cottages. Henry thumped cheerfully on the door.

'Come on Charles, you lazy beggar,' cried the Archdeacon, and barged into the bedroom.

Bartrum raised his head drowsily from the pillow. And though she sought to avert her face, there was no mistaking the corn-coloured head of his bed-fellow ducking under the sheets.

Vanessa had already reached the eggs-and-bacon stage of her breakfast when, looking up, she saw her husband gesturing to her from the hall. Frowning, she got up and went to the door. The rest of the family might have heard—if they heard anything—no more than a quiet murmur of voices in the hall. Then the pair returned to the dining room, Henry to collect his bacon and eggs from the covered dish, Vanessa, inscrutably, to resume her breakfast. Vanessa could be inscrutable when she thought she would.

'Thank you, Morag,' she said, summoning a smile for the young girl coming in with the toast.

At that moment Bartrum and Miranda appeared at the door of the dining room. It would be going too far, perhaps, to say that they made an entrance. But certainly they arrived together. It might have been a joint decision to brazen it out. That they were holding hands seemed to pass unnoticed by the breakfasters, busy with their meal. Only Millie, sipping her coffee—she never ate breakfast—cast a sharp look over the rim of her cup.

'Gosh, I'm ravenous,' declared Miranda defiantly. 'I could eat a horse.'

Vanessa's lips tightened. She seemed to be holding herself in check. The Archdeacon might have been on the point of saying something but was forestalled by his wife.

'*Pas devant les enfants, cherie,*' said Vanessa brightly.

Now the young men looked up. Nicko, who had still not quite adjusted to the Marlowes *en famille*, seemed particularly startled. The twins, with that sixth sense they had that something was amiss among the grown-ups, glanced furtively at one another.

Miranda, having piled her plate with scrambled eggs and bacon, set about her breakfast savagely. Bartrum sat with his fists clenched in his lap. He looked agonised. Meanwhile the Marlowes continued to pour coffee, ask for the marmalade, pass one another toast. Otherwise, no one spoke. The very air crackled.

'I believe Jess has had her pups,' said Marlowe eventually, seeing the twins had all but finished. 'They're in the barn. Shall we go and see?'

'Oh, I'd love to see the puppies,' cried Susannah. 'May I come too?'

The twins scrambled eagerly down from their chairs. They couldn't wait to leave the room.

Millie, though, was going nowhere.

'And what is it that mustn't be spoken of before the children?' she asked.

No one answered her. The silence was all but unendurable.

'Oh, why beat about the bush?,' cried Miranda. 'Daddy found me in bed with Charles.'

She had been sipping at her coffee. Now she set down the cup steadily enough in the saucer, yet with a hand that shook slightly.

'We overslept,' she added. It might have been in mitigation.

In the barn Marlowe stood with Susannah while the boys mooned over the puppies. He told himself he'd wanted to remove the twins from an embarrassing scene. A pretext, of course. He just couldn't wait to get out of that room. Running away. It was his way of dealing with things. Now he groaned inwardly, knowing what would follow, as he heard Lachlan saying, with a mischievous twinkle, '*Would ye like a pup?*'

Giles pushed back his chair, his breakfast half-eaten, and walked out of the room. A moment later Nicko got up and hobbled after him. Richard remained in his seat.

Henry had resolved to deal with the situation with as much dignity as could be mustered.

'I think it would be better if you left, Charles,' he said quietly.

He looked across the table, fixing his eyes upon his betrayer.

'Henry,' stammered Bartrum, 'I don't... I can't... '

'Yes,' cried Vanessa venomously, 'just get into that revolting car of yours and go.'

'If he goes,' said Miranda fiercely, 'I go with him.'

Millie cleared her throat. But whatever she might have been about to say was quietly forestalled.

'No, mother,' said Henry firmly. 'This is a matter for Vanessa and myself.'

'If he goes,' repeated Miranda, 'I go with him.'

The lovers looked at one another in the sudden knowledge that the fate of their beloved Republic was hanging in the balance.'

Now it was Richard's turn to leave the room. Out in the hall he came across Giles sitting miserably on the stairs, with Nicko at his side. He seemed to flinch at the sound of his sister's voice, now raised passionately in the dining room.

'You all think you know Charles. You think you know all you need to know about him. So you've written him off. As if he was finished with. But none of us are finished with. None of us know what we have it in us to become. Charles no less than any of you. '

Richard put his hand on his cousin's shoulder.

'Come on, Giles. We came to Skye to climb grandfather's route. Let's go and do it.'

In London that Friday morning a strange uncertainty seemed to have seized the public mood. Though every newspaper carried banner headlines proclaiming the news the principal railway stations remained no less crowded than before. Trains for Scotland and the West Country especially were full to overflowing. And while many people were still seeking to escape to parts of the country thought to be less liable to air attack, others had already sought to return their hoards of foodstuffs and perishables to the stores from which they'd bought them in the hope of getting their money back.

Praise for the Prime Minister was universal. The *Daily Mail* announced that its sister paper the *Sunday Dispatch* would be telling *'the unique life story of the man the world applauds.'*

Had the Government of the United Kingdom been in less resolute hands,' declared *The Times*, *'it is as certain as can be that war, incalculable in its range, would have broken out against the wishes of every people concerned.'*

Many of the papers published maps of Czechoslovakia showing the territories which were to be handed over to Germany. The *Daily Mail* revealed that the British Legion had raised a peace force of 50,000 unarmed volunteers to maintain order in the Sudeten districts during the hand-over. *'This bowler-hatted force of ordinary men'*, declared the *Mail*, could leave for the Sudetenland as soon as they were called for.

Yet for the wardens of the ARP *'Carry on'* remained the order of the day. The digging of trenches, the distribution of gas masks, the creation of bomb-proof shelters, and all the preparations for war continued as before. Instructions were issued for the proper care and handling of gas masks which, the public was reminded, remained the property of the Government. In the public parks, however, gangs of children were reported to have already donned their gas-masks, and were fighting mock battles in the air-raid trenches.

Theatre, of one sort or another, seemed to be all the rage. At the West End shows that night there would be standing room only.

Neither of the cousins had much to say as they plodded up into Coire Lagan. The unpleasant scene they'd witnessed earlier that morning, though never mentioned, remained with them as disagreeably as a foul taste on the tongue. So when they saw the little tent still pitched under the Western Buttress of Sgumain, and the three men in tattered breeches enjoying a late breakfast amid a companionable litter of mugs and billy-cans, they were gladdened, as at the prospect of a further world they would shortly enter. For life itself there could be no remedy. But some, at least, of its bitterness might be left behind in the negotiation of steep rock, and the absorbing business of placing a boot just so, and finding it held.

As they climbed further up the Stone Shoot, drawing closer to the tent, Richard recognised the young men they'd seen in the inn at Sligachan.

The men looked up as they approached. One of them, a fellow with a thick thatch of fair hair and eyes of Viking blue, stared quizzically at the newcomers.

'English?'

As a greeting it seemed some way short of welcoming.

''Fraid so,' said Richard. 'Sorry about that.'

'That's all right,' grinned the Viking's thick-set, powerfully-built companion. 'We don't mind the English borrowing our routes, do we Archie?'

'Actually, it's my grandfather's route,' said Giles shyly. '*Marlowe's Variation*. He put it up thirty years ago.'

'Really? How wonderful. It's a fine climb,' said the lean dark fellow who was tending the stove. Richard remembered him as 'Mr Murray'. '*He completed the traverse last year. Yes, the whole ridge from Garsbeinn to Sgurr nan Gillean.*'

'So you must be a Marlowe?'

'That's right. I'm Giles, this is my cousin Richard.'

They shook hands and fell to chatting, as climbers do.

'I think we spotted you on the *Crack of Doom*,' Giles went on. Modesty forbade that he should reveal he'd led the Crack himself the previous day.

'You might well have done,' said Murray. 'Kenneth here was making enough noise to raise the dead. I'm Bill, by the way. This is Kenneth. That's Archie'

'I'm afraid Kenneth has scoffed all the kippers,' said the Viking apologetically. 'But we can offer you a brew.'

Marlowe took the shore path following the eastern side of the loch.

He had to get away. Though the pain was too raw, too recent, to be shaken off so easily: Vanessa raging round, beside herself with fury: *I want it stopped now...* Henry's vain efforts to pacify her... Millie's attempt at intervention... Bartram, clearly appalled at what had happened, like a man coming to his senses: *Your father's right, Miranda. It would be best if I went.* And she clinging to him... *No... no...* hysterical in her passion. Then the twins dashing in. *Daddy... daddy... can we have a puppy...*

He and Millie had looked at one another with that sense of helplessness peculiar to grandparents. Which is also a release.

'I'm going to the Rubh',' he'd said quietly to Millie. 'Are you coming?'

She, though, had only looked at him. And she was right. He was running away. He thought then of Richard, and of that fresh-faced Yorkshire farm lad to whom he'd given the *coup de grace* twenty years before. It's what men do, he thought. In the last resort they run away. What else can they do? We run away only to be fetched back, one way or another, to face the music.

Three hundred feet above the boulders of the Stone Shoot Giles Marlowe had found a stance on a ledge, with a good spike from which Richard was belaying him as he inched cautiously up the steep slab above. It was the same false line that had seduced his grandfather thirty years before. Like Marlowe the two young men had failed to notice the correct continuation traversing diagonally to the right. It was not that obvious. Giles was finding the angle increasingly intimidating, and he was grateful for the good gabbro, grippy under his toes.

Then, as a little boy, he'd first heard tell of 'the island of sky' it held for him the enchantment of a fairy-tale. That his grandfather had actually been there seemed extraordinary to him. Later, as a boy at school, he read those lines about '*a magic casement opening on the foam of perilous seas in fairy lands forlorn*', and saw in his mind's eye that self-same fabulous isle, a half-legendary land of cauldrons and executioners, of mists and thrashing winds, blue mountains and black lakes, a land which was a contradiction to itself. When, later still, he read in Steeple and Barlow the description of *Marlowe's Variation*, he vowed that he too would go to Skye one day and make a name for himself.

Though it was still early afternoon the September sun cast a long shadow slanting down over the line of overhanging buttresses that had thwarted Marlowe on his first ascent, and down over the slab below. To Giles, now advancing into that shadow, the further he got the less feasible it seemed that there could be any continuation. Then he remembered his grandfather's words: *Remember, one day you may find that the rock has closed itself against you.* He looked about him now with a groping perception of the heartless indifference of rock. He was suffering the loneliness of his situation, and the searching intimacy with himself that it imposed

'I can't see this going anywhere,' he shouted down to his second.

'Are you OK?' Richard called out, after a pause. Giles hadn't moved for some time.

'I seem to have run out of rock.' Casual enough, yet there was a tremor in the voice that did not pass unnoticed.

'Can you climb down?'

Giles hesitated. He seemed to consider, though the answer was never in doubt.

'I don't think so.'

Any moment now, thought Richard, he's going to start shaking.

'Listen, Giles. There looks to be a ledge a little way below you. Just below a bulge to your left. Can you see it? '

'Yes, I think so.'

'There's a crack in the bulge. A crack that might take a piton. Could you get to it?'

'No.'

There was something unutterably lonely about that '*No*'.

Richard took a deep breath.

'OK. Now listen. Are you safe where you are?'

—218—

'I think so.'

'Right. Stay calm. I'm coming up.'

Richard delved in his rucksack, produced a piton, two karabiners and a hammer which he clipped to his waist loop. He also pulled out a short length of line, with a loop spliced into it at both ends. He tucked the line into his waist loop. Then he untied himself from the belay.

This is not good, he thought to himself. *Not good at all.* Now they were both without protection.

But he judged he had enough rope to climb up to Giles, about fifty feet above him.

'OK. I'm coming up now. '

Richard climbed with care, scrupulous to avoid Giles's rope as he moved up the slab, his own end of the rope trailing down to the neat coils he'd left at the stance.

For Chrissakes, Giles, he prayed silently, *don't come off now or we're both done for.*

The ledge he was aiming for lay six feet below Giles and slightly to his left. Richard drew level with the ledge. It would take a long stride to reach it. Holding his breath he stepped across, very gingerly, reaching the fingers of one hand into the crack as he did so. Thank God it was a decent ledge.

He slotted the piton into the crack, and drove it home. Instead of the expected *ping... ping... ping...* it gave back a dull, hollow sound. Not reassuring. Even so, it resisted his tentative tug.

Then he threaded the length of line through the eye of the piton, and clipped a karabiner through the loops spliced into the line. He clipped his own rope into the karabiner, and pulled a small loop back through his waistline, tying it in a single knot round both lengths of the rope between himself and the karabiner. Giles' rope he clipped to the line loop with the second karabiner. Now they both had a measure of protection. It wasn't convincing, but it was all they had.

'Right,' he said. 'Down you go. Remember,' he added, 'I've got you.'

He kept the rope taut between them as Giles began gingerly to descend, paying it out carefully through the karabiner clipped to the line loop, praying the piton would hold. He didn't trust that piton.

He was assailed suddenly by their precarious plight.

'Giles,' he called down urgently.

The tense face stared up at him.

'The moment you get down to the stance, tie on to that spike. Do it immediately. Then take in the rope. But do it *gently*.' Richard didn't trust that peg.

As he climbed back down the false line, now belayed by Giles, Richard wondered if it was wise to continue the climb at all. Certainly he would have to lead the next few pitches himself to give Giles time to recover. But it was a huge relief to be back safely at the stance.

Only too aware of what they had both escaped, they were too drained by the experience to consider what they might do next. The ledge they stood on was not so generous that they could afford to take their ease. Nevertheless, for some moments they simply stood there, letting the tension drain from their bodies, until they were breathing easily again.

'We'd better get the rope down,' said Richard eventually. He untied himself so that the rope could be retrieved from the piton.

'OK,' he said. 'Now pull it down... *gently*,' he warned, as Giles yanked at it.

'It's stuck.'

'Here, let me.' Richard gave the rope a sharp tug.

There was a faint metallic clatter above them as the rope came away. The two men, looking up, saw what was whistling towards them. Ducking involuntarily, Richard staggered, lost his balance, and toppled backwards off the ledge.

Giles saw him hit the rock forty feet below, then rebound down out of sight.

Marlowe drifted miserably along the shore path out towards the Rubh'.

Walk on, he told himself. For the old anxiety was flaring up again. *Walk on. There is nothing you can do. Just walk away from it.*

At the Lagan burn he came across Lachlan. He found in the shepherd a timely anchorage, the old man regarding Marlowe with keen blue eyes, chatting serenely about his sheep, gesturing with his crook towards places where a missing ewe might be found, or a dangerous ravine where the fencing must be repaired without delay. A priceless man who missed nothing that mattered. Who attended to everything.

And gradually the tension eased, leaving in its wake an inner stillness. Or was it emptiness, Marlowe wondered? Was that what he was now? An empty man always reaching after something more? For fullness? What did they amount to, the high points of a life? Isolated moments of intense experience when fullness seemed complete. Yet was there ever a time without fullness spilling over into loss?

Then, crossing the burn by the stepping stones, he continued for another mile. Where the sea cliffs steepened dramatically he took a higher path climbing to the summit of a rocky knoll. For now, at last, his sense of an objective was returning. Down below he saw the boundary wall cutting across the peninsula. He set off down, aiming for a break in the wall left of the path. Half-a-mile of tussocky hummocks and boggy hollows brought him to a small rise, beyond which a reedy lochan came into view. Below, in a sheltered hollow, were the tumbled walls and ruined gable of the ancestral home of the MacAskills. A sheep-trod cutting through the bracken led down to the lochan.

Marlowe's goal, the chambered cairn, lay immediately north of the lochan.

'It's officially listed now as an Ancient Monument,' MacRath had told him. 'Aye, they wrote to Mrs MacLeod at Dunvegan. She showed me the letter. '

Marlowe had wanted to see it since first reading of its excavation by Lindsay Scott a few years earlier.

'He had no labour,' MacRath went on, 'apart from his good lady. And no equipment. I had to lend him some tools for the work. All he had was a length of chain, some of the grass rope we use for tethering stirks, and some timber he picked up off the beach at Camas a' Mhurain.'

The greater part of the cairn remained under the mound of turf and heather which had covered it for centuries, but part of the tomb itself had been left open. Marlowe scrambled down over tumbled stones to gain the pillared entrance. A few feet in front of the entrance two massive slabs lay at right angles to the axis. Bending double under the lintel, he entered a low, short passage, leading to an antechamber opening into the burial place. Able now to stand upright, he found himself in a round chamber, seven feet or so in diameter, smelling of damp earth. Part of the roof had fallen in, admitting a shaft of sunlight into the tomb.

This was no mere heap of stones, as might have appeared from outside, for the internal walls had been constructed with great skill and precision. Massive pillars, in-filled with dry-stone walling, supported the basalt slabs which formed what remained of the roof. He thought of the immense effort it must have taken to set these stones in place. The two fallen from the roof must each weigh half-a-ton at least. He tried to imagine the men who'd set them there, but they were remote from him. There was only this space, this silence, and the stones themselves, mute witnesses of whatever it was that had happened here. He was assailed then by a sense of their isolation in this lonely place, facing the boundless sea with the mountains at their back. Whoever they were, they cared for their dead.

Bending double again, he crept back through the antechamber, along the passage and out again at the entrance. The larger of the slabs, he noticed now, had been chocked at one end, presumably to keep it horizontal. What funeral rites were held? Did they, he wondered, in their remote solitude celebrate some mystic cult of the hereafter? Did the relatives of the dead bring food to this place?

Keep watch for the prescribed period?

A slight breeze had got up, stirring the ferns and grasses growing between the infilled stones either side of the entrance. It brought with it the soft sounds of the sea washing into the little bay where Lindsay Scott had scavenged his baulks of timber.

He sat for a while lost in thought of those who had been laid here a thousand years before the fall of Troy. Who had rested undisturbed for two millenia or more. He used to imagine, in the quiet security of his study, tinkering with the *Odyssey,* that he was safe for the rest of time. Somehow or other he had managed to survive the damage of a lifetime. Surely nothing more could happen now. Only, of course, it could. It *had.*

Well, peace was here. Ah, he could have surrendered to it then. To be rid of the mess and muddle. Was it, indeed, death he was yearning for? Was it? To rest in the quiet earth? To be beyond all this? *Was* there a beyond? The worse horror, if it were so, was that it might be just the same. No, he would not wish to live again.

Wearily, he got to his feet. By now the westering sun was lighting up the whole of the western seaboard, a scene of extraordinary tranquillity. Cliffs, headlands, bathed in light, or shadowed by deep re-entrants. The light in places turned the surface of the sea to silver. Sea and islands too. Rhum and Canna the vaguest shapes, silver-blue on a silvery sea.

Marlowe walked slowly back from the Rubh' in the westering light. He fixed his eyes on the scene before him, seeing how the light enriched the colours of land and sea, the white crofts dotted about the green shores, the deep reflected blue of the sky. Had he outlived his life? No. A black guillemot was diving just off-shore. Cormorants too, in ones and twos, drifting and diving in a sparkling sea. Out in the loch a fisherman was hauling his creels amid the cries of gulls wheeling above his little boat. It was still good to be alive.

He had reached a point where the shore path intersects with the path from Coire Lagan when he saw a figure racing down from the moor. There was something horribly ominous in the urgency of that flying figure. Of course, the boys might be anywhere. All he knew was that Lachlan had said he'd seen them setting off for the hill. Again he told himself they might be anywhere. They might even have gone over to one of the climbs in Coire a' Ghrunnda. Though the likelihood was they'd gone to Sròn na Ciche. Even so, they were unlikely to be the only climbers on the crag that day. At the same time some instinct told him something was wrong. Filled with foreboding he turned aside from the shore-path, and began the climb uphill. They were the longest miles of his life.

Where the path divided he bore right towards Sròn na Ciche and the Stone Shoot, pausing to catch his breath at the burn, the water foaming white, rushing between the stones. Tired already from his walk, it had taken him the better part of an hour to reach this point.

The low sunlight, streaming into the corrie from the south-west, threw into relief the cracks and gullies seaming the huge buttresses on the side of the west ridge of Dearg. It picked out the tower of Sgùrr MhicCoinich, in which King' s Chimney stood out clearly, a steep clean corner capped by an overhanging top. And beyond it An Stac and the top of Dearg, with the Inaccessible Pinnacle sharply profiled. There was no sign of life anywhere. No sound, other than the rush of water.

He pushed on, joining the track climbing up through the Stone Shoot, scanning the crag as he went. As he drew level with the Western Buttress he made out the figure of a man standing upright, coiling a rope, then two figures sitting together a little way aside from the Stone Shoot, one of which, as he drew closer, he identified as Giles.

Only then did he notice the groundsheet draped over the stones, not quite covering a motionless figure whose out-flung arm protruded horribly.

Then the man sitting with Giles was rising to his feet. Advancing to meet him.

'Better not come any closer,' he advised in a quiet voice.

Marlowe recognised the lean, dark fellow pointed out to him by John Campbell as 'Mr Murray'.

'Giles!'

Giles, though, made no response. His eyes, fixed at a distance, seemed not to recognize who it was who spoke to him.

'D'you know him?'

Marlowe took a deep breath. Looked away.

'My grandson,' he managed to get out. 'Both. My grandsons.'

The Scot hesitated, taken aback for a moment.

'I'm sorry,' he said quietly.

Calmer now, the old man looked steadily at Murray.

'Do you know what happened?'

'We haven't been able to get much out of him. The poor chap's still very shocked, I'm afraid. We had quite a job to get him down. But it seems they unroped. I don't know why.'

'I'm so sorry,' he said, as Marlowe turned to gaze at the still figure under the groundsheet, at the outflung arm. 'This must be awful for you,' he added, at a loss.

Marlowe spoke to his grandson.

'Giles…' he said gently. 'Giles… '

At that the young man took his head in his hands, and began to sob.

— CHAPTER SEVENTEEN —

It had all been all too much for the Archdeacon. In less than three hours he'd been overwhelmed by events; first, shocked by a state of affairs of which he'd been completely oblivious, then stunned by a development which he'd been powerless to prevent.

Even so Millie believed it had been badly handled. And said as much. *All you'll succeed in doing,* she upbraided Vanessa, *is to drive her away.*

In the fraught silence of the drawing room it sounded no less than the truth. Upstairs, Miranda was already packing her bags. Bartrum had gone to load the car.

If only Miranda had never been allowed to go to that wretched art school… If only Henry had never invited Charles to Glen Brittle… Those were the least of the recriminations Vanessa hurled at her husband.

Then Miranda came clattering down the stairs clutching the last of her belongings. Her face proclaimed she had broken off relations with a hostile world.

Her father stood by helplessly.

'We'll get in touch, Henry, I promise.' Bartrum's face wore a beseeching look.

Then they were gone, the throaty growl of the Lagonda receding down the glen.

Millie never forgot her last glimpse of them at the fairy pools, locked in anguished discussion; the older man troubled, despondent, the girl passionate, pleading. The old woman was filled with compassion for them. There was something pitiful in the human condition. A wound in human nature that perhaps only love could redeem. For all its ignorance, its blindness, its downright error, human love was never anything but a finite participation in God's own love. The most abandoned of voluptuaries was, however obscurely, still reaching out to God. And always, within the man who loved, was the possibility of change, of finding at last his true object, what he was truly seeking. Yes, she believed that.

And was that worth putting at risk one's own grand-daughter?

She was reminded, then, of the radical insecurity of love. Its contingency. No, there had been no way to protect Miranda unless it be to shut her up in a tower. And all those tales of young women shut up in castles or cast into an enchanted sleep spoke of the folly of attempting to frustrate life and love. It was like bidding the sea retreat.

And what if Charles was right? His life had been a kind of shipwreck, washed up with other derelicts among the bars and drinking dens of Fitzrovia. And had he now found solid ground at last? He thought so, evidently. Perhaps Love was indeed the only hope for a ruined world. Millie sighed. No, Miranda must take her chance.

She sighed again, reflecting how far she had still to travel towards that Love which moves the sun and other stars. And so little time remaining.

Archie was all but done in when he reached Glenbrittle House. Still running, he all but collided with MacRath in the yard.

'An accident on Sròn na Ciche,' he gasped out. 'Two English climbers. One dead, I think.'

MacRath sent a man to Cuillin Cottage, another to the Post Office.

Archie, meanwhile, had set off again to rouse his friends at the tents across the river.

MacRath walked back slowly towards the house. English climbers, the young man had said, staying at the Lodge. And from the description the dead man—if, indeed he was dead—must be Mr Fleming. Shouldn't the family be warned? MacRath would have felt easier speaking to the Professor. But Marlowe had gone to the Rubh. Lachlan had met him at the old sheep fold. There was no telling when he would be back.

Shaking his head at the bitter ways of fortune, MacRath went in to speak to his wife.

'Dr MacKay is in the glen,' she said, 'visiting old Mrs Ross. I'll send Jeannie for him.'

Henry had gone up to Eas Mor just to get away from the Lodge. Of course Vanessa was upset. Any mother would be. And of course she said bitter things when she was upset.

One should try to take a charitable view of such outbursts. All the same there were times when charity demanded more than the Archdeacon could manage. Then he took himself off. Besides, he was convinced Miranda must eventually come to her senses. He was rehearsing the scene he would play out with his daughter. *You must put this behind you*, he would say gently. *Yes, sad, but without hurt or bitterness. Resolve to go on learning from life, my dear...*

Then he saw his host walking up the hill towards him.

Not knowing quite how to begin, MacRath came straight to the point. There was no way of softening the blow.

'There's been an accident on Sròn na Ciche.'

Though his voice sounded matter-of-fact Henry knew MacRath had not come up the hill for no reason especially to tell him this. Besides, a grim face tells its own story.

The Archdeacon took a deep breath.

'Do we know who?' he managed evenly. It might have been a casual enquiry, as they walked back down the hill together.

MacRath hesitated—a reluctance not lost on the other.

'An English climber, the young man said.' MacRath left it at that. After all, he couldn't be sure it was Mr Fleming. Though it seemed very likely.

'Is he... ?'

'They think so.'

'I believe my son went off somewhere with his cousin,' said Henry, very controlled. 'Do you happen to know where?'

But no. MacRath hadn't seen either of them that day.

They parted at the stile. As he watched the tall figure of the Archdeacon limping towards the porch MacRath brooded on yet another accident. The last, a year or two before, had aroused considerable unease. There had even been talk in the press of prohibiting the climbing of such dangerous summits. For his own part, if MacRath had any such misgivings he kept them to himself. For him the Cuillin remained what they always were, wholly resistant to human thought, as indifferent as whatever Power it was sent the killing frosts at lambing time, and the cold summer rains that left the winter fodder rotting in the fields: sometimes dark, forbidding, the harbinger of storm and tempest; sometimes improbable, floating on clouds; sometimes vanishing altogether; sometimes disavowing all ambiguity in the thundering spate and the surging whirlwind; sometimes aloof and silent, under a silent moon; a presence that cherished no memories, and kept no reckoning of the men who toiled in their shadow.

Henry, though, was at a loss to know what to do for the best. Ordinarily he would have wished to play his part in the rescue. But the events of the morning had thrown them all into confusion. He had no idea where Giles and Richard were. Father, too, had gone off somewhere on his own. In the circumstances he thought it his duty to stay with the family. Having dispatched the twins to play in the garden he gathered what remained of his party together in the drawing room. .

'There's been an accident on Sròn na Ciche,' he told them. 'MacRath is organising a rescue party to fetch down the injured man.'

'Do we know who it is?'

'There was a Scots party camping up in Coire Lagan,' said Nicko. 'We saw them climbing the *Crack of Doom*.'

'Where's Giles?'

'Apparently he and Richard went off together this morning.'

'I know your father was going to the Rubh,' said Millie.

'Is it an English climber?' asked Susannah. It might have been a sudden premonition.

Henry hesitated.

'Is it an English climber?'

'They believe so.'

'Oh God, no,' whispered Vanessa.

'I'm sure there are other English climbers in the glen at present,' said Millie briskly. 'It is foolish to raise fears unnecessarily.'

So, like families the world over, not knowing the whereabouts of their loved ones, and fearing for their safety, they settled themselves to wait as best they could.

The call came, as it usually does, at the day's end when, down from the hill, a climber has fired up the stove, set water to boil, and taken off his boots. They were not told of a death, only that a climber had fallen on Sròn na Ciche. And if they put on their boots again, and got to their feet it was because, next time, it might be any one of them lying up there on the hill. So, trooping in from Cuillin Cottage and the Post Office and the tents down by the river, they began to gather in the yard.

Meanwhile the long pole rolled with canvas and blankets that served for a stretcher had been brought from the barn.

At last, rucksacks packed with warm clothing, ropes and torches, Archie led them onto the moor. They had perhaps a couple of hours of daylight left. They went slowly, taking it in turns to carry the stretcher, for the pole was heavy and awkward to manage, and would be heavier still on their return.

In the kitchen, Mrs MacRath was at work with Jeannie, her niece. They had sent the men on their way with flasks and sandwiches, and were now preparing food for their return. The work went on in a sombre silence, for thoughts of the accident had robbed them of any wish for conversation.

The kitchen door opened to admit MacRath. He stood for a moment contemplating the scene.

'Where's Morag?'

'I've set her to lie down. She's very upset.'

'This is a bad business. Has Dr MacKay got here yet?'

'He's gone up the hill with the men.'

MacRath looked troubled. MacKay was not a young man, and by no means fit for the hill.

'Was that wise?'

'No, it was *not*,' said his wife emphatically. 'And I told him so. 'But he would not,' he said, 'shirk his duty on that account'.'

They were silent then as the gravity of the situation fell heavily between them.

'I thought we might put Mr Fleming in the barn,' said MacRath, at length. He couldn't bring himself to speak, yet, of 'the body'. 'I've set a table there.'

'We'll need some lanterns,' said his wife. 'It will be dark when they bring him down.'

They might have been preparing to welcome another guest.

Spread out at first over the moor the rescuers had halted to reassemble at the Allt Coire Lagan. They'd slaked their thirst at the burn, scooping up the icy water in cupped hands, and were now coming on together, boots clattering in the small scree of the lower Stone Shoot.

Murray took Marlowe quietly to one side.

'It might be as well,' he said, 'if you took him down now. He won't want to see this.'

All that time Giles had uttered scarcely a word. Scarcely moved, even.

He still couldn't believe it. It was almost as if it had happened to someone else; his own loss of nerve, Richard climbing up to belay him, the piton flying out. Again and again he heard that sudden, startled intake of breath... saw Richard plummeting backwards down the slab...

'Why?' he asked himself. Over and over again. *Why? What went wrong?*

The obvious answer was that the piton came flying down with the rope, Richard had ducked, and lost his balance. That, he tried to tell himself, was all there was to it. Richard should have tied on to the belay. Richard couldn't have fallen if he'd been belayed.

Then it seemed to him he was transferring responsibility to Richard and away from himself.

He flinched now at the memory of Richard's voice *'Can you climb down?'* He should at least have attempted it. But no. He had left the difficult thing, the dangerous thing to Richard. He felt again the wave of relief that had engulfed him at the words, *Right. Stay calm. I'm coming up.*

'Giles,' said Marlowe gently.

I should have climbed down. I should at least have attempted it. I can't understand now why I didn't. I was roped. Richard was belayed safely to the spike. It couldn't have happened if I'd climbed down as I should. Then there would never have been a need for Richard to untie...

'Giles... it's time for us to go.'

Alone now in the kitchen Mrs MacRath was stirring a great vat of steaming soup. Jeannie, acting on orders from her aunt, had conscripted the Marlowe twins to help with the milking.

'Och, what use will they be?' the young girl had protested.

'Think of it the other way round,' said her aunt. 'You'll be of use to them.'

The Marlowe women had gathered with Henry and Nicko at the stile gazing out over the moor. None of them were in any doubt now that something terrible had happened. Neither Giles nor Richard had returned from the hill. Neither, for that matter, had Marlowe.

The sun had set some while before but still they waited, wrapped now in coats and shawls, for it was chilly in the garden. Again Henry urged them to retreat indoors.

'We can do no good out here. Better go inside.'

But still they remained, as women do at the pithead or the harbour wall, dreading the worst.

Just then two figures came into view under the western flank of Sgùrr Dearg. Even with the sun below the horizon, and the first stars clearly visible, the soft afterglow lingers long along that north-western seaboard. Even so, at that distance the two figures were no more than moving shapes against the stillness of the moor. Then, for a while, they were lost to sight, swallowed up in the humps and hollows.

Then, as they re-appeared again on the brow of the hill below Eas Mor…

'It's Stephen,' said Millie suddenly.

Then, as they drew closer, the fair head of his companion became unmistakeably that of Giles.

Instantly, as realization dawned, Susannah uttered a piercing cry. Wild and high, it rang out again and again, a frantic shuddering cry. A lone face, looking from an upper window, saw it was the English lady howling in the garden, howling like a beast wild with pain or terror, and that old Mrs Marlowe had taken her in her arms. And Morag, who had fore-suffered this, began to weep again.

In twos and threes the rescuers gathered at a respectful distance among the boulders of the Stone Shoot. They stood, waiting in silence, while Dr MacKay examined the body. All had been out on the hill that day, and had scarcely time to grab a mouthful before setting out once more. In other circumstances they might have been glad enough of the good sandwiches which Mrs MacRath had provided. Few of them, though, felt like eating, subdued as they were in the presence of death. They did, however, drink from the flasks. Then, at last—for there was no hurry, and the descent would be grim—Murray's ground sheet was removed from the body, which was wrapped in the blankets. A climbing rope was used to lace it securely into its canvas shroud. Another cut in pieces to make four shoulder loops.

At last, their preparations complete, the first of the bearers hoisted their burden and began the descent over the boulders of the Stone Shoot, down past Cioch Gully and Central Gully and down under the Western Buttress, while above their heads Sròn na Ciche glowed like a furnace as the sun slipped further below the western hills.

Down and down they went, with frequent halts, changing the bearers, stopping to drink once more at the Allt Coire Lagan, then on past the little reedy lochan, and on over the flank of Sgùrr Dearg where one of them, Murray it was, turning to look back at the great precipice, saw the glow fading as the furnace cooled.

ALSO FROM RYMOUR BOOKS
https://www.rymour.co.uk

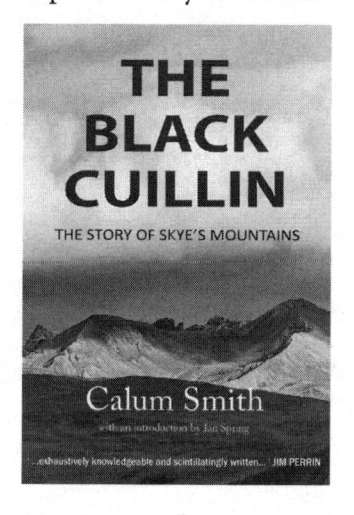

THE BLACK CUILLIN

THE STORY OF SKYE'S MOUNTAINS

Calum Smith

with an introduction by Ian Sprung

...exhaustively knowledgeable and scintillatingly written... JIM PERRIN

'Calum Smith's chronicle of mountaineering in the Black Cuillin of Skye—Britain's finest hill range—is exhaustively knowledgeable and scintillatingly written. A monumentally good book that transcends even the excellent earlier works by Humble and Stainforth'. JIM PERRIN

'A major work of research and history—not only of climbing but also of social developments and the significant personalities involved in events surrounding Skye and the Highlands over the last two centuries. A must read for anyone with an interest in the history of the island and Scotland'. DENNIS GRAY

'A book can get no higher testimonial than to be read swiftly. That's certainly what happened in my case. The book arrived on Thursday and by Sunday *The Black Cuillin* had been devoured in three bedtime sessions; testament not just to the subject matter but also the very readable style of writing'. ADRIAN TRENDALL

'An excellent and highly recommended history of climbing in the Cuillin. All in all, it is a fine addition to the literature of Scottish mountaineering'. ANDY FRASER

RYMOUR

The British Book Awards 2021

Small Press of the Year
COUNTRY FINALIST

#BRITISHBOOKAWARDS